WESTERWICK

WESTERWICK

GEORGE PATERSON

into books

Westerwick by George Paterson

First published in the United Kingdom in 2023 by
Into Books (an imprint of Into Creative)

ISBN 978-1-9163112-4-4

Cover design and typesetting by Stephen Cameron.

Typeset in Garamond.

For sales and distribution, please contact:
stephen@intocreative.co.uk

Dedication

This book is dedicated to Jim, Daphne, Ira, Muriel, Mariana, David, William, Jenni, Thomas, and Alasdair, all of whom have provided keys to chambers I possessed but never knew existed.

Acknowledgements

I would like to thank the good people at TLC Duntocher, namely Katrina, Nicola, Liz, Chloe, James and Aiden for their kindness and camaraderie. Also to Rachael Parker, Nicola Middleton and Monica Farrelly, all of whom have indulged my inquisitions with grace and patience. A very big thank you to Jimmy McKendrick, John Thomson, and Helena and Rothwell Glen for being awfully good sports. To Alan Parks, Alistair Braidwood and Julie Rea for their kind words and generosity. To Jan Kilmurry and John Welsh at Into for their friendship and continued support, my ever attentive readers, Julie Duffy and Loretta Mulholland, and the kind of publisher - and friend - anyone, writer or not, would be privileged to have, Stephen Cameron. Last but most certainly not least, the eagle eye and mighty red pen of my very own Alma Reville, Lisa Johnsen Paterson.

This book wouldn't have been possible but for the collective efforts of all of you fine people.

"One summer, my mother allowed me to stay up late but only until the sun set. As daylight hours were longer on the island, it was already past eleven when the last light had gone. On this one night, the temperature dropped suddenly so she asked if I would go into the kitchen and close the outside door. By the pantry, at my feet, sat a slug. Dark green in colour with yellowish markings, perfect for garden camouflage, less so for the checker-board linoleum which covered our uneven, hard stone floor. My grandfather had been doing some work that weekend and had left one of his tools on the sill by the door. I took it, and slipping the blade beneath its body, I lifted the slug, carefully placing it back in the long grass. The following night, as I closed up, I noticed a trail from the door frame and over one of the black squares; the slug had returned. The same slug. Again, I used the tool to lift it. This time, I walked barefoot through the cool damp grass to the far end of the garden. I put the slug down among the shrubs on the other side of the wall, safe in the knowledge that while it was not welcome in our home, I wished it no harm. That night however, while I slept, the slug returned. Through the kitchen, along the hall and under my bedroom door. I heard it come. Onto the foot of my bed, and onto my chest. Frozen with fear, I prayed. The slug raised its head, and spoke;

"Your God cannot help you now."

"What do you want of me?" I asked.

"Evil lives on Westerwick and here, it shall die."

Chapter 1 - Hidden

It has been said that Glasgow looks up to the West End but the West End looks down on Glasgow. And from the summit of Partickhill, the physical truth in that adage is undeniable. While the tight, steep wynd to the north of the clubhouse twists to its apex, the straighter, more fearsome climb from the Dumbarton Road offers a lung testing reward for all but the hardy.

At its base, the flat, high-sided blocks around the once industrious banks of the Clyde not only provide shelter from the winds which swirl up from the coast but hide some of the city's more curious secrets.

To its west, behind a barrier of corrugated rust, lies a cricket ground which conversely happened to be the birthplace of international football. If it wasn't for a miniscule plaque, a visitor might walk past contentedly, never knowing it was there. On its eastern side, just beyond the bustling, student infused streets of Byres Road sits the splendour of Kelvingrove. The park with its lush hills and mossy ponds, its ancient trees and cherubs perched on the lips of the fountains and the breathtaking gallery where a fat fibreglass Elvis and The Glasgow Boys - Henry and Hornel - act as support to Salvador Dali's interpretation of heavenly majesty. While the local adjutants of *his* Christ offered mercy to the celebrity suicides and the well heeled poisoners like Madeleine Smith, the countless stolen souls upon whose scarred backs *The Square Mile of Murder* was built, weren't afforded the same courtesy.

The cloak of the dear green place's respectability has always been mottled in sanguine. Hidden in plain sight.

While Edinburgh has a history of torturing those it considers monsters, a cursory look at any west coast tabloid will confirm that Glasgow chooses to venerate theirs. The Lord may judge but this town doesn't.

Though not its highest point, no other place in the city provides a vista so dramatic as the tarmaced, red-brick ski jump from the edge of the Partickhill Bowling Club at Gardner St. As the world watched, almost all of the curtains on the worked-on-block had been pulled back. Almost all.

"We need you to come in."

Thomas took a deep breath and clenched his fist. "Why?"

"Not over the phone."

"I don't know," he sighed, slowly releasing his grip. "Let me think about it."

"I'm sending some documents to you now."

"I didn't ask you to."

"We'll expect you at eleven."

"It's not easy for me to get around. You know that."

"I understand. We'll send a car."

"I've got a prior engagement."

"No you haven't."

"Look, I said I'll give it some thought."

"I'll send Collins."

"That's not necessary…"

"I shouldn't need to remind you but…"

"OK." Thomas understood. "I'll be there at eleven."

Until recently in a townhouse a few streets away, at around ten minutes past midnight, Thomas Leven would lay down his pencil and place a marker between the pages on which he'd been sketching. He'd whisper a prayer - usually a sotto voce version of The Act of Contrition - before placing the book on his bedside table. Every single night, without fail, he'd reach up, stretching into the wireframe of the shade, feeling his way around the bayonet casing to find the switch, while making a mental note to start closer to the lamp next time. Those rituals, repeated with the precision of a Swiss church bell, were acts which simultaneously exasperated yet comforted Milene, the non-believer. It was as though Thomas was in possession of an inbuilt cut-out, a deactivation mechanism designed for that time each night. He would nestle into the back of Milene, his right arm draped over hers and, provided that their physical nearness did not develop into something more intimate, a straight seven hours of sleep followed. If it did, six and a half. A quick shower and then on to the office. He'd eat en route. A well adjusted creature of habit, nature had been kind to Thomas Leven.

Until recently.

It was eight thirty five. On the days when he had no doctors appointments nor physiotherapy - which he hated - Thomas slept late. Not too late, but later than he used to. Around the old tenement block, there was a ring of scaffolding and for the last six weeks or so, the workers had been carrying out repairs to the sandstone brick work. Their fine pointing - the tapping and scraping of metal on stone - was mercifully intermittent but the loud, invasive blasting, beginning each weekday at nine sharp, had become an unavoidable nuisance. Since the incident, Thomas had become practised in the art of ignoring the physical need for an early morning ablution. The medication the hospital prescribed had helped with that, and with his management of the external noise. Post discharge however, many of Thomas's long established routines had been cast aside, like the musty loungewear littering the floor of his current bedroom. Milene wouldn't have approved but his poor housekeeping was no more her business than the once random clusters of her son's toys was his.

There was no clock buried among the unopened boxes that took up much of his living space, surrounding his recliner like a cardboard fortress. A handful of magazines, a hi-fi system and a single, framed sketch of a bird was all he'd unpacked. For Thomas, time and its management had become increasingly fluid. He pulled open the heavy curtains and winced. For the first time since he'd moved into the second floor flat on the corner of Gardner Street and Partickhill Road, bright sunlight filled the room. Maybe, he thought, the dark yet comforting gloom of what seemed an aeonian winter had finally outstayed its welcome. His index and middle fingers made a pair of shallow trenches in the settled stoor on the varnished wooden window ledge.

I need to dust.

As Thomas looked out onto the new morning, every window he could see was undressed, disrobed. Life continued. Planet Earth in all of its rude glory was ready for business, even if he wasn't. The distant whirr of a slow moving car syncopated with the light rhythms of birdsong. The sounds of nature and the colours of the spring morning; the crystalline sky, the lush bowling green opposite and the ruddy sandstone of the surrounding blocks with their distinctive forest coloured sashes. Too much for his unprepared senses. He gently closed the curtains and let the darkness envelop him once more.

Only his physical scars had started to heal.

He picked up the small bottle beside the amplifier and emptied its contents into the cleanest tumbler he could find. As the valves of the amp buzzed into life, Thomas swirled the contents of the glass and sat back in the recliner awaiting the crackle of the record's opening track. The neighbours won't mind, he thought, turning the volume up high. He'd spoken with them only once and it was something about bins. He couldn't remember and given his condition, he didn't need any further aggravation. Thomas needed 'Voodoo.'

'One, Two, Three, splondge!'

****

The car arrived early. Aside from a curt but civil greeting, he didn't speak to Collins, the driver. Thomas had never been one for small talk. Milene liked that about him. Don't speak unless one has something to say. Collins took the slope slowly as the firm's sleek German saloon dropped from three to two to one. Slaloming around the potholes, the gearbox joined the car's suspension in offering a prayer of gratitude to the cautious driver.

After half a year of unremitting rain, snow and cloud, Glasgow had seemingly bypassed spring and gone for an early march on summer. On days such as this, with its skies stretched beyond translucent, Scotland's biggest city can appear to be a gloriously different place. Boxfresh, almost reborn. While smiles hadn't quite reached the faces of the city's inhabitants, their shoulders did seem less stooped. As a long term resident though, Thomas knew that Glasgow could only cope with three, maybe four days of this unseasonal but welcome weather before a strange kind of heat madness would invariably infect and incapacitate its citizens. Inevitably, chaos would follow and the rule of law which he'd once worked so diligently to uphold, would be gleefully obliterated like an empty tonic wine bottle against a wall.

Collins pulled the car onto The Royal Crescent, beyond the row of amputated trees and into the private parking space, perfectly shaded by the foliage of the last remaining, untouched oak.

"Glad to be back, Mr Leven?"

Thomas didn't respond. He raised his sunglasses and scanned the street opposite.

"Didn't there used to be a couple of phone boxes over there? Beside that lamppost?"

"The lamppost with no lamp?"

"Yes."

Collins shielded his eyes from the sun and mentally retraced the area. "I think you may be right."

Thomas had been given a walking stick by his consultant but he was reluctant to use it for a number of reasons; the primary one being that of acute embarrassment. He gripped the rail outside the Kunis Clement office and took the steps slowly. Hesitating, he wiped a bead of sweat from his forehead then pushed open the freshly painted but still tacky, heavy black door, walking into the building for the first time since his sudden departure. By the time he'd surrendered his position as lead counsel, Thomas had grown tired of defending the indefensible. While the fallout from low level gangland feuds was the firm's bread and butter, their reputation was built on the defence of the country's worst; high profile child murderers, celebrity rapists, corporate plunderers and footballers. As loathsome as their client base was, for Scotland's most ambitious legal students, a chance to work at Kunis Clement, under the watchful gaze of the firm's senior partner, Rothwell Glen, remained a desirable prospect.

"Mr Leven," said Jacqueline, the receptionist, "so lovely to see you again. I almost didn't recognise you there."

Despite looking at least ten years his senior, the bony, birdlike Jacqueline - pronounced Jacque-*line*, not Jacque-*leen* - was actually two years younger than Thomas. Once, after a company function in Dunblane, she'd made an unambiguous proposition to him, in the presence of her husband who at the time was sheltering her from the elements with a large golf umbrella. Neither party mentioned the incident again but Thomas, then devoted to Milene, kept her at arms length for the remainder of his tenure at the firm. As he added his name to the visitor's register, Jacqueline reached over her desk and placed her hand over his.

She whispered, "How you been keeping?"

"I'm well, thanks," he replied as her not-so subtle scent transported him back to that Stirlingshire car park. Thomas slowly withdrew his hand. "You?"

With her middle finger, Jacqueline traced a circle around Thomas's entry in the register.

"Now that you're back," she said quietly, "if there's anything you need, just ask."

Thomas smiled, tight lipped.

"Can I go up now?"

"She's expecting you."

Outside of the lift, an oil-covered engineer dropped a heavy wrench into the worn, soft sided trunk which bore his firm's name.

"Sorry pal. Stairs only, I'm afraid."

****

Situated on the building's third floor were the partner's offices with de facto owner Rothwell Glen's suite at the end of the hall. Known to his clients as the big dog - but to his closest colleagues as the old man - Glen was neither particularly *old* nor *big* but while he tolerated the tone of the latter, his ego preferred the more aggressive weight of the former. So acutely attuned to the importance of public perception was Glen that he'd habitually order the renovation of the firm's viscera, an expense customarily passed on to its clients. Thomas found the latest design rather anodyne and very much at odds with the memorable splendour of the ornate *Bois De Rose* panelled interior, something that had both impressed and intimidated his youthful self. No one at the firm had ever explicitly confirmed it but Thomas held the view that, for a partnership which defended some of the most heinous people the country had to offer, the optics of the refurb weren't as much to do with civic image as a regular opportunity for Kunis Clement to wipe the stain of human detritus from its surfaces.

Thomas stopped outside the office. Catching his breath - and his reflection in the glass frame of a picture - he took a moment to run his fingers through his unruly, still damp, collar length hair. Do I have to knock, he asked himself. Fuck it. A short but self-conscious rap on the door and in he walked.

By the long, open window, stood Mira Berglund. As tall as Thomas in her heels, the slim, striking Mrs Berglund was dressed in a perfectly tailored cream trouser suit which contrasted starkly with her shoulder length, raven coloured hair and some heavy but tastefully applied strokes of kohl. It was a look that belied her years. Mira had been the third and final wife of Martin Berglund. The son of Norman, founder of the Berglund haulage dynasty, Martin was fifteen years her senior and since his death, she'd lived alone in the lofty house they shared overlooking the river at Kelvin Drive.

Mira took a long drag from her unfiltered cigarette and held a rogue strand of tobacco between her tongue and her lips. Drawing it from her mouth, she exhaled slowly over the passers-by below. Thomas had known and trusted Mira since he'd first arrived at Kunis Clement as an undergraduate. While others considered her blunt to the point of rudeness, Thomas found her straight-down-the-line fair. He respected her frankness. At Rothwell Glen's right hand for decades, Mira was the only one in the firm that the old man wouldn't dare browbeat. Thomas joined her at the window. Initially, neither spoke. Mira dropped the half finished cigarette into her coffee cup and continued to stare out towards the golden dome of the Gurdwara at the back of Fitzroy Place.

"It's actually quite beautiful, don't you think?" she asked. "Have you ever looked at it?"

Thomas nodded. "Sure."

"No. Up close, I mean?"

"Can't say that I have."

"Of course, from a distance, it's impressive but at close quarters, the quality of the workmanship takes one's breath away. It's all in the detail," cooed Mira. "You know, when the Temple was in the planning stages, we were very supportive, publicly of course. Behind the scenes though, the old man did all he could to block it. He still hates it but I guess it has grown on me."

Mira's voice was throaty and retained the faintest trace of her Middle Eastern roots.

"That's the pull of the almighty," replied Thomas.

"In all of its wonderful guises," chuckled Mira, ruefully. She leant over and kissed Thomas on both cheeks.

"You're looking...awful," she tutted. "The beard doesn't suit. It ages you. And that hair."

"Lovely to see you too, Mira," returned Thomas.

"And you're out of shape," she said, patting him on the stomach. "Is that a little pot belly? You've not been eating the right things. I'll have Jacqueline make up a fresh batch of her soup. With roots and kale. You like kale?"

"I do."

He didn't.

"Perfect."

"How's Milene?" Thomas blurted, unable to contain his curiosity.

Mira arched an eyebrow.

"I told her you were coming in."

"And?"

"And what?"

"Did she say anything?"

"Nothing in particular," Mira said with a shrug.

Thanks for the pep talk, thought Thomas.

"Look, I just wanted to thank you for everything…and the flat."

"Did you know that it was the first place the old man bought for the company?"

"I knew they had a few places but I didn't realise that Kunis Clement had moved into the property game."

"Diversification. The old man's idea but it's a good one."

Makes sense.

"He always had a couple on the go, just out of interest, but when the markets wobbled a few years back, he started cherry picking some more. Now we own more private housing stock than the big five agents combined."

"That, I did not know," replied Thomas.

From Saracen Street to the Gallowgate, Kunis Clement had been snapping up solid, well built but neglected buildings. A sand blasting company - in which Rothwell Glen had an undeclared interest - would clean the front of the building and once the debt collection agency - also owned by the old man - circumvented the legalities and forced out the undesirable tenants, a fresh coat of paint for the close and a new electric entry system would be put in place. Basic modifications, but always with the burden of a market rate cost handed straight to the new tenants. As for the ground floor commercial units, Mira explained that Kunis Clement raised the rents just enough to price out the low level gangsters who owned the electronic cigarette shops and the tanning salons. Once they'd completed that stage, a maintenance company would strip back the interior to brick, hang some post-ironic art and suddenly a previously unloved shop was a potential gold mine.

"You know what the old man's new favourite word is?" Mira asked, with a chuckle.

"Crypto?"

"Artisan," she replied. "Apply that silly little word to the livery of a café or an eatery and one can basically charge what one wants. Shabby chic has come to the shitholes and everyone loves it."

"Except for the e-cigarette smokers."

"Fuck them," said Mira, taking a long draw. "It's a filthy habit. Those mouthbreathers have no idea the damage they're doing to themselves."

"So you're doing them a public service?"

"I hadn't considered it a social experiment until now but I suppose when an entire city has swapped an afternoon in the bookmakers for carrot cake and a cortado, I will have a contented glow. You're welcome, Glasgow."

Thomas nodded, impressed.

"Let the golden Gods have the sky," continued Mira. "We'll control the streets. First you take Duke Street, then you take Kirklee. The Chinese may have cornered the market on the new builds but we own the rest of the West. It's true. What we do, what we've become, our business… it's all a bit pointless."

"Our entire legal system? Pointless?"

"It lacks real clout. And money will only take one so far. Without property in this city, you're just a bum."

Mira took another cigarette from her case and lit it. She offered one to Thomas.

"No offence meant…"

He declined the cigarette.

"The flat, though… it's comfortable enough for you?"

Thomas hesitated. "Em…yeah. It's perfect Mira. Again, I appreciate everything you and the old man did for me after the … you know."

"We won't consider letting it out until the entire refurb is complete so you're good for a while yet," she stressed. "Come, sit with me for a moment."

Thomas joined Mira on the low backed leather sofa.

"Your input at Kunis Clement has been missed. You do know that despite his … flintiness, Rothwell is quite fond of you. Always has been. He's not the cunt that people think he is."

Thomas, surprised by Mira's profane candour, snorted awkwardly. *He may be a cunt but he did give me a break,* he thought. *I do owe him. But why does he want to see me? And why now?*

Mira nodded then clapped her hands. "So, to business."

"Mira, as I said, I appreciate the flat, the retainer and how you cleared things up after…" Thomas paused, awkwardly. "I really do but I'm still recovering. And as much as I'd love to be considered for a partnership, I'm not sure I'm fit enough at this stage to return. I'd be happy to consult…"

Mira shook her head and exhaled.

"We…he needs your help on something in particular."

"Is he in trouble?"

"Did you read what I sent you?"

"I glanced at it," replied Thomas.

Mira knew he was lying.

"What can you tell me about Angus John MacMillan?"

"THE Angus John MacMillan?" asked Thomas, confused.

"Yes."

"Is he looking for a flat?"

Mira ignored Thomas's glib comment and took another long drag of her cigarette.

"Where to begin?" he said.

Thomas sat back and ran his hands through his hair. Given the University's association with the MacMillan case, it was no surprise that the sitting Principal and Vice-Chancellor had overruled the tutors, considering it too raw and personal to be dissected with the requisite amount of detachment and dispassion. Nevertheless, the affair was a subject most of Thomas' class was familiar with.

"MacMillan is up there with Bible John and Peter Manuel as one of this country's most notorious murderers. Two confirmed but evidence at the time suggested that he may have been involved in the deaths of up to seven, possibly eight people. The trial was front page news for weeks."

"Months," said Mira.

"It was an incredibly high profile case which didn't do the firm's reputation any harm. Naturally, I was too young to remember much about it at the time but I do have vague memories of the TV dramatisation. My mother watched it. The press pushed that whole devil worshipping, cannibalistic sex cult angle quite hard. Some of the names they gave him though were classic tabloid stuff."

"Yes," replied Mira, "The Demon of Dowanhill, The Creature of Clarence Drive…"

"Indeed," laughed Thomas. "The Merchant of Menace was my favourite but it merely firmed public opinion against him. The old man was his appointed counsel but inexplicably, MacMillan offered no defence. Declared clinically insane by the judge, Lord Ferguson, MacMillan was sentenced to three consecutive life terms, with no recourse to parole. Locked up in the state's secure unit at Kirkmalcolm from where he disappeared in 1991?"

"1992," replied Mira.

"Never to be seen again."

Mira stubbed her cigarette out and returned to the window. "Yesterday evening, Angus John MacMillan walked into Stewart Street police station and surrendered himself to the custody sergeant."

Thomas's mouth fell open. He exhaled dramatically. "You've got to be kidding?"

Mira turned to Thomas and shook her head.

"He only spoke to confirm his name and the unit he'd absconded from."

"Why didn't I hear about this? It wasn't on the news or in the papers. Not that I've been..."

"The story would've broken but for the intervention of Chief Superintendent Ames and some of our friends in the Scottish Office. The embargo ends today. By tea time, the world will know that the notorious Demon of Dowanhill is back in custody."

Thomas's mind flooded with questions.

"Where has he been? Why did he hand himself in? And why now?"

"That's what we need to find out," she replied.

"Does the old man know?"

"He does."

"And?"

"Despite everything, he still has great confidence in you."

Thomas's throat dried. "Mira, there are any number of excellent lawyers at Kunis Clement's disposal. Sam Cleary, for one. He's perfect for this kind of thing. Or Vanessa...what's her name…"

"No," said Mira, sitting down. "It has to be you."

"Why?"

"Because Angus John MacMillan has explicitly indicated that he will only speak to Thomas Leven."

Chapter 2 - Bowls

"Collins will help you with the files."

Three boxes. Easy enough for a middle aged driver to carry, less so for a younger man still nursing a number of battered bones.

"Where do you want them, Mr Leven?" the driver asked, his rolled up shirt sleeves revealing a pair of faded tattoos on his tanned, muscular forearms. Collins had been a Kunis Clement chauffeur since Thomas was a teenage intern, at a time when his school motto - *ad majora natus sum* - I was born for greater things - was a dictum he still held true.

"Over here," the younger man replied, breathing deeply. He took his stick from the door handle, and propped it against the wall. Thomas opened the curtains and cleared space on the table which perfectly fit the contours of the bay window.

The driver placed a box on the table and gazed down at the bowling green below. "That is a lovely view you've got, Mr Leven. Ever play?"

"No," replied Thomas, washing down his medication with

water. "Can't say that I have."

"Very relaxing. Partickhill's a good club, I know it well but there's plenty of quality greens around here. I've been a member over at Shawbridge for a few years now but in my younger days, Fortrose, Polwarth Street, Willow Bank, I played all over the West End. A couple of ends then a pint or twelve afterwards. Jeez, the things we got up to. I could write a book about those days."

Collins returned to the present. "Not the worst way to spend a sunny afternoon."

"I could imagine."

"Especially, if you don't mind me saying so, you need to build up your strength."

Thomas did mind but he didn't show it. His 'condition' was his business, not the company's and certainly not that of any of its employees.

"I've got it from here," he said, ushering Collins out. "Thanks for your help."

"I'm always around if you ever fancy giving it a go," continued the driver, rolling down his sleeves and buttoning his cuffs. "Just give me a shout."

Thomas smiled and closed the door. The trauma specialist had told him that even beyond those crucial early months of recovery, it wasn't wise to put his still damaged body under any undue strain. After the previous week's check up confirmed that he'd been healing well, Thomas knew that today's two-pronged nudge at his nervous system was going to be the first true test of his physical worth.

Lifting the lid from the first box, he removed its contents.

Four files, held tightly shut by pink four-way rubber bands. At Kunis Clement, anyone wishing to read material such as this would have to have good reason to do so. Even the partners, for the sake of transparency, had to sign and date an accompanying docket in order to read sensitive or classified documents. The dockets belonging to the files of Angus John MacMillan however, had been removed. Thomas looked inside the box again. Nothing.

He tugged at one of the rubber bands. It was taut, brand new. If this was the original, from thirty years earlier, surely it would be brittle? Maybe someone else had wanted to refamiliarise themselves with the MacMillan case.

Separating the paperwork into the order in which he wanted to read it, Thomas popped two brightly coloured capsules and cracked open the seal on a fresh bottle of morphine sulfate. Milene wouldn't approve, he thought as the clear, bittersweet liquid coated his throat.

Fuck Milene.

Chapter 3 - Kirkmalcolm

"Open the lines of communication, find out where he's been and what he wants. That's it. Once he's given you that, make your excuses."

"Should I push him for information on the location of the missing bodies?"

"That's more a job for the police. You remember Campbell Ames?"

Thomas did. The Chief Superintendent was one of the old man's regular golfing partners.

"He'll have a team working on that," said Mira. "Call me when you're done. I want this taken care of before the old man returns. Remember, MacMillan's dangerous so don't get too close. He was resident in Kirkmalcolm for a reason, don't forget that."

"I won't," he replied. "Who'll be joining me?"

Thomas recalled that when an inmate was interviewed by a senior counsel, it was company policy to appoint a junior lawyer to assist. In keeping with the firm's convoluted fiscal practice though, the client would still be charged prime rates for two experienced counsels. If the client was satisfied with the outcome, the firm found that they rarely returned with a demand for an itemised breakdown. Some 'fresh meat' from Kunis Clement's conveyor belt of hungry young advocates would willingly do the leg work so that Thomas could concentrate on the serious business of getting high.

"It shouldn't be that complicated but if you're struggling, we'll send someone down to hold your hand."

Thomas felt his cheeks redden. Not that his embarrassment would have mattered to Mira, he was nevertheless glad she was on the other end of the line and not there in person. "That's not what I meant, Mira. You know...it's been a while."

"The old man has great faith in you," said Mira, dismissing his concerns. "They're expecting you at Kirkmalcolm at eleven. Officially, you've been given access until two but I can't imagine that it'll take more than an hour or so."

****

Thomas placed the phone on the seat beside him, sat back and watched as the urban gave way to the rural. Collins, the tattooed chauffeur of the previous day, had been replaced. Today's wheel man was Piotr. Tall and pale, expressionless and most importantly, silent, Piotr was roughly the same age as Thomas but worked harder on maintaining his physique than his passenger did. Not only was Piotr the old man's regular driver, he was considered by the partners at Kunis Clement a handy first line in security.

Thomas looked at his watch. Plenty of time. He dipped into the inside pocket of his jacket and took another couple of capsules from the small plastic pill box. As he sipped his water, his thoughts returned to Milene. Following the crash, she had not only moved out of the house they'd shared but had broken off all contact with him. Last he'd heard was that she'd taken a post at a hospital in London. He didn't want to push Mira on it. Still too early. He closed his eyes and wished that she was back tending to his wounds instead of those of others.

****

The secure unit at Kirkmalcolm was located a few miles from the heel of Loch Ericht in the Grampian mountains. Built on nearly four hundred acres of land reluctantly surrendered by the Duke of Blair for an unpublished indiscretion, the unit, opened in 1966 and dubbed 'The Monster Mansion' by the press, was not, by design, an easy place to get to and in theory, an even harder place to escape from.

Although he wasn't the first inmate to attempt to leave the institution before the end of his sentence - that 'honour' fell to James Hamill and Thomas Cline, a romantically involved pair who murdered a guard and a nurse before being gunned down just short of the second fence - Angus John MacMillan had been the only detainee to successfully broach the unit's series of walls and evade its sensored trenches and electrified fences. How he achieved this though was almost as much a mystery as the motivation behind the murders in the first place. Given the nature of the place, men like MacMillan were kept apart from other captives. He exercised alone, he ate alone. Due to the severity of his crimes, the unit's governors insisted on MacMillan being given his own security detail. An eight man team, working in pairs, split over three shifts ensured that even his limited movements remained closely monitored.

The cell he'd occupied for the five years prior to his disappearance was, to the chagrin of the national media, surprisingly comfortable and far from standard. Six metres long and three quarters again as wide. A small, neat couch with cushions at the foot of a steel framed queen-sized bed which was bolted through the short pile carpet to the floor. In the only non carpeted area of the room was a small metal toilet and adjoining corner sink. There were skirting to ceiling radiators either side of a security toughened window which looked out towards the snow coated peak of Ben Alder.

Upon arrival, MacMillan had spoken only to request two items; a set of encyclopaedias and a television. As the cell was intended to be his accommodation for the remainder of his life, the governors agreed to both appeals. MacMillan spent a week in smaller, more spartan quarters while the solid stone walls of his permanent chamber were chipped away to accommodate a rudimentary bookcase and the housing of a small television set.

****

Rocking, rocking…

For much of the previous decade, Thomas considered himself a fit man but when the hits became harder and the appeal of the clubhouse japery started to wane, he'd swapped rugby for the more solitary pastime of orienteering. Thomas subsequently spent years plotting courses throughout the unspoilt Scottish woodlands until a misjudgment on the distance between a grounded branch and the stony earth severely strained his achilles tendon and put a halt on his regular wild runs. And without a replacement, his physique began to feel the burden. You should try swimming. Low impact, people said. Help maintain your fitness. But Thomas had always feared the water. On trips back to her native Bergen, Milene would gently tease him about his reluctance to join her and her son in the cool, fresh waters around Nordåsvannet. He never revealed to her that as a cautious, solitary child, he was thrown into a pool by his father, with the intention of teaching him to swim. Thomas froze. He gave in. That feeling, the never ending sinking sensation, watching the diminishing silhouette stand, hand on hips at the edge of the pool while darkness consumed him, was always present. Thomas didn't share his father's rugged outlook.

Rocking, rocking…

In the hours following the crash, he'd had vague memories of Milene coming to see him. Given the medication that was darting through his veins, he wasn't sure if the visitations were real or imagined. During one such 'visit', Milene wept and that was something she never did. The boy, he asked. The boy? Shhh, she said. Maybe we'll run together. When you are well. Maybe…

"Shouldn't be too long now, Mr Leven," said the taciturn driver, his voice drawing Thomas from his slumber.

Thomas rubbed his eyes and pulled himself into an upright position. His legs were stiff and where his head rested against the window, the still raised scarring felt tender. Instinctively, he reached for his satchel. Two mouthfuls will take the edge off. He looked across the water. The small stone tower of Eilean nam Fiolaig confirmed to him the location. Situated off the banks of the loch was an old cottage where he had once spent an idyllic weekend with Milene, running and fucking. But mainly fucking. The car slowed to make a sharp right-hand turn. On the grass verges either side of the road were two large squad cars making sure that the gathered media scrum could go no further.

The road to the unit was tight with space only for one vehicle and no obvious passing points. The only things that differentiated this from any number of country roads in the area were the dark green poles behind the tall hedges, upon which were mounted the security cameras.

Ahead of a large, well maintained wire fence, the driver pulled up and pressed the button on the intercom.

"Mr Leven from Kunis Clement," he said. Seconds later, the mechanical gate rolled to the side and the driver continued slowly along the route. A half mile later, there was another fence. Again, Thomas's driver spoke to confirm the appointment and again, the gate rolled open. They'd only been driving another minute or so when they reached their third gate. This time, the post was manned.

"Mr Leven from Kunis Clement," repeated Piotr.

"Mr Who?"

"Leven from Kunis Clement."

The sentry guard ran a finger down his list. He flipped over the page and repeated the motion.

"Sorry Sir. I don't understand what you're saying. If you don't mind me asking, what accent is that?"

The driver unbuckled and was about to get out of the car when Thomas reached over and stopped him. He wound down his window and asked, "Can I see the list, please?"

"I'm afraid not, Sir. The list of visitors is classified."

"Could you please check again? It is quite important."

"Sir, with respect," said the guard, leaning on the roof of the car, "everyone who comes to Kirkmalcolm is here for something important."

Pushing up the brim of his hat, he continued. "Before they put the polis at the turning, you'd be surprised how many day trippers would treat this like it was a safari park for the insane. A toasted brie panini and a frothy cappuccino, please. Keep your windows rolled up and no harm will come to you, kind of thing. And given who we've got here, I wouldn't be doing my job properly if I didn't make sure that wasn't the case, now would I?" he said, pausing for affirmation.

"Absolutely. Making sure is your business," said Thomas handing over a headed letter from Chief Superintendent Ames.

The guard's eyes enlarged. "Bringing in the big guns, eh? Let's have a look at that list again. Here it is. Eleven a.m. Mr Leven...ahhh...*Kunis Clement*. You should've said. Straight ahead, Sir."

As with the exterior of the building, the reception area had the feel of a 1960's secondary school. Burnished parquet, the smell of disinfectant and a long, wide red brick corridor which ran straight behind the horseshoe shaped reception desk, seated behind which was a man Thomas thought looked two parts guard to three parts librarian.

"A member of staff will be with you shortly, Mr Leven."

From behind a coded door, appeared Officer Rodgers. A broad, brutish looking man whose hooded lids were cast so far from the bridge of his nose that Thomas thought he resembled a suspicious fish.

"I saw from the questionnaire that the Governor sent to you that you'd prefer to speak with the prisoner face to face and not from behind the protective screen," said the guard in a brusque manner. "We'd recommend that you reconsider, Mr Leven. I have to remind you that most civilians would consider our inmates at Kirkmalcolm a touch volatile."

"Will the prisoner be secured?"

Rodgers confirmed that he would.

"Then there's no reason to believe that he'll be a threat to us."

While Thomas was used to speaking with miscreants with unpredictable behaviour, he acknowledged Mira's warning that MacMillan's crimes were on a different level. Still, he knew that any show of fear might be taken by the prisoner as a sign of weakness. Thomas needed to show that he was in charge, for his benefit as much as for MacMillan's.

The guard grunted in disapproval. "Your choice, sir. I will need you to sign a waiver though."

"Will Mr Armour be joining us today?"

"I'm afraid not, Mr Leven," said Rodgers. "The Governor has been called away on personal business. Very short notice. He does send his apologies."

"Not a problem."

As a junior guard opened the door, Rodgers entered the room alone. After carrying out his check, he nodded to his colleague.

Thomas followed Rodgers into the airless, brightly lit room. On the far wall was a table, fixed with a bolted plate. The tabletop was clear. The guard didn't look directly at the shackled man sitting opposite but Thomas did. Recently trimmed reddish brown hair, grey temples and above his jawline, a freckled but clear complexion. Around his left eye there was obvious and fresh bruising and a raw, seeping scrape on the side of his nose. Of medium height and build and hidden under a pale grey jumpsuit, MacMillan's blue eyes stood out against the bruising.

Soft blue eyes.

There was a vague familiarity but now, Thomas thought, MacMillan looked more like a hospital orderly on a break than Scotland's most dangerous convict. He made an attempt to stand but the fixed harness held him tight.

"It's all a bit much, don't you think?" said Angus John MacMillan, quietly.

"Excuse me?"

"The checkpoints and guards and this stuff. A tad over the top, if you ask me."

Despite being perplexed by the incongruous comment, Thomas didn't react.

"So you must be, the great white hope…"

"Thomas Leven," he said, taking charge of the conversation. "I'm sorry I'm late, Mr MacMillan."

"It's understandable. When the circus is back in town, traffic around here can be murder." MacMillan smiled. "A little levity to break the ice. Who said monsters can't be fun?"

"You consider yourself a monster?"

MacMillan snorted.

"Tell me, Mr Leven," he asked, leaning forward. "Have you heard of Bobs Roberts?"

Thomas glanced over at Rodgers whose shrug of the shoulders was willfully ignorant.

"By that expression I'd say that you haven't. Never mind. Frederick Roberts was a heavily decorated British military campaigner of the Victorian era. Affectionately known as 'Bobs', this Eton educated Field Marshall inspired not only unswerving loyalty from his troops but numerous tributes from luminaries of the day, including one in the form of a sentimental, colloquial poem composed by Rudyard Kipling."

"I'm sorry, I don't follow."

"During the Second Boer War, Roberts had an inspired idea to use prisoners as human shields. If that wasn't enough, he also became a prime mover in the establishment of the modern concentration camp, which led to the death of over twenty five thousand women and children in South Africa."

"Again, Mr MacMillan…"

"Today, Field Marshal Frederick Roberts sits atop his mount, proudly looking southwest over Glasgow's Kelvingrove Park, a city with which he and his family had no obvious link, yet *I'm* considered a monster?" MacMillan shook his head. "No, Mr Leven, I am the son of the barren rock on which I was born, nothing more."

"Again, apologies for my tardiness," said Thomas, changing direction. "First things first. Would you like to talk about that bump you've taken?"

"Oh this?" he said, turning his gaze back towards Rodgers.

"Did the injury occur prior to your incarceration or since?"

"Would you think me disingenuous if I said that I slipped over in the shower? Seriously, Mr Leven, it's nothing for you to worry about. I'm a very forgiving man."

"That's reassuring to hear," replied Thomas, staring.

"When it comes to my God, however, that's a different matter." MacMillan clapped his hands, startling Thomas and the guards. The steel restraints which attached his wrists to the chain wrapped around his torso chimed against the rim of the table. "Would you like something to drink? Maybe a pot of tea?"

"Excuse me?"

"Raymond, would you be so kind as to fetch us a brew? I'm parched and I can only imagine how thirsty you are in this weather with that big hat on."

"Mr MacMillan, you know we can't do that," said the junior guard.

"A latte, perhaps? Or maybe a flat white. Now, who doesn't love a flat white?"

"MacMillan," snapped Rodgers. "That's enough."

"Alright," he replied, leaning over again. "I'd expected a rise in the standards during my absence. Pity."

"Shall we start with that absence, Mr MacMillan?"

"What's the rush? Surely we should kick off with a little

'getting to know each other' kinda thing, don't you think? Hi, I'm Angus John. Fifty something year old Gemini. I love short haired cats, long walks on the beach and thirty odd years ago, I was convicted of murdering a whole bunch of very interesting people. Your turn."

"Mr MacMillan, please," interrupted the junior guard, his face reddening.

"Lighten up, Raymond. Don't worry yourself. Did you know that stress is the number one killer of men your age? Not cancer, not car crashes, not even psychopathic murderers. Stress."

Both guards glared at the prisoner.

MacMillan put his hands up and closed his eyes. "OK, you win."

"Shall we begin?" said Thomas firmly.

"Fire away."

"If it's ok with you, there's a few questions that need to be answered before we proceed. Firstly…"

"How's the boy?"

"I beg your pardon?"

"The boy. The one who was in the crash."

Thomas sat back. "That's not relevant…"

"I understand but I'd just like to know what happened."

"Eh…he's fine. Fully recovered, thank you."

"That's a relief. Terrifying for him, I suppose."

"Yeah…"

"And for you."

MacMillan's question had rattled Thomas. For someone

with a track record of being uncommunicative, the intimacy had taken Thomas by surprise. Mira had warned him to be on his guard.

"OK, Mr MacMillan," said Thomas. "As the legal representative you requested, I'm duty bound to advise you that everything you say in this room will remain confidential."

"Only in this room?"

"Why?"

"Because, to tell you the truth, I'm not feeling it here." MacMillan made a clacking noise with his mouth. "Do you hear that?"

Thomas put his pen down before realising he'd left it within MacMillan's reach.

"The acoustics in here are terrible. I presume that your device is recording?"

The illuminated red dot on his phone confirmed that it was.

"Listen back. Go on."

Thomas played back the recording.

MacMillan had a point.

"You couldn't possibly use that. No, I'm afraid this room won't do. Rodgers, get on the phone to the governor. We need another room."

"Mr MacMillan, you're in no position to demand…"

"Oh, I think that I am," replied MacMillan, his mood darkening. "Would you prefer it if I stamped my feet and started screaming indecently? That is what you're expecting from me, isn't it? Give your boys a good reason to have a proper pop at me this time."

MacMillan turned to Thomas. "Maybe, given my history, I could break out my greatest hits?"

"Mr MacMillan?"

"Some ungodly assistance, Thomas," he replied with relish. "Do you possess faith?"

"That's enough, MacMillan."

The prisoner ignored Rodgers and continued.

"And does that faith still hold true? Provided your intentions are honourable, you have nothing to worry about. Are you pure of heart, Thomas Leven? In the half dark, when you return to your home, you close the doors and draw the curtains. Do you call out to your God in the half dark and beg his forgiveness? As your chest heaves with the shallow breath of your guilt. Suspiria de profundis. For everything that you've done and all that you've lost. Does he come? If not, then who does? Who comes to your aid? Who do you see, Thomas? Tell me, who do you see? Are you a slave to the impulses?"

Thomas stared at MacMillan.

"This one is," he said genially, breaking the tension. "Aren't you, Raymond?"

A combination of frustration, embarrassment and rage told on the junior guard's face.

"Actually, Raymond's a decent sort," said MacMillan. "There's no malice in him. His colleagues though…"

Rodgers returned the prisoner's glare with interest.

"I'll give them this, they do know how to keep a prisoner in check. Some of their methods though. A little too twentieth century for my current tastes," said MacMillan. "You've read the files, Mr Leven. I'd be very interested to hear your views on my mental state."

"I don't believe that's for me to say, Mr MacMillan but…"

MacMillan started clacking again.

"Raymond, can you inform Governor Armour, that we're done?" he said, wearily. "Interview terminated at…" he looked at the clock above his counsel.

"11.31am."

Raymond nodded and turned to the intercom behind the door.

"It's the little things," whispered MacMillan. "You start by thinking that they're just the little things. And as we're all told, the little things don't matter. Don't worry about it. That's what the cards and the mugs and those mass produced works of art say, don't they? Don't sweat the small stuff. Then one day, you start to piece it together and you know what? The little things were the big things all along."

"Mr Leven," said Rodgers, "I think it's best that you come with us while we clear this up."

MacMillan rattled the chain holding him in place. "No rush. I'm not going anywhere."

Thomas stood.

"Forgetting something?" MacMillan slowly pushed Thomas's pen back across the table. "I wouldn't advise you to do that again."

After being escorted from the room, the lawyer, in bewildered silence, took a seat in the corridor.

"That was a bit…"

"Intense?" replied Raymond.

Thomas nodded.

"Just think what he could have done with that pen," the guard said with a slight shudder.

But Thomas knew it wasn't the pen that MacMillan was referring to.

As he was escorted back to his cell, MacMillan shouted back, "Bright as a button tomorrow Thomas, you understand? Your instincts are of no use to me if they're buried in a narcoleptic cloud."

Chapter 4 - Clarence Drive

"Anywhere here will do," said Thomas as the car drove up Clarence Drive, pulling into a free space opposite a cluster of shops. Waiting for a break in the traffic and still stiff from the journey back from Kirkmalcolm, Thomas hobbled across the road to Middleton's Pharmacy. The shop was small but bustling.

"Busy today, eh?" he asked, handing over a prescription.

"Lead up to the Bank Holiday is always busy," replied the girl with a smile. "How's your day been, Mr Clark?"

Mr Clark. There was a reason Thomas Leven chose to hand over his script at this pharmacy at that precise time. Mr Clark. There were chemists all over the west end of the city but Thomas had narrowed it down to the handful that he trusted. The larger chains were busier but they carried more staff which meant that they had more time and with that, there was a greater chance of a hand-written script and a fake identity being questioned. The smaller ones tended to know their patients *too* well. Middleton's was ideal.

The café three doors down from the pharmacy had been

Milene's favourite. On Sunday mornings, as her son received under nine's futsal coaching from a Brazilian libero recently freed by Greenock Morton, he'd started to forgo morning mass to join her for a late breakfast under the canopy. Since she'd left, and his week had become less structured, Thomas would find a booth upstairs, away from the counter and the kitchen, in the more secluded section of the café. When he was quite sure no one was watching, he'd double check the contents of the crisp, white paper bag that the pharmacy dispenser had just handed to him.

Note to self. Need to stop thinking of Milene.

Even the most surreal of re-introductions to the world of legal counsel couldn't prevent his mind slipping into thoughts of how good she felt. She fit his hands perfectly. Now, she was tending to someone else.

I wish her dead. No. That's too far. Incapacitated. Like me. So she'd understand. She *would* understand.

Thomas popped two pink capsules into his mouth and washed them down. He groaned as the still piping hot tea burned his tongue and throat. His stomach was empty.

"A croissant to take away, please. It's ok, I've got a bag."

Fifteen minutes and counting before the first wave of the modified release hits.

Slowing down. Legs already weighty. Home in less than ten. If the flat could be considered home. But that's all I've got. I should unpack. Tired. Tired and sore. I'll sleep for an hour. Maybe two, then I'll unpack some more. Don't want to think about MacMillan at the moment. He can wait. Need sounds. No Tubby Hayes this time though. The Mars Volta. Milene hated them.

By the time Thomas made Partickhill, the first bursts of the morphine were starting to explode into his bloodstream. The unseasonal rays burnished his tender skin as the shelter of the close approached.

"Hiya," came the voice. Friendly but needy. "Hiya!"

Thomas wasn't capable of a conversation now. Don't turn around. Keep walking. Keys. Concentrate. Don't look around.

Door opened. Door closed. Door locked. Double locked. Key in lock, turned to an angle. Bag on table. Keep the lights off. Just lie down. Jacket off. On the bed. Hand on cock. Reach under pillow. Cover face. Breathe her in. Stay awake. Finish off. Don't sleep yet. The hand which used to reach down her unbuttoned trousers, clutching the one she'd loved the most. It was always mine.

Since the incident, the headaches and the paralysis that had occasionally afflicted Thomas' sleep had taken a firmer grip, manifesting in a number of unusual forms. The milder versions would result in a brief, but tense panic which stretched the sinews of his gut. At their most acute though, they made him feel as if he was frozen, balanced on the lip of a window sill, fifteen stories high, or worse, sinking like a stone, as he had as a child, under the surface of the water. Regardless of the instance, Thomas had a foreboding sense that he wasn't experiencing this phenomenon alone. And those episodes were becoming more frequent and more vivid.

The end is the end for some. But the beginning for others. Awaken your dead people. Ask their forgiveness.
What was that?

You know, I wasn't sure but I see it now. Those eyes. Unmistakable. Your mother…

Hello?

Thomas lay in the darkness, perfectly still, his eyes adjusted to the failing light. The voices, immusical and dissonant, fell silent as the paralysis subsided. He couldn't see Milene's t-shirt by his head but he could still detect the smell of her body from it. Thomas turned to the side. How long would that scent remain? Weeks? Days? Once it was gone…

He pushed it back under the pillow and slowly swivelled his legs round. Although the Tramadol capsules, Amitriptyline tablets and bottles of liquid morphine helped to dull the sharp edge of his paralysis - and its accompanying anxiety - the worst thing Thomas had discovered about the medication was the hangovers that they delivered. The music had long stopped but his mind, still locked in, played its final strains on repeat.

His phone told him that it was gone eight in the evening but his stomach already knew that. He pulled back the curtain, took a seat at the window and ate the remainder of his croissant, dry. Thomas checked his phone. After the accident, and Milene's departure, he'd expected that the calls and the social interactions would dry up. Checking his phone was another reminder that she wasn't coming back. An unknown number? Odd. Turning his thoughts back to Angus John MacMillan, again Thomas wondered, why now and more importantly, why me?

He surveyed the street below. The soft light of the Glasgow evening beckoned to him. Perfect for a rare night time walk, among the ever living monuments to a lost life. The nebbish neighbour who tried to greet him earlier was now dressed in shorts and a brightly coloured, sweat soaked t-shirt which bore the legend; 'Atomkraft - Nein Danke'. Since he'd been forced to stop running, Thomas had grown to detest casual joggers and judging by his neighbour's physique, he was certainly that. He'd briefly met Derry - or Gerry - in the close one morning, cleaning the felt-tipped word 'cunt' from the paintwork above the tiles. Someone had used a purple marker, the kind one finds in an unwanted shoebox filled with kids toys and lost jigsaw pieces that some wronged mother had forgotten to take with her when she left. Thomas was particularly bad at remembering names. 'Derry Gerry' was speaking with an older woman.

The table vibrated and Thomas's phone shuddered. It was Mira.

"Well?" she asked.

"I don't know. It was quite surreal."

"I can imagine. Did you get anything?"

"No, not yet. Did you know that he'd been beaten?"

"Campbell Ames did mention something. How badly?"

"Looks like he took a few sore ones to the face."

"I can't say I'm surprised. I'd imagine that the authorities wouldn't have been too thrilled about his escape."

"And the fact that they weren't the ones who found him."

"Precisely," replied Mira. "Have another go tomorrow."

"Sure."

"It won't be easy but maybe try to push him a little."

"Will do."

"Just take care. Remember why he's there."

Because he handed himself in?

"Call me when you're done."

From the window, he could see his neighbour and the older woman look up in tandem. He closed the phone's cover and darkness returned to the room. Thomas leant back, out of the light. Out of sight.

Chapter 5 - Argyle

Mince and potatoes. That smell. Unmistakable. Given that he'd woken up late and went straight from the shower to the car without eating, Thomas' stomach felt as if his throat had been cut. More than the low rumble of feet on boards and the distant chatter in the corridors, the savoury bouquet emanating from the direction of the prison's kitchen transported him back to the stark, unforgiving institution of his youth.

Fish on a Friday was the only meal he'd habitually take from school. The rest of the week, a lunch box containing some fruit and a sandwich was prepared for him each morning by his mother. Seeded bread, with ham, or cheese and pickle. Sometimes tuna or occasionally, if there was any left over after one of his father's meetings, some smoked salmon on white bread, dry and curled up at the edges. Out in the yard, as a confident, detached clique of pupils with unbounded means compared the contents of their ipod playlists, among the less financially assured the horse trading would begin. Unconsciously mimicking behaviours witnessed at home, these fledgling exchanges, usually concerning externally sourced foodstuffs, often turned as nasty as the business done by their parents. Thomas, positioned somewhere in between the two camps, remained detached, focused more on sketching the uncaged avians than the human zoo below.

It cost his parents seven thousand pounds a year to send him to St Saviour's College but all Thomas Leven really wanted was the mince and potatoes.

"Mr Leven…"

In the corridor just beyond the reception desk, a young woman stood up. Petite and soberly dressed, she straightened the hem of her knee length skirt and tucked a stray, unbound curl back behind her ear. Despite her professional appearance, she was clearly not long out of one such educational establishment herself. She offered her hand to Thomas.

"Good morning Mr Leven."

"Hi," replied Thomas. "And you are?"

"I'm sorry, Mr Leven. Didn't Mrs Berglund inform you about me? She said that you might need some assistance."

"Are you a junior at the firm?"

"No, Mr Leven. Kaitlin Ramsay. I'm your paralegal."

"Have we met before?"

"We've worked together."

"On what?"

"Nothing major but when I was an intern, I did some research for you on Calderwood versus Her Majesty's Advocate."

"Oh sure. Kaitlin. Yes, I remember now," he lied.

"Can I help you with those?"

"No, I've got it," he said, clutching his satchel. Thomas stared at Kaitlin. So familiar, he thought.

She caught him staring. Thomas began to blush.

"Your hair was lighter then, wasn't it?" he said, moving the subject away from his embarrassment.

"That's right," she replied. "I was a mousey wee thing with a few piercings."

"Piercings, right…" said Thomas, still racking his brains.

"Still do," said Kaitlin. "Four, actually but I make sure they're not visible during work hours."

"Not so mousey now," muttered Thomas.

"Mr Leven?"

"Nothing. Just thinking out loud," he blushed again. Despite his appearance and his success with the opposite sex, at least with Milene, Thomas remained awkward around women. Milene once intimated to a friend that while Thomas possessed all the necessary components, it was she who'd delivered him the instruction manual.

****

"This is better, don't you think?"

Thomas didn't respond to MacMillan as he surveyed the warmer, cosier secondary interview suite.

"We'll be here for a while."

The young paralegal, seated to the lawyer's right, whispered the word, 'record'. Thomas turned the device towards the prisoner and pressed the button on the screen. He stated the date.

"Thomas Leven on behalf of Kunis Clement speaking with Angus John MacMillan. Is it alright to begin with a few questions that I think are pertinent to the current situation?"

"Pertinent…"

"I'd like to know why…"

"Let's start today with 1986," interrupted MacMillan.

"The year you left the island?"

"That is correct."

"Can I ask why you want to start there? Why not 1992?"

"Or the day of my birth? I do remember that."

"You remember being born?" puffed Thomas.

"That and before. In my mother's womb. I was perfectly happy there. Her touch, I could feel. When I wanted to hear her voice, I'd move so she'd sing songs to soothe me. I would've stayed longer but…"

Thomas tilted his head. His nose wrinkled.

"You don't believe me." MacMillan forced a cold smile.

Sensing the prisoner's displeasure, Thomas pulled it back. "Perhaps you imagined that you did?"

"Perhaps I'm atypical, Mr Leven? Is it so hard for an educated mind, like yours, to conceive of the possibility of prenatal cognisance?"

"I can't say it's a subject I'm too familiar with," conceded Thomas.

"The word that was used back then was preternatural."

"Used by whom?"

58

"The people who came to talk about my tendencies."

"People from the island?"

"No, the islanders kept away from us," said MacMillan, ruefully. "The visitors travelled from the mainland, though every call had to be arranged when my grandfather wasn't around."

"He didn't approve?"

"The thought of strangers poking and prodding me as if I was some hitherto undiscovered species, would send Auld Joe into a fury. My mother kept the worst of it from him. Vague questions, as if they were testing me, trying to trip me up but like you, they didn't comprehend what they were dealing with."

"And that was?"

"A normal healthy boy, according to my grandfather," MacMillan laughed.

"From the files I have, there is no prior mention of him."

"He was a fitful presence in my mother's life, though he'd reappear at the most inopportune moments. I remember him bringing her daffodils and balls of red wool. An itinerant drifter is probably the most concise way of describing him."

"The files say…"

"Do you know Westerwick, Mr Leven?" interrupted MacMillan.

He did not. Milene did though. Before they'd met, she'd spent time island hopping with her son's father. And while she couldn't confirm it, Milene reckoned that her child was conceived in the hotel by Port Fintan. Though he hid it well, Thomas found any mention of her life prior to his arrival an irritant.

"Then with respect, Mr Leven, I'd suggest that you take the contents of those files with a pinch of salt. I would like you to have a full and clear understanding of the person and the place you're dealing with."

"I think I've got a good idea…"

"No, you don't," said MacMillan, adamantly. "Before we continue, let's get one thing straight. You may have an intimate knowledge of your legal world but my situation, my condition, goes way beyond any temporal parameters."

"So why did you ask for me?" snapped Thomas.

MacMillan exhaled slowly. "In the fullness of time, there will be a realisation. You will come to recognise me for what I am, not what I'm perceived to have done. And you will thank me for the illumination."

"There is *so* much I want to ask you, Mr MacMillan. For instance, I want to know what drove you to do what you did…"

"Why do you think I did what they say I did?"

"That's what I'd like to find out. And why you refused to defend yourself. I've never understood why you didn't allow Rothwell Glen to…"

"As I said, in the fullness of time."

"And the reason why you returned when you did. Where were you?"

"Mr Leven, I would implore you to disregard what you've been instructed to do and trust your instincts. You didn't make your name with Kunis Clement by blindly following directives from the third floor now, did you? I can imagine that your superiors want this mess cleared up quickly. Slay the beast in time for tea? It doesn't work that way. Be patient and consider what I say very carefully," said MacMillan. "There's time. We needn't rush this."

The prisoner leant forward and grabbed at Thomas' wrists.

"Remove your hands at once, Mr MacMillan," said Officer Raymond. "Physical contact is expressly forbidden."

"Don't be afraid, Thomas."

"What do you want?"

Unsuccessfully trying to unclasp their hands, Raymond called out for assistance.

MacMillan looked Thomas in the eye and said, "I want you to join me in a sacred covenant. For your part, you'll receive an invitation none of your peers will ever be offered."

"Taser. Now."

Raymond placed his hands behind the prisoners arms and pulled, trying in vain to break his grip.

MacMillan continued. "A once in a lifetime chance to look behind the curtain. A carnet, a book of tickets into the machinations of my mind."

With MacMillan's hands still on his wrists, Thomas returned his stare.

"And what's in it for you?"

"No!" The panicked guard yelled at Rodgers, about to deploy the taser. "You'll get them both. Use the stick."

"Thomas, I'm giving you the keys to the carnival. What have you got to lose?"

"Only if you tell me what you want."

As Rodgers brought his baton down towards MacMillan's arm, the prisoner released Thomas.

"Closure," said MacMillan, pulling away a fraction before the guard's baton cracked against the table, ricocheting against its metal edge like a gunshot.

"We will start in 1986."

"You fucking…"

"Officer, it's ok," said Thomas. "I'm fine. No harm done."

Releasing his grip on the prisoner's clothing, Rodgers continued to make his displeasure felt. Thomas turned to Kaitlin, sat back in her seat, the shock of the encounter starting to subside.

"Oh, do shut up, you silly little man," replied MacMillan. "Grown ups talking."

The guard returned to the prisoner and through gritted teeth said, "We'll be having a chat about this later, MacMillan. Make no mistake."

"Half six for seven? Sounds like a plan. I'll rustle up some appetisers. You bring dessert. Let's make a party of it."

MacMillan winked at Thomas.

"And feel free to invite all of your friends this time," he added as Rodgers left the room, his face as red as the light above the door.

MacMillan took a deep breath. "Ok, let's start. I left Westerwick on the penultimate day of August. That morning, my mother boiled me an egg. Before I left, she gave me a twenty pound note and told me that she didn't expect to see my return."

"That's quite final."

"I told her that I would bring her back the thickest red wool I could find. But once the blackness settled onto her…"

MacMillan paused to consider his words.

"The melancholy. It attached itself to her like crumbs to a wet hand."

"Before this, had you ever left the island?"

He shook his head.

"The boat to the peninsula was scheduled to take precisely two hours and thirteen minutes and it rained for the entirety of the journey. Not heavy by local standards but enough to send the mainlanders and the tourists scuttling for cover. All except for one young English laddie who stood with his back to the port. His hair was quite something. Shaved just above his ear but long at both the back and the front. The downpour made no impact on his impressive thatch. He held a small transistor radio to the side of his head, and wore tight mottled jeans which, bordered by crisp white socks, ended a few inches before his tassled slip on shoes began. But his jersey. I'd never seen anything more perfect. Canary yellow with a sky blue and white diamond Argyle pattern on each side of the v-neck. It was like a vision. He noticed me staring and said he'd let me have a listen if I gave him a cigarette."

"And did you?"

"I remarked that I didn't smoke but he let me listen anyway. I told him that I liked his jersey and asked where he'd bought it. He said that it was a birthday gift but a sudden spurt meant that he'd started to grow out of it during the course of the summer. I offered him money for the jersey, there and then. Fifteen pounds. He said that his mum would kill him if he did. You could buy a lot of cigarettes for fifteen pounds,

I replied. The laddie spoke about music and football. As I had no interest in either, I nodded politely as he described in detail his favourites. After a short while, he was summoned by his mother and bade me farewell. By this point, the island was out of sight."

As Thomas listened, Kaitlin carefully documented MacMillan's memories.

"From the port, a single decker bus wound through the pale villages en route to the city. The cobbled cottages that dotted the countryside quickly gave way to boxes upon boxes of cloud-coloured domains; little stone rectangles of existence. Before long, we reached the Dumbarton Road and its rows of brightly festooned shop windows, selling jumpers similar to those my erstwhile travel companion wore. And something called button-fly blue jeans."

MacMillan chuckled at the thought.

"As fascinating as I found it all, it did not prepare me for the city. As soon as I stepped from the bus at the terminus on Killermont Street, my senses were violently assaulted by the noise of locals, the saliva, shot like bullets from the mouths of what seemed to me, the angriest collection of human beings on the planet. Broken glass, gutters full of crushed, discarded tin, not to mention the dog dirt at my feet. And that smell; tobacco from the lips of every single adult and the heavy waft of hops from a nearby brewery. I understood that it may take a while to get used to it but from my first impressions, I did not like Glasgow one bit. I took my case and, on the advice of the driver, I started walking west through Cowcaddens and across the motorway overpass. How many cars does one city need, I recall thinking. It seemed like every vehicle in Scotland was racing beneath my feet. For a brief moment, I shelved my doubts and basked in the excitement of the mechanised roar. Though I hadn't come here on God's work, I thanked Him for the purpose that was yet to be."

"And that purpose was?"

"It was yet to reveal itself. But as I reached the Great Western Road, I could sense His presence."

"You chose the West End purely because of its proximity to the university?"

"I did. Despite my initial reaction and unlike many I studied with, I arrived with no preconceived bias about the city, much less its unheralded quarters. East End, Southside, it wouldn't have mattered to me."

"Tell me about your accommodation."

"Having slept in the same room every night of my short life, I didn't know what to expect from Mrs Telfer and the share of the flat that she was providing for twenty pounds per week. She opened the storm door and invited me in. Mrs Telfer had already been widowed twice. A good wife's a godly prize, she once told me. Given her background, it was no surprise that her speech was peppered with proverbs. To my teenage eyes, she appeared old, around forty, maybe forty five but still lusty. She wore clothing that may have fit her form in earlier times but was now stretched at the seams, garments she'd had for years and were clearly a size or two too small. But she had kind eyes and a ready smile, even when, over a mug of strong tea, she informed me that until the front bedroom was replastered, I'd have to share quarters with a fellow student. It should be less than a week, she said. When I asked her if this entitled me to a refund on my first rent payment, she laughed. You Scottish boys are obsessed with money, her Welsh burr becoming more pronounced. That's as may be, I said, but I paid for a single room and for twenty pounds per week, that is what I expect. She told me that there would be no refund but in the meantime, she would provide me with a meal a day for the next month. Money is a good servant, she'd say, but a hard master. Over a plate of the thinnest beef ham and tinned potatoes, I had reason to question the parameters of her generosity. It would not be the last time."

"I have to admit, Mr MacMillan, your powers of recall are impressive."

"My father's voice I don't remember at all but button fly jeans, yellow jumpers and Mrs Telfer's welcome, I do. Strange what one retains and what one discards. You have to understand Mr Leven that, despite my reluctance and lack of familiarity, this was a novel experience for me."

"I understand. Please continue."

"The room I was to share would be comfortable enough in the short term, though I suspected the high ceilings and thin curtains would provide its long term tenant little protection during the harsher winter months. I crossed the hall and took a look around the room which would be my home for the next three years. The walls were bare and a heavy dog lay asleep on the dust sheets which covered the floor. I asked if the hearth was in working condition. Her reply didn't convince me. She told me that I might need to rod it but I'd have to pay for it myself. As we spoke, a bedraggled fellow not much older than myself, clad entirely in oil marked denim and smelling worse than he looked, walked in laden with bags of shopping muttering something about Be-Ro flour. The only thing I could determine from his coarse doggerel was how he addressed the landlady. Slightly reddened by his use of the word auntie, Mrs Telfer chided him and asked me if I thought the term made her sound old. Eager to placate, I too blushed as I remarked that she could easily pass for thirty five. Tickled by the compliment, she said, 'Better fleech the de'il than fight with her, eh? I think I'm going to like you, Angus John. Call me Cicely.'

'Like the Italian island?' I asked.

'No,' was her reply.

She grabbed the arm of her nephew and introduced us. Andrew keeps pigeons, she told me.

Not in his room, I hoped. The concern I had was placated only slightly by the news that they had a doocot on the roof. The glamour of the West End, I thought. But before I could decamp to my quarters, Andrew looked over his dense glasses and through the thicket of hair that covered his mouth, decried the teuchter who was stealing half of his room. As we got the measure of each other, our landlady informed me that Andrew was about to start his final year at the Boyd Orr. Home to neither geography nor linguistics, I suggested. There was a baffled look in his weak eyes. And for your information, I told him, I'm no teuchter. That's as may be, he chuckled, but ye sure fucking look like one. As Andrew sat down to his plate of beef ham and Mrs Telfer checked the results of the day's sport against a list of her gambling selections, I sat on her couch and stared at her television. On screen, there was a personable Irish fellow singing songs which I admit that I found oddly compelling. We'd never owned a set."

"You had no entertainment on the island?"

"Other than what we'd conjure up ourselves, there was little in the way of entertainment except for a big, box wireless that belonged to my mother. And books. But not many of those."

MacMillan continued. "Calling the name 'Fergus' through flecks of potato populating his already filthy beard, Andrew asked as to my plans for the evening. As a few of his friends were going out, an invitation was extended my way with the minimum amount of enthusiasm. After correcting him, I pretended that I was much too tired after my journey to join him. I'd hoped to take a walk around the campus in the morning after church but aside from a book which I'd planned to finish before the Bank Holiday ended, the truth was that Mrs Telfer's television set had me more fascinated than anything Andrew and the city had to offer. From the corner of my eye, I could see her motion towards him. And not just the once. I didn't let on.

Sensing my reluctance to budge, Mrs Telfer let out a sigh and Andrew shrugged. I had waited eighteen years to watch the television, I had no intention of cutting short the thrill and especially not for alcohol. So while Andrew took a bath, presumably to clean the dried starch from his person, I watched a man coax a team of small dogs through a hoop of fire and a married couple solve a bizarre riddle to win a Talbot motor car. It really was quite exhilarating.

By ten o'clock, the summer sun had set and the excitement of my first day in Glasgow had started to take its toll. As a favour to my landlady, I took the big dog downstairs for his final constitutional of the day. The animal, more familiar with oppidan life than I, dragged me left towards a tree-lined patch of grass which it clearly favoured. Between our block and the one opposite, there was deep red brick as far as the eye could see."

"I suppose that too must have been quite the culture shock."

The prisoner stared at his cuffed wrists.

"It did feel unusual to know that there were so many families living cheek by jowl. Eight dwellings in a block, sometimes more. A thousand neighbours of whom maybe five or six would become familiar. The anonymity of tenement life wasn't something that I was used to. Like a chain of lovers, each link inextricably binding a block to its partners. Back on the island, the nearest family to us was a good mile away."

"Did you miss Westerwick from the start?"

"No. While the island would forever have its hold, I'd made the decision to take to city life, however tough it might be. I knew it would take time. Let nature, of sorts, be your teacher, said …" MacMillan paused to think. He clicked his fingers as if he was summoning the answer.

Thomas knew but didn't speak.

Kaitlin, thinking he didn't, whispered the name of the poet. "Wordsworth."

"Wordsworth!" hollered MacMillan. "How could I forget? A perfect woman, nobly plann'd…"

"To warn, comfort and command?" replied Thomas, recalling his English studies.

"My heart leaps so to know that the young still hold the romantics dear. Please allow me to escort you around the urban paradise."

"Is that how you found the West End? An urban paradise?"

"Loathe as I am to sentimentalise the past, I did sense that I was now part of something greater. Upon my return, I found that Mrs Telfer had set a warm cuppa and a biscuit by my bed, leaving me in no doubt that the night's televisual feast was now over. By now, the dining table was clear but for a velvet tablecloth and deck of large cards, spread face down. I bade her a goodnight, washed my face in the basin and let it dry naturally. Mrs Telfer, and others, would later compliment me on how clear my skin was. What is your secret? No secret, no regimen, I'd reply. When she'd insist that it must be all that lovely coastal air I grew up with, I'd nod. I dressed for bed and said my prayers.

The mattress was more loosely sprung than the one I'd been used to but I told myself that there was much that I had to be thankful for. Everything is fine for today. Andrew returned from his outing sometime after midnight, stumbling into his bed a few minutes later. I could smell the smoke and the alcohol from across the room. He clearly hadn't brushed his teeth and I'm sure he didn't wash his face either though at that stage, I doubted he would've accepted my skin care recommendations. I pulled the bedspread over my face and let thoughts of the cool island winds, whistling through its long grass, send me to sleep."

"You lived there for…almost the entirety of your stay in Glasgow."

"Despite my early misgivings, it did suit my needs."

"And Mrs Telfer…she spoke at your trial."

"Yes she did," replied MacMillan. "Poor thing."

"I don't think her testimony helped your cause."

"No but I couldn't hold it against her. She was easily manipulated."

"How so?"

"In good time. Let's stick with 1986 for the moment."

"Sure."

"The following morning, I visited the large church on Hyndland Street. The parishioners were welcoming enough. However, it was not what I'd hoped for."

"In what way?"

"Its shape was not suitable."

Thomas gave the prisoner a blank look.

"A church should always be circular in design, or at least in the shape of a tear. Our Church on Westerwick was. This one wasn't."

"And that was a problem?"

"Mr Leven, do you know the significance of the circle?"

"No, I can't say that I do." Sensing that the conversation was veering off track, Thomas made an attempt to adjust the route. "Mr MacMillan, can you tell me about…"

"You should do your homework."

"I shall, Mr MacMillan but for now, would you mind explaining? Just this once."

"To most, the circle represents the perfection of God and the unbroken unity of the mysteries of life, death and rebirth under His watch. Think about the shape of the moon and the sun.

MacMillan leant in and spoke quietly.

"However, another reason is that in a room with no corners,

the seducer has no hiding place."

Kaitlin stopped transcribing, her eyes turning towards Thomas. He was unmoved but interested.

"The seducer?"

"You do understand what I'm implying, Thomas?"

"Figuratively or literally?"

"We do not mention him, lest he appear. Like that chap in Harry Potter."

"I don't think we have the time for the realms of fantasy, Mr MacMillan."

"You do not fear seduction?" MacMillan's eyes narrowed. "Despite our best intentions, and hundreds of thousands of years of evolution, we're conditioned to respond in a certain way. Can I fight it, can I eat it or can I fuck it? At our core, those reactions are innate and nothing speaks louder than the silence between connected beings. Recognising it is true liberation. But only when one reaches that state, can one move beyond the fear of desire. Look at yourself. A handsome young fellow. A few marks of character aside, you're quite a catch with your thick head of hair and perfectly straight teeth."

Thomas could feel the colour rise in his cheeks.

"Picture the scene. You're seated next to an attractive young woman. Or speaking to a young man on a ferry. Whatever, wherever, whomever, it doesn't matter. On most occasions, social convention dictates that rather than act on the urge, it's safer to quell it. However, when a look or a gesture is shared, that subtle prompt elicits a response. A connection has been made, regardless of whether it is acted upon.

During the act of devotion, we offer ourselves up to be taken by the Holy. Without guile, we are defenceless and willingly so. On our knees, with our eyes closed and our chests bared, piously begging for our host to take us and offer us eternal salvation. We are not worthy to receive you, we say. Only say the word and I shall be healed. Never are we more susceptible to domination than at that precise moment. So, Thomas, I'll ask again. Do you fear seduction?"

"It's not that I fear it…him…whatever. I just don't believe in it any more."

"A double line. A full stop."

Thomas didn't respond.

"Can I ask why?"

"I'm not here to talk about my beliefs, or the lack of them. We're here to talk…"

"Thomas, please. If we are to understand one another that bit better, at least meet me halfway. Indulge me, if you will."

"Ok, Mr MacMillan."

"What don't you believe in?"

"All of it. Heaven, hell. God, the Almighty, Beelzebub, Satan, the devil…"

"Why?"

"There is no basis in fact for it. No logic at all."

"But again, why?"

"Ancient superstition manifested in the fear of the weak. Almost every culture has a propensity for being led. It's just not for me."

"That's a fair point. But tell me, before you sold your soul to the almighty law, as it were, you were a believer?"

"I was brought up with faith."

"And now there is doubt."

"I would go further than that, but yes. I would say that these days, I prefer to remain within the parameters of the realistic."

"Speaking, as a purely legal entity, would you acknowledge that there is good and evil?"

"As concepts, yes."

"And can you accept that there might be good and evil in the same entity?"

Thomas was interested to see where this was leading.

"Yes, I could accept that. Broadly speaking."

"Then you accept, broadly speaking, that within the abstract, there is nuance? A duality. Light and shade?"

"Within that abstract," nodded Thomas.

"A profound tenet of Jewish thought is the belief that each person is born with both a good and evil inclination but that principle isn't limited to organised religions. Unbound thinkers such as William Blake contended that the nature of man was split into four manifest elements; the sensual, the imagination, the emotion and the vengeful."

Angus John MacMillan stared at the young lawyer sitting opposite. Figuring him out, sizing him

up. "You're a learned man, Thomas."

"To an extent," he replied.

"And modest too. But for all the degrees and accreditation, you've still got quite a way to go. I reckon that'll do us for the day."

As MacMillan looked at the guard, Thomas continued.

"Just to clarify, Mr MacMillan, you asked of faith?"

"I did."

"And about my faith."

"Go on."

"We've established that the broad definition of faith is the absence of doubt, have we not?"

"Broadly speaking," replied MacMillan with a tight-lipped smile.

"If I am confronted by a demonstrable truth, I would accept it. As with a mathematical equation, its empirical, factual content renders any contention obsolete."

"Well put, Thomas. Now consider this. If I say that I am an orange, you will say that I am not. Why?"

"Because you're not an orange."

"Demonstrably. But what if I claimed to be God?"

"We're back in the realms of the ridiculous."

"Answer the question. I'm God. Prove that I'm not."

"The burden of proof lies with…"

"You. It lies with you. Now, if I say that I am the man who has killed, you would readily accept that I was, wouldn't you? That would be an easier sell than to believe a claim that one was touched by the divine or the demonic."

"Your point?"

"Do you like chess?"

Thomas hesitated.

"Haven't played for a while but, yes. I do."

"I don't. As a pursuit, it is the high church of the impenitent snob. Its adherents are even more ardent than the worst religious zealot. To be honest, I'd rather golf."

Thomas snorted.

"That said, there is something about its strategic swings and sways that fascinates me. For all of its labyrinthine defences, the fact is that given the right circumstances, even an average chess player can stumble into a match winning position against a skilled practitioner. Doesn't happen too often but it can be done."

"Your point is?"

"Show me your workings."

"My workings?"

"I would like you to present to me the reasoning behind your credo that I'm the man they claim that I am." MacMillan paused. "But you can't, can you?"

Thomas now recognised where he'd been taken.

"And while you're far from average, you're no master. Still got some way to go, Thomas. But fear not, I'll do my best to guide you in."

Thomas collected his notes and stood. Not defeated, nor humiliated in the eyes of his assistant but firmly reminded. As the guard opened the door, MacMillan spoke again.

"So you know your Wordsworth, eh?"

"Beyond what I recall from sixth year literature, I wouldn't say I was overly familiar with his work."

"I do admire him," MacMillan offered, "but I get so much more from Blake. And from Coleridge. As the latter so memorably stated, 'Faith is not an exotic bloom'. The more stones that are added to the mosaic, Thomas, both bright and dark, the clearer one's picture is of God. You'd do well to keep that in mind. Here's one for you to ponder afore ye go…

Tak'a walk doon frae the crag, by the watter.
On a moonlit Samhain night,
By the sunless sea,
The diel waits.
He waits for me.
With a'thing that he doth alone
Hind the thicket or the juba stone,
He bides his time, just for me.

A'thing that he doth see.

The diel waits, the diel waits for me.

Tomorrow."

****

Thomas and Kaitlin walked through the cool brick-lined corridor from the interview suite to the exit in silence. Before the receptionist released the magnetic lock on the security door, the two stood, momentarily basking in the magnificence of the sun's specular reflection.

"With the Wordsworth thing," said Thomas, "I did actually

know it but…"

"It's fine, Mr Leven. I dabbled in literature before switching to law. Do you think it's going to be like this every day?"

"Like what?"

"You know," she replied. "Like super intense?"

"It's not too late to return to literature," said Thomas.

Kaitlin continued, "I know it's a bit full on but I have to admit, I do find him fascinating. Don't you?"

Not the word I'd use, thought Thomas. "You seem to know your stuff. Did you recognise what MacMillan was gibbering about?"

"The poem? Sorry, can't say it was familiar. Obviously the diel is the devil."

"Obviously."

"with a'thing that he doth alone,

Hind the thicket and the juba stone."

"I have no idea what a juba stone is," he said.

"I'll see if I can find out more about it."

"Just to cover the bases," said Thomas, momentarily forgetting that he always hated phrases of that ilk.

"I'll email you the notes tonight."

"Perfect."

"And if I find anything on the poem thing," said Kaitlin. "I'll send you a message. Which platform do you use most?"

"I've been off grid for a while."

As the light breeze helped extricate a lone curl from her secured bunch, Kaitlin took the phone and connected

Thomas to one more human being. He closed his eyes again and breathed in the perfume of the freshly cut grass, the dry wood chippings underfoot and that of his paralegal. Nothing speaks louder than the silence between connected beings, MacMillan had said and as Kaitlin moved closer, using his frame to shelter herself and his device from the strong glare of the sun, that fear of desire was something Thomas suspected he may need to confront.

"My number is in."

Thomas blushed again as she placed the phone back in his hand.

As Piotr the driver opened the door of the company's car, Kaitlin peeled away towards her own vehicle.

"I expect to be hearing from my lawyer," she said.

"Where to now, Mr Leven?" asked the driver.

"Home."

****

Pain woke Thomas before the car reached the city. An hour of being strapped to a seat had left him stiff and uncomfortable. That and the twisted directions in which the mind of Angus John MacMillan travelled, had gone a long way to convince Thomas that he wasn't yet ready to ease away from his daily pharmaceutical rituals. Get home, get undressed and get numb. Thomas checked his phone. He'd put it into silent mode before he drifted off. Two missed calls, both from Mira.

Damn.

Thomas played the voicemail.

"I was hoping to hear how today went but obviously you're too busy to talk right now." Thomas knew that tone. He recalled how Mira's snippy sarchasm used to agitate him.

Damn.

"Before you return to Kirkmalcolm tomorrow, come into the office for a debrief. I'll have a driver collect you at nine."

As Piotr eased the car into a rare space outside the flat, Thomas's neighbour watched on with interest.

"What the fuck does he want?" muttered Thomas, shuffling his papers, hoping not to be noticed.

Sensing his passenger's agitation, the driver glanced in the rear view mirror and asked Thomas if he was alright.

"Yes," replied Thomas tersely. "Just give me a minute."

"Take all the time you need."

Fuck.

After trying, and failing to see through the tinted glass, Thomas' neighbour nodded towards the driver. Piotr ignored the gesture.

"You alright there, pal?" asked the neighbour loudly, tapping a knuckle on the driver's window.

Thomas was certain that he heard a low, throaty growl from the normally unresponsive Piotr.

"Fine."

"Are you lost?"

"No."

"Can I ask what you're doing here?"

Thomas rolled down his window and asked, "Is there a problem?"

"Oh, it's yourself! Didn't realise it was you. Sorry."

Fuck, now I have to talk to this prick, he thought. Thomas opened the door and as he exited the car, a file fell from his grip onto the street.

"You've got your hands full there, eh?" said the neighbour.

Thomas bent down and picked it up. He strained to return to a standing position.

"You should really bend with the knees," he added, unhelpfully.

"Aye, sure thing."

"While you're here, can I have a wee word about something?"

Thomas sighed. "Fire away."

"I didn't want to bother you until you had a chance to find your feet, so to speak."

"Go on."

"As you're now a fellow top of the hill resident, I was wondering if you'd be interested in joining our Otter Drive?"

"Your what?"

"Our Otter Drive. Every year, The Citizen and the PHTA highlight and sponsor an endangered animal which inhabits the area around the River Kelvin. You may have already read my column?"

Thomas shook his head.

"As well as contributing to our 'Ten things to do this weekend' section, I cover local interests and the environment. This year, it's otters."

Thomas once had Milene doubled over, convulsing with laughter when he claimed that…

"Otters are just wet cats, aren't they?"

Reacting to that observation, the neighbour's head jerked to the side. "That's quite an odd way to describe them but…"

"I'm sorry, maybe next year."

"No bother. It's not for everyone. I get that. We've been here for twenty two years and we didn't get involved for the first couple but you'll find that most of us who live up here have been residents for a considerable time and as such, are very keen to become involved. If I may be blunt, one of the reasons we've stayed in this part of Partickhill is the lack of students who rent up here."

"You don't like students?"

"Don't get me wrong, we were all students once upon a time but this is a quiet, residential corner. We like it here."

"Good for you."

"If you're interested, we'd love to make you a member of the PHTA."

"The what?"

"The Partickhill Tenants Association. It's a collective and I'm the…"

Thomas interrupted him.

"Surely that should be the PTA not the PHTA?"

"I'm sorry?"

"Partickhill is one word, isn't it? Which should make your collective, just the PTA?"

Juggling both the correct and the misconstrued concepts, the neighbour continued unabated.

"I was wondering if you would like to get involved in the

PH…collective?"

"What are the benefits?"

This was not what the neighbour was expecting.

"Ehhh…"

"I mean, there's got to be some reason for me to join. Do I get a t-shirt? Or a badge?"

"There's a Silent Disco in the clubhouse on the first Saturday of the month…"

"And the wet cat thing."

"The Otter Drive, yes."

"But apart from that?"

"We're a collective…"

"So you said. Is there anything else I can help you with?"

"Frankly, yes there is one more thing. I live directly above you…flat three stroke one…and for the last couple of weeks, my wife and I have been struggling to sleep at night because of the music that's coming from your place."

"Oh."

"As I said, it's a residential area, not a short term letting place. We know that one needs to let one's hair down, on occasion but we'd really appreciate you keeping the music levels to a minimum. Especially during the night. We're all professionals here so…"

"Got you."

"Thanks for being so understanding."

"Happy to help," said Thomas, making a mental note to write *otter cunt* above the tiles next time.

"And the glass bottle bins go out on a Thursday. We all

take turns doing it. I think I mentioned this to you before. I can send you a revised schedule, if you'd like. It'll cover the entire year. Brown bins every second Tuesday, black bins on alternate Saturdays, green bins as and when. All the bins, all the bins."

"Yeah, just put it through my door."

"Derek Stobbie, by the way," he said, offering his hand.

"Thomas. Thomas Leven."

"Really good catching up with you, Thomas. Take ca…"

Thomas slammed the door behind him and headed straight for the bedroom.

Derek. For some reason, Thomas hated that name but until this moment, he didn't realise why. There were two Derek's in his class at St Saviour's. Big Derek was an unctuous arsehole and the other, Bigger Derek even more so. The man who owned the fish van that drove from Anstruther every Wednesday morning when he was a kid, he was a Derek too and he was the worst. Always reeking of booze and asking after Thomas's mother. He'd never met a Derek that he liked. Derek. Dereks. He thought about the name some more. Derek. There was nothing about that name which suggested honour, decency. Derek. Like a gull clearing its throat. Derek. Like a Slavic curse. Derek. Or a manic stabbing motion. Derek, Derek, DEREK. And this one. Was he ever a Deek? Or a Dirk? A Degsy? No. Just fucking Derek. Wet cat loving, column writing binfluencer Derek. Definitely in the 'prick' category.

Thomas took two yellow capsules and lay down. He reached under the pillow. Maybe Milene could stop him from sinking tonight. Free him from the spell.

Incantations. Oh Lord, my God...

Watch over me. In everything I say and do. In the darkest moment and in the light. I love you. And I fear your wrath. Your eternal law.

****

This doesn't make sense. Sixty, seventy pages. Charge sheets, records, pictures. God, the pictures. Where are the notes? Check the other boxes.

Mira,

Can't find the old man's notes.
Or MacMillan's statements.
Do you have them at the office?

T

Revisiting the files on MacMillan had Thomas stimulated more than he'd wanted to be so a mouthful of morphine at 2 a.m. helped pull him back over the line. A single pink capsule with his morning coffee would be undetectable, he thought, even to someone with MacMillan's eye for detail. He reached the hi-fi remote and pressed repeat on Jackie Mitoo's 'Drum Song'.

Volume up.

Chapter 6 - Cordon

A pitiful amount of sleep meant that Thomas was in no mood for anything other than the basics that morning. Thankfully for him, Piotr was driving again and not the more sociable Collins. The seemingly never ending stretches of cabling work and its associated 'quick red' traffic lights at the Partick Cross junction also weren't helping Thomas's mood. Superfast broadband had become shorthand for super fucked roads. He'd thought about calling in sick but he knew that would only antagonise Mira, not to mention leave MacMillan feeling put out. Kaitlin would be paid regardless so she'd be alright but Mira - and the old man - had brought him back in from the cold. The retainer they'd set up was basic but as with the accommodation, it was a lifeline. Without that, who knows where he'd be. His mother was dead and once the grand family house, a stone's throw from Wemyss Bay was sold to pay off debts accrued by his now infirm father and his spendthrift second wife, Thomas was bequeathed precious little. Not that he wanted anything from him. Their relationship, fractious before, had broken down completely following his mother's passing. He did feel however that he owed Mira and Rothwell Glen something. They trusted him, and believed in him, the way his mother did. He missed her gentleness.

By the time they reached Derby Street, the car had slowed to a halt. From his window, Thomas could see that the road ahead was blocked by two police vans each side of the line. Traffic heading east towards town was being diverted towards the tighter streets of Finnieston.

Piotr rolled down the window and asked the police officer what was going on.

"Follow the diversion, Sir," he replied. "Keep moving folks. Nothing to see."

Thomas opened his window. There clearly was something to see. Between the vans, opposite the Kunis Clement office building, a tent was being erected.

"My office is literally there," said Thomas.

"Nothing I can do about that, Sir. The road is closed now so nothing will be coming down here for the foreseeable. Please take the diversion."

Piotr spun the car around and headed back from where they came.

"Where are you going?"

"I was asked to bring you to the office so I'm bringing you to the office," he replied matter-of-factly.

Taking a sharp right onto Derby St, Piotr manoeuvred the company car down a tight lane between the buildings. Thomas held on as his driver sped along the cobbles, traversing the loose brickwork and potholes. As Piotr attempted to get into the lane behind the Kunis Clement building, ahead another police van slowed to a crawl. The officer stepped out of the moving car and started placing cones along the side of the car park, preventing them from going further.

"I'm sorry Mr Leven, this is as close as I can get."

Thomas got out of the car.

"I'll take these for you," he said.

Rather than argue with a man who looked as if he didn't take kindly to being argued with, Thomas handed over his backpack and satchel. "Must be serious if they're blocking off the street."

"Not my business but they do that with crashes," replied Piotr, less curious. "The really bad ones."

On the front steps of the Kunis Clement building, surrounded by police officers, sat Wee John Thomson. Hired by the old man for reasons seemingly unknown, the moustachioed, barrel chested security custodian with the strike first, ask questions later approach, was on first name terms with a number of the firm's more earthy clientele. As with most things, only Mira knew the finer details of the story. Because of a bet between Rothwell Glen and a notable Southside gangster, a wager the old man lost, Kunis Clement had been finding gainful, if incongruous employment for Wee John since the mid nineties. Despite that, with Mira looking to modernise, the deceptively intuitive sentinel - with his raspy lack of a filter - knew that his days at Kunis Clement were numbered. As the oil soaked lift engineer asked around for a light for his cigarette, away from her reception desk and angling for a better view, stood Jacqueline.

"There's definitely a body," said the lift engineer. "Wee John saw it first."

"I did," said John, gulping down a cup of tea. "The boy was hingin' aff a fucking lamppost."

"Seriously?" asked an incredulous Thomas.

"Mr Leven, you think this is the first fucker I've seen hingin' aff a lamppost?"

Given the amount of law enforcement officers in proximity, Thomas thought it best not to push for detail.

"I just couldn't get near the poor cunt."

As ever, the choice language of Wee John drew daggers from Jacqueline. His regular phrase of atonement - pardon my French - rarely cut the *moutard* with the permanently affronted desk jockey.

"Why?"

"There were a couple a' dogs just gnawing at his feet. Up on their hind legs. They must have chewed right through to the bone. I tried to shoo them away but they were right nasty cunts," he said, catching the receptionist's rolling eyes again. "Pardon my French."

"Whose feet?"

"The boy a'hind the tent. Hingin' aff the fucking lampost."

"Question is," asked the engineer, squeezing the end of his roll up, "what was the daft cunt doing hanging off a fucking lamppost?"

"Fuck knows," he said, removing his cap to wipe away the beads of sweat, "but he's fucking deid now."

Before Thomas had the chance to thank Wee John for his detailed forensic analysis, Jacqueline took him by the arm.

"Mira's stuck in traffic. Should be here soon, though it's anyone's guess when they're going to open the road up again."

"Well they'd better do it sharpish," said the eavesdropping lift engineer, " I've got to be in Paisley by ten. This heat is playing havoc with my motors."

"Stairs again?" asked Thomas.

"Sorry pal. Should be back up and running later this afternoon."

Stairs.

"You need help, Mr Leven?"

"I'll be fine."

The staff break room was situated on the first floor and was where the non-directorial staff warmed up their ready meals, compared notes, and generally gossiped about the proclivities of the clients, television personalities and their workmates. Thomas stopped on the landing momentarily, listening out for chatter and noise. There was none. Slowly, he took the flight of stairs to the second, then third floor.

Mira's office was unlocked so Thomas went straight in. As a rule, Mira never smoked at home but at work, she did so continuously. To freshen the room, every morning, regardless of the weather, Jacqueline would crack open a tall sash window for approximately half an hour before her arrival. The warm gust from the door coupled with that from the window made the curtains billow and the draw chain rattle. Mira's late husband liked a cool breeze and given the years she'd spent in Scotland, it hadn't taken Mira's Persian blood long to adjust to climes fresher than she'd been used to. On the street below, a number of mobile response units snaked along the centre of the road with a plain white car and two ambulances on the apron of the hastily erected tent. Overhead, a pair of police helicopters patrolling the area between the Gurdwara and the park, kept a third, the one belonging to the local radio station, hovering at blades length from the site. From his third floor vantage point, Thomas could see over the high sided blue tarpaulin that surrounded the scene.

Using the curtain as cover, he knelt down and peered over the window ledge. Behind the enclosure, bright bursts of light from the cameras of the police photographers illuminated the scene.

Fucking hell...

To the left of where the phone boxes once stood was a man of similar age to Thomas, impaled on the damaged, decommissioned lamppost.

Though Wee John's vivid if unmannerly description of the scene had provided a clue as to what grim reality lay within, it bore scant resemblance to what Thomas had just seen. A man, stripped to the waist, with a metre long stretch of the lamppost protruding from his bare, riven chest. The angle of the tarpaulin however meant that Thomas couldn't see the man's feet. As his shock moved from revulsion to curiosity, Thomas looked again but given the distance between the window in Mira's office and the body, the more intimate details of the incident eluded him. Delving into his jacket pocket, Thomas removed his phone. Still out of sight of the investigating officers, he used his camera to zoom in.

White male.

Slim to medium build. Thirty, possibly thirty five years old.

Jagged edge of lamppost pushed through torso, skin on

throat, also lacerated. Eyes, bloody. Left arm draped over the crossbar.

Swiping his finger against the screen of his phone, Thomas's clammy hands began to shake. As the camera adjusted to the distance, he used the window sill to hold position.

A score…maybe a slash. V shaped. One on each side of his stomach. So much blood. It had already started to clot. Like he'd been branded.

As soon as Thomas captured the image on his screen, the man's head returned to position. His lifeless neck, previously snapped and serrated, had inexplicably regained its limber. Thomas gasped as the dead man's eyes, already open, suddenly turned their gaze towards the third floor window with the billowy drape.

"Up there. Look."

The young lawyer slid down the window and faced away. With his heart pounding, Thomas failed to detect the presence of a nearer, more acute threat.

"A terrible thing," said Mira standing in the frame of the door.

"Jesus!" exclaimed the startled Thomas.

"Would you prefer it if I knocked?" Drawing from her cigarette, Mira continued, "I know you have grand designs, Thomas but this still is my office."

Before he could speak, the shrill trill of Mira's office phone broke the silence.

"You don't mind if I answer?" asked Mira cooly. She exhaled and picked up the receiver.

"Yes, Jacqueline. Put him through."

Mira put a finger to her lips.

"I'm sorry, Sergeant. Yes, that was just me," she said, glaring at Thomas. "Nothing untoward."

Fighting an aberrant urge to look again at the impaled man, Thomas picked himself up off the floor. Mira continued, her tone at odds with her expression.

"...not at all. I've told the staff at reception to extend any courtesy towards you. You're most welcome. Anything we can do for your officers, please don't hesitate to ask."

She replaced the receiver and said, "Another uneventful morning at Kunis Clement."

"Did you get my message?"

"About?"

"The files."

"Yes."

"And?"

"I'll look into it." Motioning Thomas to sit, Mira stubbed out her first cigarette of the day.

"Tell me, Thomas. What's he like?"

"MacMillan?"

Thomas took Mira's sharp grunt as a yes.

"Physically unremarkable. He isn't out of shape but he's not been spending the last twenty odd years in the gym."

"No, his manner, his behaviour, that kind of thing."

Thomas leant back in his seat and closed his eyes.

"Very weird."

"How so?"

"I can't determine whether he's yanking my chain or mentally ill."

"Maybe both? Do you have transcripts of the interviews yet?"

"No, I'll get them to you by the end of the week."

"Naturally, I'd like to take a look at them as soon as possible."

Thomas understood. This was Mira-speak for 'I want it yesterday.'

"Of course."

"Still no insight into why he returned?"

"Not yet but I'll start guiding him towards an answer later today."

Mira, satisfied with the response, lit another cigarette.

"Sorry for skulking around in your office. I just wanted to know what was happening over the road."

The sheer net curtain parted, and as the plume of smoke swirled around her as if part of the fabric, she said, "Suicide is a such a waste."

As nothing about what he'd seen would suggest that this was self-inflicted, Thomas replied to Mira's assertion with a question. "What makes you think that this is a suicide?"

"There's a lot of it about," she replied. "Does make me worry about you, Thomas."

"Why?"

"The pressures of the modern world are so great. So many young men of your age feel as if they have no option but to take their own lives. Despite everything, you still have so much to offer."

Nice to know.

"Anyway, have those transcripts sent to me as soon as possible."

Thomas picked up his phone and headed for the door. "You'll let me know when you find the original case notes?"

"Naturally," replied Mira as her desk phone rang again. She picked it up and pressed the mouthpiece against her shoulder. "Is there anything else?"

Thomas shook his head and waved goodbye.

"Send him up and hold my calls," he heard her say as he closed the door.

On the landing between the first and second floors, Chief Inspector Campbell Ames and Thomas greeted each other. As an old friend of Rothwell Glen, his was a familiar presence around the corridors of Kunis Clement. Yet despite taking a personal interest in his development, Thomas never felt anything but uneasy in his company. His form tutor once stated that vice was most dangerous when donning the garments of virtue, and each time he was in the presence of Campbell Ames, it was a sentiment Thomas couldn't shake.

Grinning, his front teeth healthy but misshapen, the Chief Inspector's default manner oscillated between excitable and dissolute, traits Thomas also found at odds with the office he held. As he'd done on numerous occasions, Campbell Ames gently squeezed Thomas' hand, feeling his way around the contours of the younger man's knuckles.

"Good to see you back," he said, leaning in. "Nice break?"

You know that it wasn't, thought Thomas. He nodded nonetheless.

"You on your way to visit W258RF?"

Thomas's perplexed look drew clarification from the senior policeman.

"Our friend, Mr MacMillan."

"Yes," he replied. "I'm leaving now."

"What do you think of him?" asked Ames, with a look bordering on the lascivious.

Not as weird as you, thought Thomas.

"Yeah, we're getting there."

"Wee heads up," said Ames, leaning in. "Might be worth your while phoning ahead today."

"Why's that?"

"I hear there was a bit of a...scene, shall we say, at the Kirkmalcolm facility this morning. Don't know all the ins and outs but your man MacMillan was involved."

****

Before he'd reached the final set of stairs, Thomas was struck by the resounding ping of gibbering inanity reverberating through the high-ceilinged reception area. A pair of interns stood on the sill, stretching and straining as if they were angling for a glimpse of a teen idol hidden behind the tarpaulin. By the water cooler, a similarly fresh faced police officer was interviewing the increasingly agitated lift engineer but in the role he was born to play, Wee John utilised all of his rough charm to herd the reporters back towards the door.

"Have you got an appointment?" he barked. "Naw? Well

fuck off then."

With his chance of a quiet, unimpeded exit diminishing, Thomas was forced to consider his remaining alternative; the fire exit situated in the corridor behind Jacquline's desk. In an attempt to curtail any uncomfortable small talk, Thomas issued the receptionist a direct instruction.

"Jacqueline, call Kirkmalcolm and tell them that I need to speak with my client immediately."

The manner of the receptionist's response was uncharacteristically muted. Flighty? Yes. Flirty? Incessantly, but in the time that he'd known her, Thomas had never seen Jacqueline look so unnerved.

"Piotr said he'll pick you up at the corner of Derby Street, by the park," she added quietly.

Before Thomas could ask if she was okay, Jacqueline stared into the middle distance and said, "I think I know him."

****

"And as his lawyer, I'm going to have to insist that I see him for myself."

"Mr Armour has given strict instructions that no one is to be allowed access to the inmates today. No therapists, no ministers and specifically, no lawyers. I'm sorry Mr Leven." The sentry lowered his voice. "I shouldn't be saying this, but I've been here for nearly fifteen years. What occurred up there this morning was unprecedented."

"Can you at least let me know what happened?"

The sentry sighed, "I'm afraid I can't."

"Then I'd like to speak with Mr Armour himself."

Kenneth Arnott Armour had been in charge of Kirkmalcolm since being headhunted by the Chief Executive of the Scottish Prison Service and the then Cabinet Secretary for Justice eight years previously. Like many men of his background, he'd dropped his Christian name in favour of the other two. Arnott Armour had built a reputation as a strong governor at the lower security but highly volatile Quarry Moss prison near Falkirk, a spell which moved him ahead of his contemporaries in the race to oversee the country's most challenging inmates. Thomas had been in Armour's company once before, at a Kunis Clement event at Muirfield Golf Course though neither man had any recollection of the other. Business obliged them to be there. While Thomas had dutifully smiled through another of Rothwell Glen's interminable travelogues, the dour Armour sat alone, picking slivers of cucumber from his sandwich.

"Do come in, Mr Leven." Armour stood and extended his hand across his desk. "Please, sit. Sorry for the heat. It's caused the windows to swell and I can't open them."

"Mr Armour, I've been led to believe that my client will not be available to me today."

"That is correct, Mr Leven," he said, daubing the sweat from his head.

"Would you be so kind as to explain why?"

Armour sighed. He flattened the frontal wisps of his thinning hair before guiding each side to the front of his forehead. "He is currently sedated. Heavily sedated, in fact."

"And why is that?"

"Prior to breakfast, there is a rotation for certain prisoners to exercise or in the case of our religious inmates, to pray. Mr MacMillan is allocated a fifteen minute spell in the yard beside the hall."

"Ok," said Thomas.

"Well, at seven, when the guard opened his cell door, MacMillan wasn't there."

"I don't understand."

"He wasn't in his cell. Naturally, this led to the alarm being sounded and an immediate lock down protocol initiated."

"Naturally."

"Minutes later, he was located by our most experienced dog handler, Officer McKendrick, close to an unused checking station on the edge of the inner perimeter."

"Did he resist?"

"No, that's the thing. He was entirely untroubled by their presence."

"So, what was he doing?"

"McKendrick reported that he was sitting by a fence post."

"Just sitting?"

"We're not in the business of letting our inmates roam free but if sitting by a fence post had been the extent of the incident, Mr Leven, we'd have chalked this one up as a freak occurrence and returned him to his cell, post haste. As the handler approached, he noticed the prisoner carving something into the fence post. Some numbers."

"With what?"

"The prisoner had a knife."

"Jesus."

"Indeed. Of course, McKendrick issued the prisoner a warning. Stand up, drop the knife, hands in the air. Standard stuff. If he didn't comply, his dog would be released. MacMillan however remained fixated, unresponsive. This left the officer with no option but to follow protocol."

"Which was to set the dog on MacMillan?"

"His last act before issuing the command was to radio in his location. Instantly, all available personnel raced to the station only to find McKendrick's dog tearing into its prone, overwhelmed handler. As the deputy's animal had started to turn on him too, Officer Rodgers took charge. He drew his firearm and exterminated both dogs. Although the deputy suffered a broken wrist and multiple lacerations, McKendrick's injuries are expected to be life-changing."

"And MacMillan?"

"He continued to carve."

****

"I take it they wouldn't let you see him?" asked Kaitlin, sunning herself by the gate.

Thomas didn't answer but his agitated gait suggested that her assumption was correct.

"Do you need me to head back to the office with you?"

"No," replied Thomas. "I need you to go straight to the Mitchell Library. Pick up every single thing you can on MacMillan. Articles, features, books. Anything."

Chapter 7 - Hurtwood

The doorbell woke him abruptly. Disorientated, Thomas' palate was bone dry from sleeping face up on the flat's burgundy leather sofa with his mouth open, while his naked lower half was stiff from the position he'd held for the last few hours. As the morning sun cut through the scaffolding and curtains of the bay window, Thomas remembered that moments earlier, he was deep in a dream where he was laying in the mouth of a giant. As the delusion involved wedging his penis into the median sulcus, the groove on the giant's tongue, Thomas quickly checked himself and the couch's upholstery for signs of the fantasy's extent.

Maybe I do need to cut back a little.

The doorbell rang again. This time for longer.

Thomas pulled on his shorts and tiptoed stiffly towards the door. He peered through the spyhole.

It was Mira.

The doorbell rang again and Thomas slid back along the

wooden floor and from a safe distance, he shouted out, "Coming."

Mira walked into the hallway and stopped. She took a breath. The air was stale and musty.

"You're aware that windows in this flat operate in a number of different positions, aren't you?" she asked, coughing and shaking her head in disapproval. "You should try to open one sometime."

"Sure thing," replied Thomas, unconvincingly.

Mira ran a finger along an empty shelf on the bookcase in the hall. "And once you get around to dusting, Thomas, you really need to start filling these shelves up. I'd start with the Russians."

When she'd left, Milene took all of their books, even Houellebecq. The novel about Michel and Valerie in Thailand was the one he most frequently masturbated to when she was away. Upon her return, Milene determined which paragraphs had kept his attention by checking which pages had detached most from the binding. She figured that it was better for Thomas to be lost in the imagination of a writer than buried deep between the legs of another.

"What's up? I'm not late, am I?" Thomas picked up his phone. The music he'd decided to share with his neighbours had long since stopped. The time showed 08.34.

****

The short drive along the Hyndland Road, took considerably longer than it should have, due in no small part to the slow moving daily procession of considerably tiny school children being ferried considerably short distances by considerably stressed parents in a convoy of considerably large cars.

When not on company business, Rothwell Glen himself preferred smaller, more highly sought after vehicles. Sleek, Italian and low. Given his position as head of the country's best known law firm, he could easily afford the prohibitive costs of purchase and usage. The older he got, the less interested Glen was in the grim minutiae of the firm he fronted, so he surrounded himself, as many successful but unsatisfied men do with objects that other men desire. No one was entirely sure how many times Rothwell Glen had been married. In a rare, unguarded moment, Mira once joked that she'd had cigarettes that lasted longer than some of his unions. She'd stopped counting at four. Paintings, artefacts, women. The old man had built for himself, Thomas thought, a barrier of beauty. Seductive, empty hedonism aside, as loathe as he was to admit it, he did admire the old man's eye for the refined. Spending a bonus on snapping up a classic Jaguar, in British Racing Green with fawn leather interior, might have irritated Milene but it made the old man purr with approval.

"I thought he was supposed to be back by now."

"He decided to extend his stay. And why wouldn't you? The wine is perfect and the *cigalas* are in season. Everything about the Côte is delicious at this time of year."

"Do you have any idea who did it?"

Mira shook her head.

"I take it that the house is alarmed and recorded."

"Alarmed, certainly but even when he's away, his staff maintain a presence."

"And no one saw anything?"

"Apparently not."

Set back from the Great Western Road - Hurtwood House - Glen's elevated, four storey, double pillared blond stone mansion remained as impressive as Thomas had remembered it. Every detail was precise, from the cornicing down to the immaculately matched lead-bordered, stained glass inlays which skirted the windows. The old man could have easily afforded a larger, even grander residence, like any number of the more private buildings on Cleveden Drive, one road back. But he chose Hurtwood for a reason.

Rothwell Glen wanted to be seen.

"Nice porthole," said Thomas.

"It's not a porthole," replied Mira. "It's called a borrow light. It's a term taken from before the days of electricity when the light which illuminated the hallway came through that window, hence the term."

"For a lawyer, you sure know a lot about architecture."

"I don't and I'm a chemist, not a lawyer."

"Which reminds me, it might not be the best time to ask but could you possibly get me another few prescriptions?"

"About that…"

.Thomas had anticipated that there may be some resistance. "I'm only using what I need."

Mira glanced to the side and shook her head slowly. "What you *need* is to start weaning yourself off the medication."

He knew he had no comeback.

"The last time, Thomas. You understand?"

"Appreciated."

As they waited on the old man's domestic chief to open the door, Thomas' eyes were drawn to the leaded glass semi-circle above the raven glossed wooden door. Overlapping the stylised monochrome digits that formed the number eleven appeared to be a red marking.

"This is number eleven, right?"

Mira didn't respond. As the door opened and Clara, from the old man's staff, greeted them, the same sun which had already illuminated his morning now suggested to him that the marking was more liquid than solid.

"Show me," said Mira as Clara led the way.

Only once had Thomas been inside Rothwell Glen's house; on the occasion of the old man's sixtieth birthday, three years previously. Already drunk on Malbec, Thomas had been keeping Milene company during a damp cigarette break. As they'd scurried in out of the rain and onto the polished but now wet marble of the hallway, Thomas lost his footing, narrowly missing a fifteenth century Hispano-Moresque vase but sliding into a table, overturning the old man's bronze cast of Pan.

As Clara continued to brief Mira, Thomas spun the cast

around and inspected it. The indentation he'd made on the satyr's rear was still there. He carefully returned it to its base before slowly following Mira up the staircase. More bloody stairs, he cursed under his breath as stiffness mixed with pain. He'd never been beyond the ground floor of the old man's house before, never mind the upper echelons, but its scent - sandalwood and the faint smell of a coal burner - took him back.

"Jesus," he said, looking at the artefacts on the walls on the approach to the landing. "That's a bit disturbing."

"A man must have his recreational pursuits," replied Mira, ascending the staircase, "and for the old man, it happens to be golf."

"No, not the trophies, those masks."

As Thomas followed Mira up the stairs, suspended on the walls between the inscribed plates and impressively gilded third placed medals was a collection of masks. Some covered with wiry horsehair, others with stained pelt, but each one appeared more hideous than its predecessor.

"Oh those? He must have picked them up on his travels."

Thomas followed Mira and Clara into his private office.

Backing onto the window was Rothwell Glen's oak desk. Large, carved and empty but for neatly stacked, unopened correspondence, Thomas pictured his diminutive boss buried behind the half tree of office furniture, tapping away like a tight lipped, grey haired, priapic beaver. Maybe a lower dose next time.

Facing the windows was a wall of ornately bevelled

bookcases. Residing behind the glass and the criss-cross lead piping was the old man's personal collection of antiquated volumes. In the centre of the study, complimenting the inlay of the desk, was a matching pair of oxblood Chesterfield sofas. While of similar design to the one Thomas had just woken up on, both were in better condition and neither showed signs of recent sexual congress.

"Nothing was taken, Mrs Berglund, but this doesn't make sense," she said, pointing to the bookcase.

"I don't see any damage," said Mira.

"It's not that, Mrs Berglund. It's the key."

Jutting from the barrel of the lock was a small key with a circular loop. "This wasn't there yesterday."

"Are you certain?"

"One hundred percent certain," replied Clara. "I'm the only member of staff who attends to this room and when Mr Glen isn't at home, I keep it secured. The book case only has the one key and Mr Glen has that with him at all times."

Thomas took a look at the antiquated books behind the lead lined glass:

'The Handbook of Lies'
'Daemonologie'

"An original King James version?" he said. "Must be nearly five hundred years old."

"As I said, a man must have his hobbies," said Mira. "You said there was something else, Clara?"

Clara leant into Mira and whispered.

"Thomas," said Mira, "I need to go upstairs for a moment. Wait for me here. And don't touch anything."

Looking around the room, Thomas ran his hands across the polished surface of the old man's desk.

Not a speck of dust.

He sat on a sofa, spreading his arms out. The scent of sandalwood had given way to that of leather, beeswax and a distant but lingering hint of cigar smoke.

I've always wondered…

Thomas peered out the door. But for the faint click of Mira's heels on the floor directly above, there was silence.

He pulled out the old man's chair and sat down behind his desk. Mira wouldn't be pleased if she saw him there but when she cooled off, even she'd understand. This was where Thomas Leven had always wanted to be. Everyone who was hired by Kunis Clement had ambitions, desires. Most of them, realising that they couldn't fulfil those dreams at the firm, moved on, embittered, sometimes scarred, but proud that they had a Kunis Clement tour of duty on their résumé.

Thomas gently placed his hands on the desk, looked around and for a moment, allowed the fantasy to play out. Like the bit part players who had unrealistic designs on a starring role at the firm, he'd forgotten how much he'd craved this. The ambition, the power and the trappings. It all came flooding back. And now, he was in the holiest of the holies. Fuck the bedroom, he thought. Any number of long legged whores could access that. *This* was the old man's most intimate chamber.

If I was Rothwell Glen, thought Thomas, what would I keep in here? Papers? Sure. Documents? Probably. Cigars? Definitely. There were six drawers of equal size on either side. If one of them was unlocked, he might be forgiven for accidentally taking a look. Nothing sinister, of course. Just curiosity. Thomas reassured himself that he wasn't looking for anything in particular. No angle, no leverage to be used. Just curious.

With both eyes on the door, he placed his hands on the handles of the nearest drawers, left and right. A creak above his head. He has time. The slightest tug. Nothing. Hands down to the next two. Same again. Locked. Quickly to the bottom two. Firm. Damn, he thought. Another creak above, then another. Moving away. Shit. Thomas reached over and tried the three furthest to his left then same again with those to his right. Not one. Motherfucker. Better get up and out. As he did, his knee caught the lip of a narrow central drawer. Unlike the others, this one wasn't locked. Thomas slid the shallow drawer towards him. Three compartments, identical in size, each with photographs and passports. Surely he's got his passport if he's in the Côte, Thomas thought. Footsteps at the top of the stairs. Another compartment, this one covered with a thin layer of wood with a hole near the back. Thomas quickly placed a finger in the hole and slid it open. Inside was a manuscript:

Westerwick - The Unholy Isle
Final draft - Innes Guthrie, 2002

"Mr Leven," said Clara, slowing down to see Thomas rise.

"Beautiful desk," he said, gently pushing the drawer closed with his legs.

"Mrs Berglund would like you to join her upstairs."

Thomas followed Clara up yet another set of stairs to the old man's private quarters.

On the walls were paintings, fifteen to twenty in total, all exquisitely framed. Portraits, landscapes, classic style. The faces of the subjects had been blurred out. Mira leant in close.

"Turpentine," she said. Thomas sniffed then nodded in agreement.

"Wasn't there some Irish fellow a few years back who punched a hole in a painting? I think he got five years. Maybe we should call Campbell Ames?"

"And he'd do what?" asked Mira dismissively. "No, we'll deal with this ourselves first."

"So who would do this? Does the old man have enemies?"

Mira raised an eyebrow.

"Wait," asked Thomas. "What's this? It's on that one too."

Daubed in the bottom left hand corner of each piece was what looked to be two chevrons.

"That's what I was talking about, Mrs Berglund. I don't know what it's supposed to mean."

"And they weren't there yesterday?"

"I've never seen them before."

But Thomas had.

Chapter 8 - Sturnus Vulgaris

From its belly, you can't rise. You can't rise. Lounge while you can, in its mouth, on its tongue.

From its belly, you can't rise. It will own you, devour you, end you. Lounge while you can on its tongue, trouble it not, lest it taste of you and suck from its teeth from whence you shelter. Suck from its teeth and grind. And swallow. Into the pit, the belly of the beast. Say your prayers and keep still.

Spit.

"Mr Leven…" came the voice.

Thomas didn't stir. When he'd left Rothwell Glen's place, he returned home to get changed into his suit. Piotr waited for him in the car. Thomas deliberated as to whether he could afford to take a capsule, to get him through the process of figuring out whether what he'd seen seared onto the chest of the impaled man was in any way related to what had been crudely added to the old man's art works and daubed on his front door. And equally important, who was Innes Guthrie?

"Mr Leven, Sir…"

"What's happening?"

"Not sure but we're being stopped." Piotr turned the ignition off and unclipped his belt. "Just stay seated, Mr Leven. I'll find out what's happening."

Once Piotr was out of the car, Thomas checked his phone. He'd sent Kaitlin a message after he left the old man's house but though she was online and had seen it, she hadn't yet replied.

Does the name Innes Guthrie mean anything to you?

T.

At the end of the turn off, the driver of the car directly in front had finished his conversation with the yellow jacketed police officer and had returned to his vehicle. He slowly reversed then quickly spun round to his left and drove away, leaving a gap between the company car and the two unit vans which were blocking the road at the junction. Facing the turning, a three person film crew angled for a better position, shining a fluorescent arc up the narrow road which led to Kirkmalcolm. As the mix of light, real and artificial, filled the windscreen, it was hard for Thomas to see what was going on with any clarity. He stepped out of the car to get a better look. Hearing Thomas approach on the gravelled path, Piotr turned to him.

"What's going on?"

"Birds. Thousands of them," replied the driver.

From the start of the road to its first turn, the length of a football field and more, the path was filled with a legion of fallen birds.

Thomas hoped that the youthful police officer standing at the turn might provide some insight.

"They just fell from the sky," he said. "It happened so quickly, I didn't have time to get my phone out."

Thomas knelt down. At a glance, he could see a collection of birds that by nature wouldn't be together; finches, magpies, robins. He knew that while the latter might care for the young of say, a song thrush or a willow warbler, most birds of this type tended to be fiercely territorial.

"These ones," said Thomas, "definitely starlings."

Of the five hundred or so breeds native to this island, the common starling was the bird of which Thomas was fondest. It was also the one he had sketched the most. As a child, one of the few gifts given to him by his father was a well thumbed copy of Hollom's 'Popular Handbook of British Birds', and its companion piece on the rarer breeds, that he'd found while on a business trip to Morecambe. Both volumes bore a small blue sticker of their original stockist; *Waghorn & Son, Booksellers.*

The things one remembers, Thomas thought, cupping a tiny bird in his hand.

"Are they dead?" asked the officer.

Thomas could feel its heartbeat. Not as strong as its normal rate but steady. "This one's alive."

"These too," said Piotr as the policeman's radio crackled.

"They're dazed, but still alive," added Thomas. "Something stunned them."

Catching sight of his approaching superior, the officer's tone became more dictatorial. "Sir, I'll need you to get back into your vehicle while we clear the road."

Thomas was in no mood to be brushed aside. "And exactly how are you going to do that?"

"One of the local farmers is on his way with a team of lads and some shovels."

"I can tell you right now that they're not being shovelled into a ditch," Thomas stated forcefully. "Especially when they're not dead."

"Don't worry. No one will touch them. And that is an order."

Deferring to the command, the junior officer barked the word Sir and stepped back. The quietly spoken sergeant knelt and in his hands, cradled one of the stunned creatures. "Thou was not born for death, immortal bird."

Bypassing his colleague, the sergeant addressed Thomas directly. "Sturnus Vulgaris, if I'm not mistaken."

The baffled officer chimed in, "Sir?"

"The common starling," he replied before returning to Thomas. "Any idea what might have caused this?"

"Could be a few things. Magpies and starlings are considered to be bullies, yobs, and as they have a tendency to feed on overripe fruit, they could be drunk."

Eager to get back onside with his superior, the younger officer laughed. "Is he serious, Sarge? Mangled magpies? That's a new one."

"Isn't there a hedge you should be guarding?" said the sergeant in a hushed tone.

As the chastened officer walked off, Thomas continued. "Overripe fruit may account for a handful of birds, but not thousands."

"An electromagnetic field might though?"

"Could be but as someone who appears to know about the species, I'm sure you'll understand that birds of this type are almost never together. A phenomenon such as this goes against nature."

The sergeant nodded in agreement. "As perceptive as starlings are, did you know that they're also incredible mimics? Mozart had a pet starling which could sing one of his piano concertos."

"I'm betting that Mozart didn't have to deal with a couple of thousand of the little buggers, did he?"

"My guess would be the sudden presence of a determined predator."

Speaking of which...

"How far do you reckon?"

"Sir?"

"To the main building. How far?"

"You're talking one and a half...no, probably just short of two miles."

Two miles it is.

Thomas returned to the car with Piotr.

"You sure?"

"Been a long time since I went for a walk around these parts. It'll do me the world of good."

"This is not a problem, Mr Leven," said Piotr. "I can drive through. It's only birds."

"Absolutely not," replied Thomas. He threw his jacket on the back seat. "And anyway, they're not just birds, they're starlings."

Once Thomas had navigated his way through the stretch with the birds, he hit the turn. The momentary temptation that the privacy of high hedges offered was strong. Pop a capsule now, he reasoned. Help with the stiffness. No one will notice. No. It's too close. MacMillan would pick upon it. Later. When I'm home. Save it for then. After the turn, the height of the hedges diminished and the road was less narrow. Since he'd been coming to Kirkmalcolm to question MacMillan, Thomas realised that he'd never properly paid attention to the vista. He took a deep breath, mopped his brow and counted off the first of three dips and matching inclines. On one of the latter, atop a weather-beaten fence post, Thomas spotted the tiniest robin, perched and alert. For a moment, he stopped and listened to its cry. Sweet yet misleading. Knowing that the bird wouldn't have dared wait around so long had the murmuration of starlings not been indisposed, Thomas reached into his pocket for his phone and opened up the camera. Holding as still as he could, he failed to capture the bird before it flew off out of view.

****

"How are you feeling today?"

"I'm fine. Though a little sluggish," said MacMillan shaking his head from side to side. He made a point of widening his eyes. "I would say that I prefer my restraints to be physical rather than medicinal."

"I'll be conducting the interview alone today."

"As opposed to…"

"My paralegal, Miss Ramsay, has been otherwise detained."

"Oh, that is a shame. And I was getting on so well with her too."

"Would you care to talk about what happened yesterday?"

"Not particularly but I suspect that you would."

Thomas considered the tone of what he was about to say. "Where should we start? Absconding from your cell or the incident that hospitalised staff and left two dogs dead?"

"Death, as you know it, is just a door to another room."

"Is that where you went?"

"In a manner, yes."

"According to the Governor, you were in a state of apoplexy."

"A trick any number of illusionists may use."

"Is that what you were doing? Playing a trick on the staff?

"Not quite."

"Mr MacMillan," said Thomas, exasperated, "I'm at a loss as to what is going on here. I genuinely don't understand what you want."

"I needed to communicate with someone."

"During the period where you were…"

"No longer of this world, yes. And for reasons I cannot expand on at this time, I'd like you to trust me."

"Trust's a two way street," replied Thomas. "You need to tell me what happened."

MacMillan leant back and closed his eyes. "If you insist."

"I do."

"I needed to communicate with someone."

"You said."

"Someone in particular," said MacMillan. "I needed to speak to your mother."

Thomas felt his chest tighten and his focus narrow.

"My mother's dead."

"Eilidh Broome."

"Pardon?"

"I'd like to talk about Eilidh Broome today," said MacMillan abruptly.

"You mentioned my mother."

"Eilidh Broome."

"No. You're not doing this," Thomas said, the anger rising in his voice. "Why did you mention my mother?"

"You're not ready, Thomas. I'm sorry."

Thomas lunged for MacMillan, grabbing him by his prison issue t-shirt.

"You sick fuck," snarled the lawyer. "What is wrong with you?"

"Mr Leven, please let go of the prisoner."

As he held on, Thomas stared into MacMillan's eyes.

"Mr Leven, please," insisted the guard. Thomas released his grip. MacMillan's eyes remained focused.

"Maybe take five, Thomas."

"That might be an idea, Mr Leven."

Officer Raymond took Thomas into the hallway and poured him a cup of water from the fountain. "He's like that, Mr Leven. I try not to bite but it's hard, especially when it becomes personal."

Thomas didn't respond. As his breathing slowed, he took a sip of the water.

"I'll be just down the hall. Give me a shout when you're ready to go back in."

Thomas offered Raymond a chastened nod and checked his phone. While Kaitlin's status still showed that she was online, there remained no response.

Damn.

Practically, he had no minute taker but the roots of his frustration lay deeper. For the first time since Milene left, Thomas had started to allow himself to enjoy the nearness of another. And by catching her glance his way, he suspected that the delight he felt was mutual. Thomas understood that workplace infatuations, even trysts between colleagues were not uncommon, and at Kunis Clement, this was no different. While her presence - and her wide and welcoming smile - was something that he was growing accustomed to, Thomas was increasingly aware that as MacMillan's innumerable threads weaved tangentially in his mind and around his feet, the young paralegal's sobering influence had been keeping him on a firmer footing. Professional considerations aside, the realisation was dawning that he looked forward to being in Kaitlin's company.

After refilling his cup, Thomas felt ready to return to the interview suite.

"Apologies for the earlier outburst, Mr MacMillan. It was unprofessional."

"Perhaps I was lacking in the requisite amount of tact, Thomas. No harm done."

Although his curiosity demanded a clear explanation, Thomas thought it wiser - and safer - to allow the prisoner to dictate the direction in which to proceed. Though hoping for a quick resolution to the affair, he hadn't anticipated the matter of Eilidh Broome to be broached so soon. From the conversations they'd already had, Thomas expected MacMillan to reel around the subject for a bit longer before he started to open up about the girl whose demise captured the imagination and spurred the ire of the Scottish public.

While the information MacMillan was about to share could prove the key to unlocking a mystery which had stumped observers for decades, Thomas decided against using his phone as a recording device lest the seemingly unprofessional deviation from the norm again derailed proceedings.

"Within days of my arrival at Mrs Telfer's, I'd started to warm to my flatmate, Andrew…"

Thomas interrupted. "I thought you wanted to talk about Eilidh Broome?"

"I do. And if you'll allow me…" added MacMillan with a pause, "I will."

He wants to talk, so let him talk.

"The floor's all yours."

"You're too kind," said MacMillan with a pointed lack of sincerity. "Andrew may have been slightly coarse and lacking in social graces but he appeared to be a solid fellow. And less of a philistine than I'd originally thought. He didn't have to take me under his wing but he took on that responsibility."

"Why do you think he did?"

"As quare as he was, Andrew was more of a people's person than I. You could place him in almost any company and he'd make a connection. I admired that quality in him."

"What did you talk about?" asked Thomas, "I mean, you didn't appear to have a great deal in common with one another."

MacMillan paused before answering. "Everything and nothing."

"Such as?"

"Mechanics, politics, sport."

"You bonded over sport?"

"Not quite but we did make a point of watching television together on those Sunday afternoons that Mrs Telfer would be off on her visits. I'd return from church and he'd be just stirring, usually recovering from the excesses of the previous night. We'd cook up some sausage and eggs for our rolls and perhaps watch a detective serial or a game show. I imagine that at some level, we both had a need for companionship that was fraternal and non competitive. Like me, Andrew was an only child. His parents, well meaning sorts, had christened him Hector, after the Trojan warrior but as I'm sure you can imagine, it was far more acceptable to be named after an ancient apostle than it was to share one's name with a mythological prince. Seemingly, it was a name that had caused him no end of grief at the hands of the primary school bullies, unfamiliar with the classics. So, in the interests of a less combative school experience, he began to use his middle name: Andrew."

"Did you socialise with him beyond the flat?"

"Not immediately. When he was home, he spent most of his time working on his motorbikes, to the mild annoyance of Mrs Telfer, or with his pigeons which irked her more."

"How so?"

"Poor Mrs Telfer had a mortal fear of birds. Particularly dead ones."

Recalling the birds on the road to Kirkmalcolm, Thomas asked, "Can you expand on that?"

"I shall," said MacMillan, "but in good time. As Mrs Telfer's flat was situated at the top of the building, she benefited from having a narrow but private roof terrace. Her first husband, Andrew's uncle, kept pigeons in a doocot he'd built on the left side of the terrace. Even though it was a sun trap, she refused to spend any more time on the terrace than she had to."

"Was her husband around?"

"Sadly for her, no. He was killed on the building site he'd been working on. A crane operator lost control of the crossbeam he was lifting and down it came."

"And that's what killed him?"

"Actually, no. It struck a labourer who was holding a nail gun. It was he who shot a flurry of four inch nails into his

126

head."

"Christ almighty," said Thomas aloud. "Wasn't he wearing a helmet?"

"This was the nineteen eighties, Thomas. Back then, attitudes towards matters of health and safety tended to be a little laissez-faire. Anyway, the doocot he'd built was about ten feet tall by four feet wide. It was quite a structure. Mrs Telfer couldn't bear to look at it as it reminded her of him so for years it had stood empty. Her second husband, in an attempt to rid the house of any trace of his predecessor, wanted to tear it down but she steadfastly refused."

"He died too?"

"Working on an unearthed street light with a heavy hangover apparently brought to an end his tenure as man of the house. Mrs Telfer swore herself off marriage for life. To make ends meet, she started taking in lodgers, students from out of town, mainly. When Andrew was accepted into the University, it was understandable that he'd return to the place where he'd spent countless weekends with his father's brother and his Welsh wife. And as her late husband and Andrew loved the pigeons, she eventually relented, took her washing line down and allowed him to reopen the hut."

"That was very decent of her."

"She did charge him five pounds a week for the inconvenience though but between the auto repairs and the occasional spot of delivery driving, he made that up quite quickly. It was from the doocot where I first saw Eilidh Broome."

Thomas consulted his notes.

"I'd watched her before I met her."

"In what way?"

"I'd been spending more time with Andrew, up on the roof. I'd read from the mountain of text books I'd been given while he'd occasionally need someone to pass him a wrench. He was always tinkering with an engine or something. Mrs Telfer often had people over. Afternoon women, who like her, had lost a husband or a loved one. Whatever."

"Is that where the cards came in?" asked Thomas, consulting Mrs Telfer's paperwork.

"Right. When they came over, we'd head out to the doocot. Remember Andrew, she'd say, safe is the owner of a clear conscience. Keep your nose away from Edelweiss Terrace."

"Edelweiss Terrace?"

"The block that backed onto ours. She was insistent that bad energy surrounded that building. As with most things, Mrs Telfer trusted her own instincts but Andrew was a young man with a thick head so he paid little notice to the rantings of his eccentric aunt. Anyway, in the lower nook of the doocot, Andrew did his smoking. He said that it kept him focussed but mainly he'd talk nonsense, giggle then fall asleep. He kept a selection of drinks, left behind by the more sozzled of Mrs Telfer's groups. Pernod and Advocaat. Those were big favourites. They'd always arrive with a bottle but would rarely leave with one. I was not much of a drinker back then but I'd accept a swift tot on a cold day. There was also a collection of magazines of an adult nature which Andrew claimed were left there by his aunt's second husband. We joked about asking her and her ladies to reach out beyond the ether for confirmation. I wish that we hadn't now."

"Why is that?"

"She was just a poor abandoned soul, ill-equipped to make sense of the madness that followed. It was unfair to mock her in that way. I am sorry for that."

MacMillan continued. "Among the few possessions that the late Mr Telfer had left behind were an air rifle and a pair of binoculars. As there were many students living in the area, the mess behind the blocks could be foul. It's not like today with all your colour coordinated recycling and the like. Back then, one shovelled all of one's rubbish into the big metal bins and left them in these stone middens. Which were always full of takeaway boxes and chip wrappers. And if you didn't put the lid on tightly, as anyone who'd ever lived in these communal blocks will attest, vermin would become attracted to the area. When he'd had a few, Andrew would fire off a few pellets in the direction of the feasting rats. His eyesight and the weapon's poor calibration meant that the animals were rarely in danger. He urged me to try it. I was reluctant but he insisted. So I cocked the barrel, inserted a ball bearing and took aim. Andrew watched on through the binoculars, guiding me to where the rodents were gathered. Crack! Jesus, he said excitedly. First time! Beginners' luck, I said, hiding my disappointment."

"Disappointment?"

"I had no intention of killing the creature. As unappealing as vermin may appear, I wished it no harm."

"See, this doesn't make sense. You've shown remorse for the fates of Cicely Telfer and the rat that you shot but not for Eilidh Broome? The girl you murdered."

"The girl that the authorities *claim* I murdered."

"The girl the authorities *convicted* you of murdering."

"You say potato and I say, check your notes."

MacMillan leant over to look at Thomas's sparse paperwork. "You do have those notes, don't you? Or is your opinion based on some scurrilous reportage or a ludicrous television dramatisation?"

Thomas didn't bite. He urged MacMillan to continue.

"Andrew said that I was a natural and given my prowess with a rifle, he suggested that maybe I should think about joining him in the T.A."

"The Territorial Army?" asked Thomas.

"He'd been a member for a year or so but he'd made up his mind that he saw his future with the Royal Engineers. A few months and he'd be off to Harrogate for his training. Insisting I take another go, I went through the motions again and rattled the projectile off the iron lid of the bin, sending an echo around the back court which set a few curtains twitching. Andrew put his hand on the barrel and quickly pulled it back inside, lest any neighbours saw and called the police. He picked up the binoculars and looked at the windows. Most of the twitchers had a quick look then returned to their business. Then Andrew spotted something. 'There!', he'd said. 'Second floor, ten o'clock.'

He didn't know her name but he said that she was quite something. Andrew passed the binoculars and urged me to take a look. He was right. She was. Curtains back, her brown hair tied up, almost wearing a flimsy gown, stradling the window ledge with one long, bare leg dangling over the edge. That was Eilidh Broome."

"Did she notice you?"

"No but she didn't care who saw her. In fact, she demanded that one did. A few days later, during a break from studies, I returned to the flat. I'd forgotten to pack a sandwich that morning so rather than waste money, I thought that I'd relieve Mrs Telfer of some of the cold cuts left over from her gathering the previous evening. As no one was home, I took my selection out onto the roof terrace to eat but shortly afterwards, the weather took a turn for the worse so I quickly sought shelter in Andrew's hut. After I'd eaten, and fed a few crumbs to the pigeons, I undid the hatch and looked out over Edelweiss Terrace, hoping to catch another glimpse of the girl who had taken up residence in my every waking thought."

"Was she there?"

"My luck was in. Again, the curtains to her room were back and she stood at the window. There was someone else with her but I couldn't make out exactly who. I took the caps off the binoculars and adjusted the sights. She turned away from my view then a moment later, turned back and pressed against the window frame, she stood like a star. The other person in the room held her breasts and slowly began to thrust, pushing her against the pane. As the act continued, she showed no obvious signs of pleasure. Her gaze was fixed. On where I was? Perhaps. A multitude of feelings and emotions engulfed me and my heart felt as though it was rising through my chest and into my throat. I was glad no one was home that day."

"When did you first meet her?"

"In person? I'd started to go with Andrew to his local, near the bottom of Byres Road. It wouldn't have been my choice of recreation spot to frequent but once I got used to the debates and the ribbing, I didn't find it too unpleasant."

"Is this where you started drinking?"

"The odd doocot shot aside, I was pretty much teetotal. Given that I was polite and sober, the proprietor took a liking to me and offered me some shifts behind the bar. He'd employed a few students in the past but they always helped themselves to his wares when he wasn't around. A teetotaller might eat a few packs of nuts and crisps but that he could handle. Although I lived a very spartan lifestyle, my bursary and my savings were wafer thin so I accepted his offer. Most Friday and Saturday nights, I'd work there and it was perfectly agreeable."

"You met Eilidh there?"

"No, that kind of place wasn't her style."

"Where did you meet her?"

"A few of the pub's patrons were going to see a friend of theirs playing with his band, at an invitation only, after hours event, and asked me if I fancied coming along. I had little interest in popular music but Andrew had already left with a female friend. I was in no rush to go back to have my sleep disturbed by hours of their primal moaning so I agreed. I joined them at midnight after the pub closed and we walked to the venue which happened to be a large residence near the Botanics."

"Who was 'we'?"

"A couple I knew from University, Iain and Gill and their friends. Barry was a photographer and Jemma had just started to work in television, I think. Anyway, we went into this long room where the band played. Apart from the ear splitting volume at which they performed, there was nothing memorable about the drone they created but going by the looks on the faces of the small crowd, I was in a minority of one. The way the room was laid out meant that the musicians played with the ornate windows behind them, surrounded by tall candles on stands. It looked better than it sounded, I thought. Everyone was on the same level except for a few perched on the staircase to the band's left. And that is where I first saw Eilidh Broome in person."

"Can you tell me what your thoughts were on that?"

"If I said that she was the most beautiful thing I'd ever seen, I'd be lying. There were at least half a dozen women in the faculty that were more pleasing on the eye than Eilidh Broome. The way that she has since been beatified would be laughable if it weren't so tragic. Some sort of patron saint of the fallen. No, it was how she made me feel."

"And that was?"

"I felt drunk and I hadn't touched a drop. I couldn't take my eyes off her. There was something about the way she existed that spoke to me in the most primal of ways. I was clearly not alone in thinking that. In plain English, being in her presence was akin to receiving a charge of pure sexual energy, something I was ill prepared for."

"So you were smitten?"

"I'd say it was more primitive than that. Seeing her against the window of her flat was nothing compared to being within touching distance of her."

"Did she notice you?"

"Heavens, no. Her eyes were closed as she swayed to the rhythm of the music. I wish I could turn back the clock…"

"You'd do things differently?"

"I'd burn every last inch of it to the ground."

"Like you did with Mrs Telfer's house?"

Displeased by Thomas's comment, MacMillan sat back and turned his head to the side. "Again, you seem to be placing an inordinate amount of trust in the testimony of those who weren't there."

"Is there a reason why I shouldn't?"

"Not so long ago, you warned me about the dangers of blind faith and now…"

"The findings of the Scottish judicial system in this case were based on fact, Mr MacMillan."

"And again, we return to the start of the song."

"Meaning?"

"You have cast iron proof that those facts are irrefutable?"

"Well, yes…"

MacMillan smiled and replied slowly, "I would very much like to review a copy of those documents."

So would I, thought Thomas as he rifled through the few notes he did have.

"Would you like me to continue?"

"Please."

"After the music ended, I presumed that we'd head out into the cool night but Iain said, this was where it was going to get interesting."

"What did he mean by that?"

"From the mezzanine, staff with trays of filled glasses circulated but you weren't allowed to take one. Doing that meant you'd be immediately and forcibly removed. It was all a bit dramatic, I thought. The waiters received their cue from those on the balcony. A nod from them, you took a glass and you were allowed to move into another room."

"Was Eilidh still there?"

"She'd come down and was embracing the guitar player from the band. His hair was dyed black but he was as pale as she. And so painfully thin that he looked as if a slight gust might topple him over. I took a few steps to my right with the intention of doing just that. The girl was so near to me that I could detect her scent."

"How did that make you feel?"

"What makes the plants move and the blooms shake, Mr Leven."

Wind, thought Thomas.

"Desire. I couldn't hide it and I didn't want to. I asked who she was and who the musician was to her. Iain told me that it was Eilidh and her brother Archie. Ah. Just then, a waiter stopped by our party. As he did, they all looked to the balcony for confirmation. The taller of the two motioned, signifying that a drink was to be offered to Iain. His excitement though was curtailed somewhat when his partner wasn't chosen. Barry too missed out, but Jemma made the cut. Another nod and another drink was offered. Barry and Jemma remained silent but it was clear that the former wasn't happy at his partner's invitation. Naturally, I was nonplussed about the whole thing even though Gill insisted that it was the most desireable after party in town. It all seemed a bit arbitrary to me, I thought as Jenna and Barry continued their sniping. I asked Iain just who made the decisions. That would be Sand, he said. This is Sand's thing."

"Who is Sand?"

"You don't know who Sand is? That is surprising, Thomas."

"Must be in my other notes. For the benefit of clarity, could you refresh my memory?"

MacMillan leant forward and snorted impatiently. He shook his head, "Are you toying with me?"

"No, Mr MacMillan, I am not. I just don't have…"

"You really don't know about Sand?"

Thomas again realised that he wasn't as prepared as he should've been. "I'll be getting the remainder of the files later this week. Tell me about Sand."

"As Iain said, this was Sand's event. And as I was about to find out, the planets revolved around Sand. As the recriminations, the guilt and the excitement built, I was drawn to a large landscape hanging over the mantelpiece. I left the squabbling couples to take a closer look. As dark as the painting was, I could tell in a heartbeat that it was Scharr Point."

"Haven't heard of that."

"Only islanders refer to it by its former name. The point now carries the name of the architect who brought light to the area. On the south western tip of Westerwick, below its elevated soft rock crags, is an inlet. As with the more dramatic coastal edge, a number of unfortunates unfamiliar with the terrain have perished there. On the island they say that a person who knows their rock from their chalk is a person who knows what they're doing. Considering myself one of those, I'd climb down to the cove and provided I remained alert to the loose stones and the rising tide, it would be a perfect place to spend an hour or two in blessed seclusion away from the domestic maelstrom. Often, I'd gather pieces of driftwood and build a fire in the shallow cave of the inlet. At its mouth, there are two fossilised trunks, the significance of which have been debated in churches and in parlours for centuries."

"Tell me more about the painting."

"Given the time I'd spent there, it was instantly recognisable. I'd know that coastline and cove anywhere. And this was quite a representation, painted in the days before the construction of McLennan's lighthouse. I wouldn't pretend to be a great art lover but seeing the moon reflected on the black waters of the bay, gripped me in ways that no other secular piece has ever done before. Or since for that matter. Have you ever heard of Stendhal Syndrome?"

Thomas shook his head at MacMillan's digression.

"An inexplicable condition which occurs when an individual is confronted by phenomena of great beauty. Confusion, rapidly racing heartbeat, even hallucinations. Had it not happened to me, I would not have believed it possible."

"Do you think that it was triggered by the painting or by Eilidh?"

"That is a fair point, Thomas." MacMillan took a moment.

"Perhaps it was a combination of both? I don't know. But standing in front of that painting, in an instant, I was home, by the sunless sea, lost in the beauty of the brushwork, in the depth of its colours. I wanted to dive into it. As I stood admiring it, a voice, rich and unfamiliar, asked if I recognised it."

"Was that Sand?"

MacMillan nodded.

"I replied that I recognised the location but not the piece

itself. Sand told me that it was Edward Scrimegour. 1875."

"Can you describe him to me?"

"Dark clothing, taller than me, thin, bony face with an aroma of anise and smoke that wasn't cigarettes. Measured but a little unsettling. Sand said that Scrimegour had painted a number of island landscapes but none with the bleak majesty of this. I couldn't disagree."

Thomas searched for the image on his phone.

"That's the one," said MacMillan. "Look at those heavy strokes. I so wanted to touch the painting but hadn't the courage to do so. Sand did, though. Tips of the fingers following the outline of the paint. Sand was interested in my accent and narrowed it down to either Boquarran or South Fintan."

"He was able to pinpoint where you were from?"

"Almost to the croft. When I said that I was born just north of Struan's Field, Sand motioned to one of the staff and said that we should talk some more about that most sacred place. As I was handed the small shot glass, I could see my party gawping at me. I mentioned that I wasn't keen on alcohol but Sand quelled my concern. Curare was a little exotic for most tastes but enjoyable nonetheless. Don't worry, Sand reassured me, it's quite mild. The stronger stuff was kept for later. My ignorance in such matters was tempered by how flattered I felt. As bitter as the curare was, the jealousy from my party was surprisingly sweet."

"Curare is some kind of alcohol?"

"Far more addictive, Thomas. You're a man of the world. Consider a sedative that combines lysergic with the euphoric."

Sounds intriguing, thought Thomas.

"What Sand offered me that night was the substance in its least potent form. Just a taste to encourage me to join the gathering in the Red Room. So I went along."

"Against your will?"

"No. Of my own accord."

"If he was so disturbing, may I ask why?"

"I figured that Sand might be the gateway to…"

MacMillan paused for thought. Eyes closed, his head swayed gently from side to side.

In the silence, Thomas watched the prisoner, stripped of artifice, lose himself as if entombed in a memory, immersed in a composition only he could hear.

"To Eilidh?"

"Correct," said MacMillan.

"Did your relationship with her begin that night?"

"Our spiritual connection, yes but our physical coupling happened soon after. After partaking, the more relaxed I became. As with alcohol, curare forced one to strip back long held inhibitions, however unlike booze, one neither fears the possibilities nor frets over the ramifications. Sand called it the true liberation of one's soul."

"And you agreed?"

"I did."

"Can you elaborate as to what happened in the Red Room?"

"My first physical impression of it was that it was a repurposed parlour. Dimly lit and very warm. Including Sand and myself, there were about ten to fifteen people present.

At the end of the room was an open fire and cushions were strewn over the floor. Music played. Tonal, rhythmic but from elsewhere."

"And Eilidh was there?"

"She was. Sand took the high backed chair and directed me to a seat on the floor, close to where Eilidh was. Jemma from our party was already there, on the other side of Eilidh, passionately kissing a man whose hand was massaging her exposed breast. On the floor at her feet, was a woman I didn't recognise. She placed a hand on each of Jemma's knees and slowly prised open her legs. Without wishing to appear crude, I was extremely aroused. Behind her another man, entirely exposed except for a grotesque animal skin mask, pulled at his penis while in the corner, a completely naked young woman suckled on Iain's bare chest as a man fellated him. I'd had no experience of anything like this before but the sensation I had was not one of shock. In fact, as my own penis became distended and uncommonly heavy, I felt no compunction or shame. So I too disrobed. As I did, Eilidh stood up and danced. For me and me alone. While this was happening, Sand was watching me."

"How long did this orgy last?"

MacMillan leant back and shook his head.

"Thomas, once again, you're labouring under a misapprehension. If you think that the Red Room played host to a common or garden swingers session, then I have to ask in all seriousness, whether you're the right man to be speaking to me now. I had real hopes for you."

Thomas looked back at MacMillan, impassively. "The notes that…"

"I'll return to the subject of your notes and the case files that your esteemed colleagues have passed on to you in a moment," interrupted MacMillan. "Heavens, even those who made that laughable dramatisation have a firmer handle on the events than you. And their take was riseable."

Thomas' eyes darted around the sparse interview room. He had nothing and MacMillan could sense it.

"We opened up on faith earlier, Thomas," he said quietly. "But maybe it's time we talked about trust. I accept that it may be hard to put one's trust in someone like me. You only know me from what you've been told, or what you've read. But whether you want to accept it or not, you can take this as a cast iron guarantee. What you're getting from me is as real as that magnificent nose on Mr Rodgers' face."

Upon hearing his name, the guard glared at the prisoner.

"Take a moment, Thomas. Ask yourself this. Who can you turn to with absolute certainty? Who can you trust?"

MacMillan's words hung in the air "Have a think about it. I'm not going anywhere."

Thomas took the advice of MacMillan and again stepped out of the room. Why did Kunis Clement send him here, unprepared? Again, he checked his phone for signs of Kaitlin. Untouched and untainted Kaitlin. As MacMillan did with Eilidh Broome, Thomas couldn't help but obsess over Kaitlin Ramsay.

Lemonade. Her calves, like upturned hearts. Twice as tight. Unblemished. Defined yet not sculpted. On the right side of angular.

He thought of her serious, then at play. He preferred the

latter.

Like a star. Against a window. Eyes like sin. That's how it goes, right?

He wanted to trust her. He wanted to taste her.

****

"The exploration of one's physicality was simply the appetiser."

"The main course was?"

"Something very different. As matters became heated, Sand stood and clapped. Everyone stopped what they were doing and moved back towards the walls. Unaware of the room's protocol, I followed suit. The small man in the mask stood and moved to the now cleared, centre of the room. He continued to flail at his penis as Sand started a low mantra. I couldn't make it out initially but the louder it grew, the clearer it became.

'Shall we?' they said.

'We shall.

Shall we?

We shall.'

At this point, a young woman was led into the room. Naked but for some binding around her head and torso, she appeared to be in a state of stupor. Before they laid her down, her bindings were removed."

MacMillan paused to consider his words.

"My first impressions were that she was covered in welts but as my eyes adjusted, I could see the reality. On her forehead, and all over her torso it appeared that she had patches of missing skin. Then Sand spoke and the mantra changed.

'God is dead and magic is afoot.'

As it built to a frenzy, the masked man ejaculated and Sand motioned for me to be brought forward. I knelt down and penetrated her. As I did, using a thin blade, the masked man removed a small slice of her skin. God is dead and magic is afoot, the mantra continued. Placing the sliver onto Sand's tongue, the masked man encouraged the congregation to approach and suckle from her open wounds."

"Did you partake?"

"I did. As the mantra built, I could feel Sand's hands reaching around to my genitals. Black nails digging into my groin. The warm breath on the back of my neck as I too was penetrated.

'God is dead and magic is afoot.'"

MacMillan slowly lifted the paper cup and placed it to his lips. "Must have been eight or nine in the morning before the doors opened and we left."

"And the effect it had on you was?"

"As if I had been reborn into light. At the time of the experience, it seemed as if each connection one made with another living being was as if one had connected with the entire planet. Sand said that who I was and what I wanted could no longer be denied. On that point, Sand's assertion was astute. Don't fight it, feel it."

"But later?"

"I realised that I wasn't alone in having misgivings."

"The others?"

"For the couples who came with me that night, life was irrevocably changed. Gill left Iain soon afterwards and he never received another invite to the Red Room."

"Why was that?"

"He did the one thing we were told not to do."

"And that was?"

"He talked about it."

"Did you maintain contact with him after he was exiled?"

MacMillan looked away. The shrug that accompanied it was non-committal. "Jemma didn't. She moved to London soon afterwards and her career exploded."

"But you returned to The Red Room?"

"To the chagrin of my tutors and my landlady, I returned at every possible juncture."

Thomas drummed his pen on a line he'd made earlier. "You said you'd return to why Mrs Telfer had a fear of birds."

"I did," replied MacMillan. "Just before she received the call that her beloved first husband died, two birds fell from the sky and landed at her feet."

"On the balcony?"

MacMillan whispered, "A harbinger of doom, she said."

Calling for the guard, the prisoner stated, "That'll do us for today."

"Already?"

"I can only take you so far, Mr Leven."

"One more thing, Mr MacMillan," asked Thomas, opening his phone. "Do these mean anything to you?"

He clicked on his photo gallery and opened up the image

he'd taken of the impaled man outside of the Kunis Clement building. Swiping right, he showed MacMillan the markings daubed onto Rothwell Glen's paintings.

"Show me the first one again," he said.

MacMillan then placed his hands on the table top. With the digits of both, he made two large v's. He then crossed his index fingers to fashion a third, smaller v.

"Indulgentia, invocatio, vindicta."

While MacMillan knew that Thomas would easily be able to translate the words from the Latin, the prisoner could tell that the lawyer remained perplexed by the context.

"It means that his Christ cannot help him now. Looks like you've got homework to contend with this weekend."

As MacMillan was led away, Thomas collected his belongings and checked his phone.

Sorry! Birds, eh?

Wow. I'm here now.

K

Any annoyance he'd felt about being ghosted by his paralegal was now checked by the fact that she was again nearby.

****

"How did it go?" she asked, her voice skipping.

To that, Thomas didn't respond. He wanted to ask her where she'd been and who she'd been talking to when she was online all fucking day but as his deep seated need for reason narrowly exceeded any incipient yearning, quiet acceptance was the path taken.

If I'm going to take a chance on Kaitlin, he told himself, I'll have to be quick to forgive. As her direct superior though, it was perfectly appropriate to ask as to her movements for the rest of the day.

Kaitlin explained that as it was Friday, she'd made plans for an early dinner with a friend. Thomas had no right to be feeling any sort of jealousy. He knew that but he still did.

"I need you to copy every single thing you found at The Mitchell then get over to the University before five. Ask for Lynne at the Law Workshop and tell her I want everything she has archived on this case, files, photos, literature, anything, as a matter of urgency. I also want you to check the relevance of the words indulgence, invocation and vengeance. English and Latin. Cross reference those words with everything you get."

"What about you?"

"I need to speak with Mira."

Chapter 9 - Noticed

"It's not as easy as that, Thomas."

"I don't understand," said Thomas, his irritation palpable and growing. "Why not?"

Mira sat on the edge of her desk and tucked her hair behind her ear. She lit a cigarette. "We need to show some patience."

"That wasn't what you originally said. Straight in and out. Get the explanation and take it from there. Well, that's clearly not happening."

"I can understand your frustration," she said.

Thomas' senses told him that something wasn't right.

"Just keep your cool. So what if it's another week or two? You've not got any plans and besides, isn't this the ideal way to prepare you for a return to Kunis Clement?"

Thomas reached into his jacket pocket and removed a silver coloured sleeve of capsules. He popped the last two and tightly crushed the now empty packaging into his hand.

"Motherfucker," Thomas spat, dropping the metal sleeve. Instinctively, he shook his hand and stretched his fingers wide, checking his palm. A sharp edge of the compressed foil wrapping had sliced through the outer, fleshy layer of tissue at the bottom of his thumb. Small droplets of blood ran down onto his wrist and past the cuff of his shirt.

Mira put her cigarette down and exhaled. "Let me take a look at that."

"It's fine, Mira," he replied. "Just another one to add to the collection."

Her look suggested that she would brook no argument. "There's a sliver of the foil lodged under the skin. Here let me..."

Mira took Thomas's hand and squeezed either side of the incision.

"There it is," she said. Before he could react, Mira placed her mouth over the cut. As her warm, fleshy lips suckled on his wound, Thomas was filled with an almost overwhelming urge to slide his free hand behind her ear and grab her thick hair. Until this moment, he hadn't realised just how starved of physical contact he had been. So intense an ache, he could feel it in the pit of his stomach and below.

As the tip of Mira's tongue traced the wound on the palm of his hand, this barely functional, but highly visceral act reminded Thomas of how blurred the lines between the personal and the private could be for Mira. An intimacy which triggered memories of a night at a Perthshire lodge as Mira, after checking on her grandson, placed herself by the unlatched door and watched as her naked step daughter straddled Thomas. Milene had her back to the half light, where Mira stood. She hadn't seen her step-mother but Thomas had.

It never happened again nor did they ever mention it but reluctant as he was to admit it, the reality of being watched by his middle aged boss - and prospective mother in law - was an erotic memory Thomas occasionally returned to.

With her teeth, Mira removed the sliver. A smudge of Thomas's blood remained on her lips. She took a silk handkerchief from her inner pocket and pushed it tightly against the wound.

"You'll ruin that," said Thomas.

"I'm more concerned about ruining you," she said tenderly.

Thomas exhaled. Despite her detached public demeanour, and her voyeuristic interest in her step daughter's carnality, Mira's instincts had been, in the main, predominantly maternal towards Thomas.

"It's been a very hard year for you. I know that. But you need to focus. Your recovery is very important to us."

"Us?"

"Kunis Clement, of course."

Oh.

Mira smiled.

"I know that I have to let go of the past but I'm finding it hard to move on."

"I can understand that," said Mira. "After Martin died, I too found myself adrift but I had to hold it together for the company, and for Milene. She'd already been through the

death of her mother and the abandonment of her son's father.
Then Martin. All within three years. That's why I was glad
that you stepped in. Someone reliable, someone she could
trust. You were exactly what she needed at that time."

"Just at that time?"

"Perhaps," replied Mira, bluntly.

"I thought we had a good thing."

"You did. But sometimes a relationship lasts a lifetime or it
runs its course by the time one takes to finish a starter."

Thomas pushed. "Does Milene consider it over?"

Mira patted the silk square on his palm.

"I think that it's best that you don't dwell too much on what
Milene thinks."

"Why?"

"It's not helpful."

"I still love her."

"I know. And I'm sure deep down, she cares for you."

"Surely that's enough?"

"Jesus!" snapped Mira, "You almost killed her son."

Though the echo of her words faded, the room suffocated
in silence.

He was more than aware of what he'd done but Mira's
verbal reminder felt like an unnecessary kick to his gut. From
promising trainee to a potential future partner of Kunis
Clement within a very short space of time and groomed by
the Big Dog himself, Thomas's instincts, his tenacity and
his attention to detail had helped the firm triumph in a
handful of cases which were hitherto thought unwinnable.

Drinks with grateful clients over lunch became habitual. The invitations to dinner from relieved offenders increased as did the celebratory trips to the nearest toilet cubicle. Those in the deepest of trouble asked for him by name. It had felt good to be Thomas Leven, the sharpest blade on the block.

Then on one nondescript Tuesday, his world came crashing down.

With Milene on call, it was down to Thomas to pick up the boy from school and take him to archery practice. When he didn't show, his tutor called the boy's mother. Agreeing to put him into the after school club until contact could be made with her absent partner, Milene eventually located him, ordering another round of drinks at a golf club in Bearsden. He claimed it was a short notice meeting that he couldn't get out of but it was an occurrence that had been happening with increasing regularity. Milene, clearly angry, ordered him to get there immediately and that they'd talk about this later.

Enraged at being called out in front of his clients and colleagues, and already over the limit, Thomas got in the car. Another wee bump would sharpen his focus, he thought. For those who were familiar with Kunis Clement's third floor, behaviour like this was as common as the ordering of a sandwich. Speeding down the Maryhill Road, cutting cars and skipping lights, Thomas picked the boy up at the Academy. If there were any issues, and there rarely were, he knew that he had a direct line to Campbell Ames who at this moment, was out of uniform and standing three feet from Rothwell Glen at the same bar.

As the archery class was taking place a couple of miles away at the High School, Thomas took what he presumed to be the quickest route. Mum is never late, the boy whined. Thomas' half hearted apology bounced off the unimpressed child as he crawled his way through the slow moving traffic on the Great Western Road. Mum always gets me there on time. An even slower moving, wide loaded dump truck taking up most of the outside lane meant that he was going to miss another chance to get through the junction so Thomas swerved around the truck and 'floored it' with the light on red. I don't like this music, said the boy.

Thomas failed to see the postal van until it hit the Mercedes side on. The impact sent his car careering onto the pavement and into a lamppost. It was only luck and some quick thinking by the pedestrians at the nearby crossing that prevented the collision from being a fatal one. Thomas's side took much of the initial impact but Milene's son, in the passenger seat, hit the crossing pole. Miraculously, he escaped with a broken arm and a few cuts. The blameless postal worker suffered a concussion and facial lacerations but Thomas himself was knocked cold. Torn ligaments, a sliced cheekbone, broken pelvis and a skull with a three inch crack was the physical price that he paid.

All three were pulled out of the smouldering wreckage by concerned passers by. The emergency services arrived shortly afterwards taking all parties across the river to the old Southern General. When Mira broke the news to Milene, she promptly collapsed with shock. As Collins collected her from The Royal and took her straight to her son's side, Mira, assisted by Campbell Ames, dealt with the immediate practicalities of the incident. Although handed a three year driving ban, it had taken a considerable chunk of Kunis Clement's powers of persuasion to convince the authorities not to hammer Thomas for reckless endangerment and for driving under the influence.

In fact, with the assistance of a sympathetic prosecutor and a helpful 'eye witness', charges were drummed up against the injured postal worker, who lost his job after being convicted of dangerous driving. To rub salt into the postman's already deep wounds, the firm sent him a bill for the repair of the company Mercedes. If Thomas hadn't known it by that point, he now knew that Kunis Clement played for keeps.

"Listen," said Mira softly, "maybe we need to slow down a bit. After all, you've been away for quite a while. I can get Sam to go in tomorrow…"

"No," snapped Thomas. His tone took Mira by surprise. He instantly reigned it in. "I can do this."

"If you're sure that you are up to it," replied Mira with a shrug.

"I want you to be able to rely on me again. To trust me."

Mira nodded contentedly.

"So, did you have any joy with the files I asked you about this morning?"

"Didn't Collins take three boxes to you?"

"He did but there were almost no notes from counsel, no tapes nor transcripts in what was given. Surely, that can't be correct?"

"Doesn't sound right," said Mira, opening up a file on her desktop.

Thomas walked around the desk and hovered over Mira as she clicked on the icon. She looked up at him as if to say, too close but he didn't read the sign.

"Password protected," she said.

"Ah, ok," replied Thomas, still hovering.

"Do you mind?" said Mira sarcastically.

It took Thomas a second to realise that while she considered him close enough to watch him fuck her step daughter, sharing password information was a little too intimate.

Mira typed fast.

A sound.

She repeated her action.

The same sound.

"Not good?"

"There is an internal lock on this file," she said. "Let me try the old man's password."

"You know his password?"

"How much work would get done here if I didn't?"

Fair point, he thought.

Mira picked up her phone.

"You going to call him?"

"That's so twentieth century, Thomas."

Of course.

Before she had the chance to take the first drag of her latest cigarette, her phone buzzed. Mira slowly rubbed her brow and sighed.

"Nat Sen Notice. It means that the documents have been declared nationally sensitive."

"I know what it means, Mira but why in the name of fuck is there a notice on these files and more importantly, why is this the first I'm hearing of it?"

Mira's phone buzzed again. "As I thought," she said. "Need

to apply for a temporary lift. I'll make a few calls and see what we can do."

As her laptop screen snapped shut, a different alert sound emerged from her phone. Mira peered at the screen then answered.

"The old man?" whispered Thomas.

Mira shook her head.

"Can I call you back in two minutes, gullet mitt?" she said, softly, "In the middle of something."

Thomas's eyes lit up. From her greeting, he knew it was Milene. In Norwegian, gullet mitt meant 'my gold'. It was how her late father had addressed her since childhood.

Mira put the phone down and looked straight at Thomas, daring him to react. He didn't.

"Go home and have a relaxing night. There's nothing we can do until I hear back from the Scottish Office."

"The other thing I asked you about this morning…"

Again, Mira sighed. But for this, Thomas knew he could handle another mild display of exasperation. She reached across the desk for a small bunch of keys and using a thin, unremarkable skeleton, she opened the drawer which contained the panacea he needed. A few years previously, after a gathering at her house, an acquaintance who happened to be a consultant at the private clinic the old man used for his urinary issues, had left one of the other guests in such a state that she needed hospitalisation, albeit at the state hospital. To keep this away from the desk of Campbell Ames, the old man instructed Mira to take care of it personally. A steady stream of blank prescriptions was only the tip of the reparations.

She scribbled a signature and passed Thomas a blank prescription.

"The last one," she said.

Thomas took it and left without a word.

Chapter 10 - Sex Magick

The Good Health Pharmacy on the Hyndland Road was smaller than Middleton's, Thomas's first choice chemist. Unlike that pharmacy, he found the staff at the GHP talkative and more keen to ask about his well being than their competitors did. But as Thomas had handed over a script at Middletons only a few days earlier, he felt the risk was too great. Next door to the Good Health was Niro's fish and chips, which had been undergoing a refurbishment, turning it from old fashioned takeaway into a modern delicatessen with space outside for alfresco dining. Good health, thought Thomas, was everywhere.

Almost everywhere.

Maybe after this script, I'll see if it works for me.

At the shaded side of the pharmacy, by the entrance used by tradesmen and delivery drivers, the big yellow skip was close to overflowing with broken tiles, indented chrome and splintered wood. Thomas sat on the lip of the wall and removed the script from his jacket pocket.

What's on the menu today? Two hundred millilitres of liquid morphine. No, the weekend starts tomorrow. Best make it three hundred. And a box of prolonged release Tramadol capsules. Just the fifty milligrams, not the hundred this time. Don't need any more voices in my head.

Once he'd filled in his pharmaceutical order, Thomas started to write his name. His own name. He stopped suddenly and realised that he couldn't remember by which name he went at The Good Health Pharmacy.

He was Mr Clark at Middletons and at the big chain on Byres Road, he alternated between Stevens and Scott. They never remembered him anyway. But here, they most certainly would.

Jesus, Thomas. Think.

"Alright?" asked a cheery, familiar voice. "We were just talking about you the other day, so we were. Karen was saying, 'We've not seen that nice Mr Jamieson in for a while.'"

Jamieson, that's it. Thomas quickly tucked the script back into his pocket. He smiled at the pharmacy dispenser who offered him a cigarette. Thomas shook his head.

"I never thought I'd say this but we really could do with a proper downpour to cool us off."

"It is pretty warm."

"If you think it's warm out here, wait until you come inside," said the dispenser, fanning herself. "Absolutely roasting."

"A bit of fresh air will do you the world of good," said Thomas, desperately trying to remain calm. "How's you, anyway?"

"Same as ever," replied the dispenser, "though I don't know how fresh the air will be when I spark up."

"Working in a chemist's, I didn't think you'd be allowed to smoke."

"Ach fuck 'em. Tell you the truth, I've had enough. And the pharmacist is a bit of a prick."

"Really?"

"Really. We're the ones who do all the work. The dispensing, the checking and the counter work yet all he does is sit in the consultation room, watching ten second videos. Tik Tok? Prick Tok."

"I hear that."

"Anyway, I'm leaving at the end of the month."

"Sorry to hear that…it's Kimberly, right?"

"No, Stacey."

"My apologies. If you don't mind me asking, apart from working for a prick, why would you want to leave? It's surely a good job with decent pay?"

"Decent pay?" she laughed bitterly. "Aye, right you are!! Twelve years in here and I'm still not a kick in the arse off minimum wage."

"Seriously?"

"Seriously. The way I look at it now is this. Minimum wage? Minimum effort."

"I guess that's fair," reasoned Thomas.

"And besides, between you and me, he's turning into a fucking weirdo."

"A fucking weirdo on top of being a prick?"

"Aye. Don't get me wrong, he used to be alright. A prick but no' a bad prick, you know? But between the motorbike videos and the conspiracy theories, he turned into a right off-the-farm, fucking weirdo. Nae wonder his missus binned him."

Thomas shared his pain. "What happened?"

"She left him for a guy fae Arnold Clark."

"Which Arnold Clark?"

"Springburn. The one beside the KFC."

"Got you. Was there a reason behind the split?"

"The guy fae Arnold Clark offered her merr options, if you know what I mean," Stacey laughed, "but seriously, she'd lost patience with all his weirdness."

Thomas was intrigued. "Like what?"

"Well, when you start believing that your postman is a serial killer you either need some psychiatric help or…"

"Or you need to get your mail redirected," countered Thomas.

Stacey cackled then lowered her voice.

"Seriously though, after she moved out, he lost it. For a while, he went into full mid-life crisis mode. Bought a motorbike so big that he barely has the strength to hold it up. And a hot tub."

"A hot tub?"

"A fucking hot tub. He organised a wee party at his place for all the staff that supported him through the break up. Mexican food, pizzas and booze, nothing fancy but nice all the same. Then he says to me, 'Stacey, just say the word.' I said 'whit?' And he said, 'Anything you want, it's yours.'"

"You should've asked him for a pay rise."

Stacey laughed. "Then, wait til you hear this, he says that he's learned all about something called sex magick and that he wants me to join him in his hot tub so that he can tell me more about it. I telt him tae bolt, so I did."

"Not a fan of the hot tubs?"

"Depends who's asking, Mr Jamieson," she said coyly before adding, "Just as well I didnae tell my Davie."

"Why's that?"

"Cos he'd have fucked him."

"He'd have fucked him?"

"Aye, fucked him round the heid with a fence post. Away ye go wi' yer sex magick," she snorted.

Sex magick indeed.

"You're from around here, aren't you?"

Thomas took a moment to remember the fictional Mr Jamieson's address. "Not originally but I've been here for quite a while."

"Is it just me or is every guy in the West End either a walloper or a weirdo?"

Thomas laughed. He couldn't disagree.

"You want me to take your script in? The weirdo's with a

patient at the moment but I could get it started for you?"

"No it's good, Stacey, I'll be in with you in a minute. Thanks."

"If he's still got that heating on, I'm going to blow, I swear to God."

The dispenser stubbed her cigarette on the Good Health sign, flicked away the butt and returned to the shop. When he was sure no one was watching, Thomas removed the script and filled it in.

The shop front was small with room enough for one patient at the counter and one in the adjoining consultancy room. A little bell rang as Thomas entered the pharmacy.

"Well hello, Mr Jamieson," said Stacey, "Haven't seen you for absolute ages!"

"And hello to you too, Stacey. I have a prescription to present. Just saw the postman there. Did you know that he's the spitting image of Charles Manson?"

Stacey laughed and tried to shush Thomas.

"It might have been the beard," he added. "Or the swastika on his head?"

"The pharmacist is in the back at the moment but we'll have this ready for you shortly."

"No worries, Stacey. I might take a wee spin around the block on my Ducati until it's ready."

"You're terrible," whispered Stacey, enjoying the banter. "I'll get it made up for you, Mr Jamieson."

Thomas smiled and took a look at his phone. He opened up the messages from Milene. There was nothing new but he liked to see if she was 'live'. If she was and she saw that he was, then maybe…

Wait. A message from Kaitlin.

Got a box of docs from Lynn.
Do you want me to leave them at the office for you
or bring them with me to Kirkmalcolm tomorrow?

Thomas replied.

I'd like to take a look at them ASAP.
Could you bring them to me?

Kaitlin responded immediately.

I'm meeting a friend in ten minutes but
I can bring them over to you after I finish?

Fuck.

OK.

Thomas typed out his address and sent it. He added…

Does the name Innes Guthrie mean anything to you?

Before she could answer, the consultancy door opened. The voice on its other side was one that was familiar to Thomas.

"So I should just apply a liberal coating of the ointment to the area?"

"Yes, it's very straightforward Mr Stobbie," said the pharmacy's other dispenser in a voice similar to Stacey's. "Make sure the area's clean and keep an eye out for recurrence of the infection. Change your wife's dressings every forty eight hours. And please pass on our best on to her. That must have been a hell of a shock."

"Aye, seemingly they rarely attack humans. We both got

quite a fright," said Thomas's neighbour, Derek. "How much do I owe you?"

Thomas turned away from the counter so that Derek couldn't see him but in a shop this small, he knew that this was a practical impossibility.

Could make a dash for it, he reasoned. But I'd have to shuffle past Derek in order to get out the door. Maybe just stay and don't turn around. He doesn't know me well enough to recognise me from the back of my head.

"Thomas? Thomas Leven, I thought that was you there," said his neighbour.

He closed his eyes in the vain hope that the ground would open up. Can't escape now.

"Stuart Jamieson?" called Stacey, leaning over her colleague at the cash register. "Can you just confirm your address?"

"Stuart Jamieson?" muttered Derek, confused.

"37 Lansdowne," Thomas said softly.

"That's you," replied Stacey as she handed over a white paper bag with Thomas's medication.

"No it's not."

Thomas grabbed the bag and left the shop.

"See you later, Mr Jamieson."

"Mr Jamieson?" asked Derek.

"Aye, do you know him?"

"Not as well as I thought."

Chapter 11 - Black Mezcal

"Motherfucker," growled Thomas, slamming the close's heavy door behind him. Suspecting that Derek would be following sharply behind, he loosened the buckle on his belt and pulled down his zip before emptying his bladder onto the recently mopped floor. Within seconds, the scent of scrubbed pine was overpowered by a bouquet altogether less aseptic. Swinging his penis around as if he was Jackson Pollock signing off on a work, Thomas' mood was briefly raised by the thought of Derek storming through the door and submerging his awful mesh training shoes in some fresh squeezed - and slightly bloody - urodynamic juices. The nurse with the Bichon Frisé who lived on the ground floor would undoubtedly cop the flack for the puddle of pish but

165

Thomas reckoned that was the price she'd have to pay for leaving one's yappy little bastard home alone all day.

Thomas took the stairs two at a time, the agony of each step, each stretch met with the dread realisation that he was about to bring some unwanted attention his way. The door's deadlock tolled like a bell. Thomas slammed it shut and threw his keys into the wooden bowl at the head of the hall.

I can't believe I was so stupid, he thought. And to be caught by that…

"Motherfucker."

He pulled back the curtains in the living room and opened the window a crack. A cool gust blew the right sided drape up and as it billowed, it tipped over a paper coffee cup that had been left there for days. A trickle of stale liquid quickly spread across the table.

Motherfucker.

Thomas scooped a jumper from the pile of discarded clothing that lay at the foot of the table and mopped up the coffee. Depositing the sodden top - and other junked items - into the overflowing hamper in the hallway, he hastily returned to the living room to peer out of the window. There was still no sign of Derek but Thomas knew that this wasn't over. For now though, the imminent arrival of Kaitlin meant that he had something more pressing to contend with. Thomas used his feet to push a handful of unopened boxes up against the wall to the left of the window. Instantly, the room appeared bigger but in desperate need of a vacuum. He gathered up his medication and took them into the bathroom. The first choice hiding place, the wall unit, he deemed too obvious. He'd noseyed enough in other people's bathroom cupboards to know that this was too risky. If Kaitlin was half as curious as he'd been back at the old man's place, he'd have some explaining to do. No. Bottom drawer, beneath the hand towels and the face cloths. The ones Milene left, the ones that he'd never used.

Done.

Once that was taken care of, there was the small matter of the toilet bowl. Since Thomas's tenancy began, the only chemical it had encountered was intermittent mouthfuls of toothpaste, spat out while he relieved himself. For the first time since he moved in, Thomas cracked open the hopper window.

He sniffed.

This will not do.

Under the kitchen sink, the previous, more house proud tenant had left some rags, wipes and cleaning products.

"Fuck this." Thomas picked up his phone and began to message.

Kaitlin, don't bother about bringing the files over.
I'll get them in the morning.

T.

He returned to the living room, unbuttoned his collar and slumped down on his recliner. With his heartbeat steadying, Thomas pulled the chair's lever, simultaneously sending the top half of his body back while shooting his feet forward. To the side of the recliner, he remembered that there was an almost finished bottle of black labelled Bruxo Mezcal. A colleague of Milene's at the Infirmary had sworn blind that this particular drink not only contained mild hallucinogenic properties but that a couple of shots of the citrus infused spirit, greatly enhanced the art of lovemaking. For Milene, that was all she needed to hear. Her Scandinavian approach to the pursuit of physical pleasure initially differed from his though it hadn't taken the willing pupil long to catch up. As a reticent, awkward teen, Thomas had been reluctant to ask either of his parents for guidance on the matter. When he first left home, his father in particular had expected a modicum of experimentation but when the looks turned to gazes and those gazes became desires, Thomas knew that holding hands and weekend fumbling weren't going to be nearly enough. As for the Mezcal, that was another taste his palate enjoyed developing.

As Thomas drained the bottle...

No bother, at all.
Already in the cab.
Two mins away.
K.
Motherfucker.

****

Kaitlin breezed in. Thomas had only ever seen her in work attire; sober clothing, hair scraped and tied back, minimal makeup but tonight, he almost didn't recognise her. She was taller, due in part to the thin, metallic four inch stiletto heels which stemmed from the heel of her black ankle boots, plunging into the flooring like a barely tipped rapier.

"For you," she said, handing over a small box, secured with a red ribbon. "Cannoli. I made the driver stop to pick them up."

"You shouldn't have gone to all that trouble," he said.

"No trouble. Aren't you going to take my coat?"

"Sure…"

Thomas gently took the oversized tuxedo jacket from Kaitlin's shoulders. She placed her fingers under her natural, shoulder length hair and shook. A couple of curls sprang down over her eyes. The back of her flimsy, loose fitting blouse was split from the collar to just above her waist, revealing in part, a pair of tattoos either side of her bare spine.

"West End flat, eh? Nice," she said. "I always wanted to live here but I guess everyone goes through that phase."

"I hope I'm not keeping you from anything exciting," said Thomas.

"Nothing that can't wait," smiled Kaitlin. She took a thin file from her bag and handed it to Thomas.

"Was that all there was?"

"Afraid so," said Kaitlin, peering into the living room. "Lynne said that someone from Police Scotland had taken everything else they had last Monday."

That would explain the Nat Sen Order, he thought.

"Excuse the mess," said Thomas.

"She said that the office was made aware of it."

"They may have been but they didn't inform me," replied

Thomas. He deposited the cannoli on the counter and hung Kaitlin's coat on the cupboard door handle.

"Shall we have a drink and look it over?"

Outside, a solitary slate grey cloud blocked out the remainder of the day's sunlight. From the kitchen, Thomas asked Kaitlin what she wanted. Her answer - coffee, black with no sugar - was neither what he expected nor hoped she'd say.

As he closed the door on the bare cupboard, there was a rumble of thunder.

"Did you hear that?" Kaitlin shouted. Before Thomas could answer, she continued. "We could do with a proper downpour. It's been so hot, I've been taking cold showers every evening."

Kaitlin's wet body. Shivering. Hold it. Fold it like a fitted sheet. Difficult. I could never manage that. White linen, stretched tight like glass. Better. Cleaner. Dry with a warm, thick robe wrapped against her shivering skin, loosely tied with red cord, the horripilation on her firm, sinuous husk retreating with each thawing touch. Lay her down. Lay her down. The Mars Volta. I will ask her. Seduce her. Succle on *her* pink flesh. I am not in a hurry this time. I am in charge. I am in control. Lay her down. Lay her down.

Shit.

Thomas grabbed a handful of paper towels to soak up the gallon of water he'd just poured into his quarter litre coffee cup.

'Quite a mess you've made," Kaitlin said, standing by the door. Having dwelt on Kaitlin's form longer than was decent, Thomas instinctively turned away to cover his modesty.

"I hope you don't mind but I had a quick look."

"No problem," he said, dabbing the splashes of coffee on his trousers with a towel. "Find anything of interest?"

"That's the thing," said Kaitlin. "There's nothing here that I didn't already know. Do you have the rest of the files?"

"Yeah, but unfortunately they're pretty worthless. Some booking sheets and medical examinations but…"

"But no notes?"

"Nothing."

As Kaitlin took a sip, Thomas asked if the beverage met with her approval. She coughed and nodded but her grimace suggested otherwise. Returning to the living room, and having gulped down the contents of his mug, Thomas took a seat. He wiped his lips with the edge of his hand, "Innes Guthrie. Any joy?"

Kaitlin knelt down and stood her phone on the arm of his recliner. "Searching for 'Innes Guthrie', naturally there were dozens of results but once the word "Glasgow' is added, it narrows down to three notables."

"Go on," replied Thomas, distracted.

"The most searched 'Innes Guthrie' is a basketball player. Played for the Rocks last year."

"I'm listening," he said, reaching over to his left. He couldn't see it but he knew there was at least one other bottle down there. His knuckles knocked against one but before it fell, he grabbed it by its neck. He didn't need to pick it up to know that it was almost empty.

"The second is a yoga instructor from Thornwood."

"Unlikely."

"Thought you might say that," she said. "So that leaves us with Innes Guthrie, a writer and occultist who happened to be a Lecturer in Esoteric Philosophy and Symbolism at Glasgow University."

"Bingo," said Thomas, picking up a half full bottle.

"And this is where it gets more interesting," added Kaitlin. "Remember that verse that MacMillan recited last week?"

"The 'walk with the diel' thing?"

"The very one. When I was looking online for the poem, I searched exactly for what MacMillan said." Kaitlin turned the volume up on her phone.

"Need to move it forward to around the forty minute mark," she said, scrolling. "Right, there."

As she pressed play, all Thomas could distinguish was the sound of glasses clinking and the low hum of chatter from a dimly lit room.

"Is this a pub?"

"Keep watching," she said as the camera unsteadily zoomed in on the face of an elderly man.

'Tak'a walk doon frae the crag, by Westerwick watter, nie lag.
On a moonlit Samhain night, by the sunless sea
The diel waits. He waits for me.

Hind the thicket or yon juba stone, sure he waits alone.
With a'thing that he hath done.
With a'thing that he doth see.
The diel waits, the diel waits for me.'

"That's it!" said Thomas.

Kaitlin shushed him. "Watch."

*'What a treat for the Ottoman Coffee Club
to have the wonderful Innes Guthrie with us tonight
and to celebrate the Samhain with an authentic piece of lost
island culture,
a reading of Manus' 'The Diel Walks on Westerwick.'*

"Fuck," he said.

"Indeed," replied a very pleased Kaitlin.

"I'll need you to make contact with Mr Guthrie as soon as possible and schedule a meeting."

"Official or off the books?"

Now she's getting it.

As he poured a generous measure of Mezcal into the cup with the cracked glaze, Kaitlin's feet drummed on the wooden floor. When there was a subject she was reluctant to broach, Milene used to do the very same thing. Thomas recognised it then as he did now.

"What's bothering you?"

Kaitlin hesitated. "I feel a bit odd bringing it up actually."

"Fire away."

"What do you think about MacMillan?"

"Seriously?"

"Seriously."

Choosing his words carefully, Thomas replied, "He's not what I expected."

"That's exactly how I feel," said Kaitlin, relieved. "I get that he's done bad things…"

"I'd say it's a fair bit beyond 'done bad things', Kaitlin."

"I understand that but there's something…I just can't put my finger on it. None of this is what I thought it was going to be."

Thomas nodded, glad that they at least shared this one instinct. He urged her to continue.

"I've just started rewatching the TV series," Kaitlin continued, "you know, the one about the murders and the trial and…"

"And?"

"It doesn't remotely reflect what I've been hearing from MacMillan every day."

While Thomas agreed with Kaitlin, there was no denying the effect the prisoner had on men like those who operated Kirkmalcolm.

"Have you seen it?" she asked.

Thomas shook his head as Kaitlin reached over to her bag. As she did the parting on her blouse opened more to reveal more of the artwork on her back. She turned back and caught him staring.

"Watch it."

Snapping out of the moment, Thomas drained his cup.

"The programme on MacMillan. You really need to watch it. I can cast it to your TV," she added.

"My TV's not in the living room."

"Where is it?"

Thomas bit his lip. "In my bedroom," he said.

Kaitlin smiled. "Let's do it."

As Thomas and Kaitlin sat on the edge of the bed awkwardly,

his heart started racing.

Signals…

"Do you mind?" she asked, unzipping her boots.

"No, not at all," muttered Thomas in reply.

Kaitlin stretched out. "It's been a long day on my feet," she said, looking deep into Thomas's eyes.

Signals…

Fighting his angst, Thomas moved closer. He held Kaitlin's stare until a sound from the hallway broke the moment.

"You expecting company?" asked Kaitlin, pushing herself up.

Frustrated at his inability to rewind this live event, Thomas answered. "Probably another fast food flyer."

"Good. I'm starving," said Kaitlin heading for the door.

Jesus, what am I doing?

By denying an attraction to this captivating presence, Thomas knew he was working against every instinct.

"Denied," said Kaitlin, her mock sniffy tone confirming his hunch. "Addressed to you. No postage stamp and no markings either."

Playfully she added, "Perhaps it's a note from another one of your admirers…"

A pensive Thomas opened the letter.

"I'm just messing with you," Katilin continued. "Who is it from?"

Judging by the angular cursive, he knew exactly who'd composed the handwritten note. In a passive aggressive style, similar to that of the bin schedule, the note said simply…

We should talk.

"Top up?"

Kaitlin smiled weakly and shook her head. As she pressed play, an ominous sounding chord emanated from the TV.

Dark Worship

"I'd forgotten what a terrible title that was," said Thomas.

"I know, right?" replied Kaitlin. "Sounds like a special edition ice cream."

As the pre-credit titles appeared on the screen, Thomas asked Kaitlin which actor was playing MacMillan.

"James MacKenzie Sill," she said.

The name wasn't familiar to him. Kaitlin explained that the actor was a popular face on TV, usually playing psychopaths; however as the contents of Kaitlin's blouse were holding far more of his attention than the contents on the screen, Thomas needed a liquid distraction. His offer to Kaitlin was met with an ambivalent response.

"Have you got anything stronger?"

"Try this," said Thomas, handing his mug over to Kaitlin.

"Woah," she spluttered, wiping the traces from her lips. "What is that?"

Black Mezcal, was the answer.

"Might need to line my stomach before I have any more of that. What have you got?"

Thomas headed to the kitchen. On the counter, the ribbon which tied together the box of cannoli was unbound. He looked inside and found it empty. Despite the lingering taste of distilled agave, his palate had no recollection of eating the crisp Italian pastries. Confused, Thomas checked the contents of the fridge. He shouted back,

"I've got soup and ….soup. That's about it."

"What kind of soup?"

Jacqueline's soup.

As per Mira's instructions, the Kunis Clement receptionist had started to make regular if unwanted drops of her bitter mélange at the flat. Ever cautious, Thomas would steadfastly ignore the intercom and her intermittent busy buzzes. After a safe period, he would open the door and, with the mandatory amount of care, hold his nose so as not to allow her scent to invade his nostrils before taking the container in and away from his fellow close dwellers.

Thomas opened the lid and took a sniff. He needn't have bothered.

"It's got kale," he called.

It's always fucking kale.

"Kale's good," replied a less than convinced Kaitlin.

Neither dwelled long on the soup. Thomas took both bowls back into the kitchen and without rinsing, he dropped them into a plastic basin filled with water the colour of chocolate milk.

"Right, time for the good stuff," exclaimed Kaitlin.

Thomas went to the bathroom with Kaitlin's cup and rinsed it under the tap. Taking the note from Derek out of his pocket, he forced it into the already full waste bin. He went into the drawer and rooted around for a yellow capsule.

Just the one. His hands shook. Was it the lack of medication or something else causing it? His sex drive, once healthy, was now sporadic and triggered only by the most inane things. It'll come back, he convinced himself. Kaitlin will see that it does. Thomas swallowed the capsule with a mouthful of tap water. He wiped his lips and watched the water spiral down the sink. Though the effects of the drug had yet to kick in, the knowledge that it would - and soon - meant that he could feel the qualm start to leave his body. Thomas doused his face in the cool water and ran his wet fingers through his hair.

Kaitlin called out, "You OK in there?".

"Two secs," he replied, stepping into the kitchen. In the tall cupboard beside the breadbin, there was a collection of half drained bottles. The unopened Black Mezcal was at the back.

Thomas returned to the room to find Kaitlin lying front forward on his bed, her chin resting on the bridge of her clasped hands. The slashes on her blouse had fallen to the side leaving the birds on her back exposed.

"You ready?" Kaitlin asked.

Huh?

"Should I press play again?"

Thomas handed a glass of the Mezcal to Kaitlin then sat a comfortable distance from her, on the edge of the bed.

As they debated the exact location of the filming - long shots Glasgow, close ups Bristol, according to Kaitlin - Thomas could feel the slow acting medication starting to take effect. Playing the local detective who pieced together the case was a serious looking actor with a gravelly voice. His accent suggested that he might have once spent a night, or at least part of an afternoon on the periphery of the city.

Another ominous atonal chord sounded and the actor

playing MacMillan appeared on screen.

"I *do* know him," confirmed Thomas.

"Told you. He's been in tons of things."

"He was in that comedy about the shop, wasn't he?"

Kaitlin, still rapt, replied, "Might have been a bit before my time, boss."

"My mother liked that."

"So did my dad," replied Kaitlin. "My real dad, that is."

"Is he still alive?"

Kaitlin forced a smile and shook her head.

She knows how it feels.

"You don't look too comfortable," she said. "There's plenty of room…and I don't bite."

Thomas shuffled across the bed. As she plumped up the cushions under his arms, he was again drawn to the inkwork on her back.

'Give in to the desires,' said the actor to an equally fictitious character in a tight t-shirt.

Thomas poured another large measure for Kaitlin.

"I don't talk to my dad," he said quietly. "But tell me about yours."

As the MacMillan dramatisation flitted from the predictable to the contrived, and their attention to its perfunctory cast and potholed plotline started to wane, Kaitlin relayed to Thomas some scenes from her own story. Of an estranged father who, tired of reaching out to a family who'd moved on, simply gave up. Yet despite her willingness to open up and share the most intimate of family details, Thomas continued to hold back. A cocktail of embarrassment, guilt and vulnerability, every bit as potent as the combustible Mexican spirit he'd been drinking, meant that he was reluctant to let Kaitlin know that the trigger for the slide into his own still very personal mire was actually detonated weeks before the crash. With each hastily imbibed glass of the Black Mezcal though, the more freely they spoke.

"Look at this arsehole," Thomas sniffed. "He's nothing like MacMillan. How fucking wrong can they be?"

'A slave to the desire. Surrender to the urge,' said the voiceover.

"This is the first big sex scene coming up," said Kaitlin. "At the time I think it was considered quite gratuitous. Seems a bit tame now. We can fast forward this if you'd like."

"No," replied the curious Thomas. "I want to see what happens next."

Kaitlin rolled her eyes, "Sure you do…"

Thomas shot her a serious look.

"Is this what sex was like in the 80s?" she asked, mischievously.

"I wouldn't know. I was still in nappies at the time."

"No chance," replied Kaitlin, almost choking in disbelief. "How old are you, anyway? Forty?"

"Cheeky cow," snorted Thomas, his ire as simulated as events on screen. "I'm thirty one."

"So you were born in…"

"1987," he replied.

"This took place in 1987, didn't it?"

Thomas shouted "1987!" before gulping the remainder of the Mezcal straight from the bottle.

"A truly momentous year," added Kaitlin. She raised her glass and smiled coyly at Thomas.

"Amen to that."

As Kaitlin finished her drink, Thomas was willing to take a chance that he wasn't alone in believing that the connections off screen were offering a charge unmatched by those on.

"This friend you were meeting…"

"Yes?"

"What would he think if he knew you were lying on another man's bed watching pornographic material?"

"Did I say that the friend was a 'he'?"

Thomas tilted his head back. Before he had the chance to process the nugget of information, Kaitlin continued.

"Not that it's any of your business but it is a he."

She spun her legs around and stood up.

"So?"

"Toilet," she said.

"No," replied Thomas. "The friend."

"We've got an understanding."

"Right…"

Kaitlin stood by the door. She undid the clip on the side of her skirt and it fell to the floor.

"Besides, it can't be wrong if we only touch ourselves."

As Kaitlin disappeared, Thomas unfastened the remaining buttons on his shirt and unzipped his trousers.

Dark impulses.

The words echoed along the hall.

Dark impulses.

In the half light, Thomas gripped his penis and looked at himself in the long mirror, propped up against the wall. He grimaced and his face changed shape. Unnatural. He forced his face into a smile and bared his teeth. Thomas held the pose until his cheeks started to cramp.

Who is this? Is this me?

His own intense, rictus grin frightened him but he continued. His penis, more dense than usual, moved in his hand, like a beast of independent purpose, straining for Kaitlin, unconstrained and manifestly uncontrollable. The sounds that came out of his mouth weren't his.

He's here.

Chapter 12 - Skelmorlie

Coronation Park. Thomas always breathed a sigh of relief when the bus passed Coronation Park and no one boarded. There was a boy. A boy with the tight curls and the grey tracksuit. Even now, many years after their last encounter, he felt relieved when the pneumatic suspension levelled out and the bus pulled away. There was no reason for Thomas to be scared of him back then. The boy may have been slightly older than he, perhaps by a year or two but Thomas was bigger and undoubtedly had more strength. Still, the youth possessed an innate aggression, one seemingly triggered by the crest on Thomas's blazer. Quite different from the random acts of blunt force violence perpetrated at St

Saviour's. Those Thomas could handle. The boy with the tight curls and the grey tracksuit was simmering, seething resentment. A product of the environment in which he was brought up? That's too easy. The boy's anger came from the dark undercurrents of a deeper reservoir. That fifteen minutes between Coronation Park and West Stewart Street was a test of nerve, one which Thomas habitually failed. Sensing a win, the grey tracksuit would leave the bus and either spit on or slam the blade of his hand against the window. Thomas didn't make eye contact.

Kaitlin left a note. Atop the freshly folded blanket on his couch, it read;

Off to find Innes Guthrie.

Talk later.

Kx

P.S. Speak with your father.

****

Thomas checked his phone. He'd received no messages since he'd left the flat, took the Subway then boarded the bus.

West Stewart Street ... Branchton Station ... McInroy's Point ... breathe. We're all going to die. I accept it but I'd rather it wasn't now. But if it has to be, better make it a quick one. Like mum. Slow but then sudden, violent. Before the angels know you're gone. Before I remember exactly what I did last night. Come on driver. You know you want to. It's a Saturday morning. The roads are as dead as your chances of a promotion. Take your bus past the bend, too sharp, onto the flats, the flats with no purchase. So sink. Like a fucking bollard has just dropped from the sky and landed in the mud and the seaweed. Race to the bottom. Me, the driver, the teenage goth with the bassy thrash bleeding from her cheap earphones, the cheery auld boy with the cap who won't shut up. The stressed dad taking his three demanding kids down the coast for the day.

But mum lets me use her phone, mum lets us do that. Well too bad. Your mum is in Craig fucking Tara this weekend with her latest neck-tattooed, Turkish toothed, bearded gym monkey ride so you'll have to do with me…

One hundred percent certain that he'd take the blessed release of suffocation by sand right now if it was offered.

When Thomas took the call to say that his mother, weakened by twenty months of chemotherapy, had stepped in front of the 538 Ayrshire flyer, the first breath he took without her being in his world brought back the scent of the coast to him. He closed his eyes and held onto the happier memories for as long as he could. Long walks to Seamill. Longer ones to Largs. Its rough, jagged coastline he knew like the bones in her hands. The hands that once held his. Tight but tender. But that was then. The last time he was here, her lifeless appendage was pained, bent and knotted, already slipping away. Ice cream. Birds, hundreds of birds. The carousel with the bus. Never the sports car or the jet fighter, always the bus. In Thomas' little mind, he was the conductor. No one could come near. He'd drop his voice and speak like his father. Brusque, curt commands to the other children. No. Not this.

Keep away. I'm in charge. Beat it.

Following her first, invasive procedure, Thomas' mother told him the truth about his adoption as a month old baby. A burden she was too weak to carry any longer. Insisting that their love was as genuine as any between a mother and a son, she tearfully begged his forgiveness. Wishing to spare her feelings, Thomas acquiesced, though in private it led him to question whether his entire life to that point had been one great lie.

Lunderston Bay … Inverkip … Wemyss Bay. Ring the bell. I'll take it from here, driver. The walk might clear my mind of death, even temporarily.

It had been years since Thomas had been inside of the train station and the instant he entered, its wonder had him transfixed. As the heat from the morning sun split the glass canopies above, Thomas stopped a while and bathed in the restorative rays. He was not on the clock, nor was he expected anywhere so he ordered a fresh coffee from the vendor, sat on the wooden bench and checked the forecast. A meteorologist will confirm that three to four days is the most that they can predict with any degree of accuracy. Mid twenties until Tuesday, perhaps Wednesday. Thomas closed his eyes and once again, let his senses paint the scene. For a moment, he was gone. Thoughts of Mira, MacMillan and Kirkmalcolm ebbed away. Milene too. He realised that since they'd met, this was the first morning that he hadn't woken, thinking about her. Kaitlin though. What was he playing at? Making a move on the paralegal might have been the norm for senior counsel and partners but this wasn't him. Thomas checked his phone again. Still nothing from her. If she'd been aggrieved then surely she wouldn't have returned to his room and fingered herself as he came. And she wouldn't have left an 'x' at the end of her note either.

About last night…

Thomas didn't know how to broach the subject. This was one of the few times where he'd rather be speaking to someone face to face. He deleted the draft and closed his eyes again.

Skelmorlie. Or Scare More Lee as he used to call it. Thomas watched his mother's nose wrinkle and her eyes close in delight as he deliberately mispronounced it. Scare More Lee. He couldn't help but love her.

The familiar sound of the train announcement stirred Thomas from his stupor. I can't stay here all day. Or maybe I could, he thought. Pick up something from the small second-hand bookstore situated in the roundel, have a sandwich and stay out of the way. Haven't done that for ages. Is the bookstore still there?

It was.

Thomas dropped the remnants of his coffee into the bin outside the shop and went in. At the desk, a heavy, middle aged lady with a red cardigan was bagging a book for an old man with a grip stick. The only other people in the small shop were a sportswear-clad mother composing a lengthy text message and a child, seated at her feet, immersed in a colourful book about a lost dinosaur. Thomas nodded to the plump clerk and started to rifle around the fiction bins which were filled to the brim with copies of gritty capital-based detective novels and well thumbed romantic fiction. At the end of a display shelf that doubled as the 'local crime' section, one book caught his attention. On its lurid cover was a stylised picture of the Necropolis with its title in a large jagged, gaudy blood red font:

'Ghoulish Glasgow'

Its subheading, typeset in a font called 'broken typewriter', made clear the content of the book:

'A History of Death and Murder in the Dear Green Place.'

The author's name, soberly printed in pale blue, bottom right, was partially covered by a sticker which bore the price; £2.99.

"I'll take this, thanks," said Thomas.

****

On the coastal side of the Shore Road, a number of adjoining blocks had sprung up; namely Meursault and Vermillion View, his father's dwelling. They hadn't been built by the time Thomas left for Glasgow but the ads, he remembered. Purpose built accommodation, said one. Unless the marketing was aimed at enticing bears from caves or birds from trees, he thought, wasn't *all* accommodation 'purpose built'? Typical property bollocks. Thomas never had any intention of following his father into business. Property, and any imperceptible increase in its value, had become an obsession greater than religion for the less imaginative inhabitants of the country.

On the face of things, Leonard Leven appeared a successful, self-made man who held a number of prominent positions. A surveyor to trade and a partner in a local real estate company, he was also the local Councillor who, for a five figure sum, cast the decisive vote which saw the demolition of the much loved Skelmorlie Hydro. That he was the prime agent for the characterless development which replaced the hotel was merely financial fortuity. Happenstance. Leven and his associates made a good living spouting the same kind of self-perpetuating nonsense that filled half of the North Ayrshire Weekly News. Horses and whores. That's where Thomas's father's true passions lay. Commissions paid the bills. The family? That was for gala days but even as his wife slipped away, Leonard Leven continued to spend more time with other men's wives than with his own.

End of life flats said his father once, scornfully. Watch the tide crawl out then back in again. The water, black as the oily feathers of a crow and the chunks of obsidian flow that would wash up on the shore. A fucking useless view, he'd add, dismissively. A view for mugs with no fucking vision.

Ironic then that he ended up here.

Desolate.

I'll make it quick, Thomas thought as he approached the wooden door on the main road.

Either side of the stone arched entrance was a wall, no more than two feet high which in truth, rendered the doorway redundant. Who designed this? Still, he turned the circular handle clockwise and the bolt lifted.

Number Six. Flat F. Thomas pressed the buzzer beside the names Aird and Leven. There was no answer. Behind the glass panel, Thomas could see a figure move. The front door opened and standing in the doorway was a middle aged woman wearing a pale blue, medical style tunic, squeezing a washing basket under her arm.

"Can I help?" she asked suspiciously.

"I'm here to see Mr Leven. Leonard Leven, Six F?"

"What do you want with Mr Leven?"

"I'm his son."

"Mr Leven has never mentioned a son."

"I can assure you that I'm his son, Thomas. And you are?"

The woman looked him up and down. "Nope. I don't see it."

Thomas laughed, "Do you want to check my drivers licence?"

The woman scanned the card, then Thomas' face before exhaling sharply. "Mavis. Home help."

"He never mentioned he had a home help."

Mavis shrugged, "You want to check my home help licence?"

Thomas shook his head. He asked if his father was keeping well.

"He feeds the birds."

"That's good, eh?"

"He shouldn't feed the birds. They make a mess. Sometimes I have to do the washing two, three times. Big mess." As Mavis turned away, Thomas asked if there was a lift. Her response, a single 'ha', indicated to him that he'd be climbing again.

Taking the first of the soft, springy stairs, the familiar odour of fresh pine lingered, triggering in Thomas a Pavlovian urge to relieve himself. Ahead, the unimpressed Mavis was wedging the back door with a brick.

Better tie a knot in it, he thought.

From the window on the first landing, Thomas could see directly across the bay. He stopped for a moment and took a mental snapshot.

On the third floor, the door to flat F was slightly ajar.

Thomas knocked as he entered.

"Hello?" he called out as he stepped into the hallway.

Directly ahead were stacked a number of sealed cardboard boxes and the walls were bare except for a pair of matching canvas prints featuring some colourful livestock. Above the phone table, there was a picture of Thomas' father with a woman, not his mother. Carved into its frame were the words; live, laugh, love.

With the blinds raised and the door to the Juliet balcony open, sunlight flooded into the small but pristine open plan living room and kitchen. Sat in an old high backed armchair with an open newspaper on his lap, Leonard Leven stared out of the window. Behind the plumped cushions at the back of the untouched couch was a small, square table with a single place setting. Covered by a plastic lid, the plate of food underneath remained ignored but for the attention of a single bluebottle which darted irritably around the living room. Careering repeatedly into the cracked stucco, it was the winged vector of disease's misjudgement to not only refuse one of the clearly marked exits but to continually disregard the ever present threat of a bitter man with nothing but time on his hands and a weekend's supply of rolled up newspaper.

"I brought you scones," said Thomas.

"Did that stupid cow wedge the door open again?"

"Mavis?" Thomas placed the paper bag on the small table beside his father's chair.

"She's an idiot," he said. Using the arm from his glasses, Leonard Leven pried into the bag. "Are they fresh? They don't look fresh."

"They are. Got them this morning in town. From that bakery you like."

As Thomas rolled a cushion to the side and pushed back on the sofa, his father picked at the crispy edge of one of the scones.

"Still scrimping on the raisins."

Thomas looked around the room. "I take it that Meryl's out?"

"She spends the weekends over in Gullane."

"Without you?"

"What is this? Twenty fucking questions?"

"Twenty one," replied Thomas. "So, the boxes?"

"I can't do the stairs anymore because…you know."

"You should've told me, Dad."

"Do I need to run everything past you?" his father bristled. "A fucking stranger?"

Refusing to bite, Thomas asked, "Do you want me to put the kettle on? Butter you up one of the scones?"

"No."

"Suit yourself. I'll leave them in the kitchen for you to have later then."

"I don't want them."

"Well I'm not bringing them all the way back to Glasgow on the train."

"The train?" he sniggered. "You still haven't got your licence back?"

Before Thomas could respond, his father continued.

"I thought your boss would have sorted it by now. You

know, one of those Rothwell Glen favours," he said, with an exaggerated wink. "But I guess you're not their golden boy anymore."

Leonard Leven picked at another edge and dropped it onto his tongue. "Probably for the best. You were as good with cars as you were at looking after weans."

Thomas sunk his fingernails deep into the palm of his hand.

"I will say this for him though, he knows what he's doing. Buying up all that property. Smart man."

"You've heard about that?"

"I should've kept hold of some myself…"

"You've still got this, haven't you?"

"Aye and I'm not selling it yet, if that's what you're getting at."

Thomas had little interest in what was left of his father's holdings. "What about the lock up? You still have that, don't you?"

A crooked smile broke across Leven's drawn face. "I knew you were here for something."

"I just wanted to drop by and say hello," said Thomas, less than honestly.

In the two years since his mother had walked out of the hospice and onto the main road, Thomas hadn't once 'dropped by' on his father. Two full years since Leonard Leven, more dead than alive and realising that there was no room on his son's coattails, finally absolved himself of the minimal parental concern he'd once shown. Two years since the trajectory of Thomas' life altered in ways he was still struggling to deal with.

Unwilling to skirt around the issue any longer, Thomas pushed his father for an answer on the status of his lock up garage.

"It's still mine but I've cleared it out."

Thomas' confused expression demanded clarity.

"I gave the keys to McEwan's boy a few months ago. He's been using it to store that old Jag of his."

"And all my stuff?"

"What about it?"

"What have you done with that?"

Leven shrugged.

"All of my coursework, my files were there."

"Aye, well they're not there now. I told him to dump what he couldn't use."

Seeing the look of impotent rage on his son's face was another score in the twisted win column for Leonard Leven.

"Looks like we're both fucked now, eh?"

With his first wife dead and his second now sixty miles away, scorching the earth for any potential third, he savoured the moment. Horses and whores may have been his passions but twisting the knife was the endeavour in which he excelled. "I think I will have one of them scones now."

Thomas grabbed the bag from the table and made for the kitchen.

"Fucking bastard," he growled to himself, hastily slicing through the scone, scattering crumbs over the edge of the wooden chopping board and onto the worktop. Behind him, the low hum from the freezer's motor suggested that it needed defrosting, something his mother would've done without thinking. For all her obvious charms, Meryl, his present wife, wasn't blessed with practical bones, and caregiver Mavis was too stretched to attend to any need beyond what she was contracted to do.

Thomas shuffled the freezer away from the wall and switched it off at the socket. Its motor slowly chundered to a halt. As Leonard, with help from the racing channel, shared vital information about the going at Uttoxeter and Fakenham at a neighbour-bothering volume, Thomas looked in the cupboard above the sink.

Medication and tea towels. Macy's of New York. They'd started their honeymoon there on the Friday following Thomas' mother's funeral.

Meryl wouldn't be happy, but needs must, he thought as he pushed the folded towels against the lower edges of the freezer.

With Thomas consulting the table of contents of the pill box, his father shouted from the living room. "Two sugars and use the real butter, not that spreadable shite."

Attached to the box, in a clear plastic sleeve, was a supply of pain relief patches. Thomas opened the sleeve and counted out five. He placed three in his pocket, one back in the sleeve. The fifth, he opened.

Peeling off the covering, Thomas unbuttoned his shirt and pressed the patch against his side. As steam billowed under the cupboard, the switch on the kettle flipped upwards and off. Using his thumbnail, Thomas sliced into a loose strip of painkillers and immediately swallowed two. He opened a third and pulled the capsule apart, emptying it into his father's mug.

Make it two and a half sugars this time, he thought, covering his tracks.

As his knife slowly stroked away at the softer edge of the knob of butter on the dish, the flying buzzing irritant from the living room, exhausted by the twin perils of Leonard's newspaper and the opinions of high pitched men on horseback, joined Thomas in the kitchen. With the pain relief starting to take effect, Thomas watched the fly hop from crumb to crumb as it too took a break from its torment. Not wishing to startle it, Thomas slowly reached out an upturned finger. Though the fly moved away, it remained close.

"Nothing here to be scared of," he whispered, holding perfectly still.

The fly brushed against his finger then buzzed back to its place of safety. Undeterred, Thomas continued to hold his position.

You could take your chances. Or you can stay and give your fate over to me.

The fly returned to Thomas. An ephemeral entity, turning, picking at the unique, infinitesimal print cut into the grooves on his finger.

"You have chosen me as your master."

"I have," said the fly.

"Sometimes we have to make sacrifices for the greater good."

The fly understood that it was better to die with purpose than to live with none.

"Who will mourn me?"

"I shall."

"Shall you?"

Thomas nodded. He brought his fingers together and as he

pressed tight, the grief he felt was sudden and necessary.

"What are you doing in there?" called his father.

"I'm almost done."

****

"Careful…"

An unsteady Leonard Leven held the railing with both hands as his son moved away from the final step. Resting against the wall opposite, he took a puff from his inhaler.

"We should take the wheelchair," insisted Thomas.

Leonard shook his head and handed over a skeleton key that had a small length of red twine tied through its eye. As he unlocked the door to the narrow cellar, Thomas asked if there was a light.

"On the right," replied Leonard. "But you've got to reach up to it."

Stretching, Thomas felt around the sticky wall for an electrical plate. Finding it, he pressed the switch and behind him, a spun silk covered bulk-head light flickered, bringing a dim illumination to the area.

"Jesus!" he blurted, flinching at the sight of an old doll's head, just inches from his face. As the sound of his father's phlegm-filled laugh echoed around the close, the missing patches of lacquer on the doll's cracked face turned Thomas' thoughts back to events at The Red Room.

"Once a shitebag, always a shitebag."

From inside the doll's depressed eye socket, the thick bristly claws of an arachnid deliberately skimmed the edges of the cavity. Unaware that this unwanted visitor had recently diminished his food supply by one, the compartment's eight-limbed guardian nonetheless kept Thomas under close watch.

"Keep going," shouted Leonard.

Onward.

For what felt like two full minutes, Thomas marched through the almost empty cellar, past the heads on the floor, its walls gradually narrowing to the point where the brickwork on either side squeezed at his shoulders, and his hair brushed against the throbbing orange egg sacs hanging from the ceiling. At the angle where he could go no further, Thomas found his father's outdoor walking stick, hanging from a handle without a door. To the side, was an uncased break-barrel rifle and small pair of walking boots, balanced atop a dusty pile of periodicals.

"Grab my hat as well."

Frustrated by the realisation that his now discarded work would have taken up far less space than his father's forgotten Racing Post collection, Thomas gently toed the centre of the pile. As the boots toppled onto the stone floor, rolling like hollow, misshapen dice, he heard a soft voice from beyond the fan of spilled paper.

"Don't wake them."

"I won't," whispered Thomas.

"Are you our master?"

Thomas didn't reply. He turned and headed for the light, conceding that the liberation of his father's medication was perhaps not the most judicious choice he'd made that morning.

"Lift it, then turn it."

I know how to close a fucking door, Dad, he thought but the order mattered more to Leonard Leven than it did to Thomas. The order meant control, the continuation of a narrative, decades in the making, now hanging by the finest of spun threads. As he shook the dust from his cap, Thomas carefully ignored the tuts that echoed through the close like one of his father's ball bearings being air propelled at close quarters.

Reacting was weak. Excuses were weak.

Man up.

From the first moment Thomas heard that command, the approval of his father remained as distant and as unforgiving as *A'Chreag*, along the coast. Leven straightened his back and zipped up his anorak. Filling his narrow nostrils with the warm littoral air, a gust of wind swirled up from the shore and snatched the handle from his son's hands, slamming the door shut. Before he could react, the very same gust lifted the newly dusted cap from the former Councillor's head, depositing it in a creamy grey pile of fresh pigeon shite. It took every ounce of Thomas' resolve not to laugh in his father's face.

Refusing his son's offer of assistance, he took his stick and slowly set off down the winding path to the wall by the shoreline. Two paces behind, Thomas pushed the empty chair. With the tide hours from returning, Thomas parked the chair and stepped down onto the impacted sand and pebbles. Finding it firmer underfoot than he'd expected, he called for his father to join him.

Leonard shook his head.

Thomas stamped his feet. "See? Solid."

Whether it was the effects of the loaded infusion, that one abnormally juicy but bitter raisin in his scone or the realisation that this moment might well provide the final burst of sunlight onto his stony features, Leonard Leven's resolve wavered.

In Thomas' experience, he knew that a correctly worded question at the right time could open a vacillating defence like a blade through fruit. "You're not scared of a wee bit of sand, are you?"

As Rothwell Glen once told him, even the sharpest shark cannot resist appropriate bait.

While the sea birds warred overhead, a tacit truce was called as the Leven men combed the beach in silence. Using his stick, Leonard poked around the surface for some smooth, flat-edged skimming stones, once the only thing that could get his son close to the water.

"See that?" Leonard lifted his stick and pointed in the direction of the two almost interlocked landmasses ahead. "Over there. Between Cowal Kirk and Craigmore."

Thomas nodded.

"The best wee bit of water on the planet, that is."

I seriously doubt that, thought Thomas.

"Before you came along, I had a wee cutter. A simple, single mast kind of thing but it was as fast as fuck."

Leonard continued. He spoke of a hair-raising excursion to East Belfast and how jealous Benny 'The Butcher' McGregor had been once he found out that he'd brokered the deal to get the Swedish the hangar he'd been eyeing up at Prestwick. McGregor was so angry, he wouldn't sell as much as the thinnest slice of beef ham to him for months.

Though he seemed happy reanimating encounters, Leven's audience of one was less than entertained. If Thomas had any expectation that his father's reminiscences would act as a preamble to some level of insight into the complex behaviours of a seemingly irredeemable soul, his worst suspicions were about to be confirmed.

"I'm tired now. Get my chair."

No contrition, no confession. Leonard Leven answers to no man.

Thomas steered his father's chair into position and stared out to the lush patchwork of the peninsula and beyond. The blues and blacks and yellows. Like the bruises on the inside of his mother's arm.

Anger is an egregious, unpredictable emotion. Like mercury in a thermometer, it will creep as slowly as a curly headed boy sneaking home early from school, rising until the temperature moves beyond the point of comfort, such as the sight of his mother being pinned against the kitchen door, with one bare leg wrapped around the slowly thrusting hind muscles of Councillor Leven, an event which lit the fuse for a period of instability in that impressionable young mind. Before he discovered self harm, intimidating the oblivious son of the man who helped his mother compose that unnatural symphony was the only outlet for the rage that the boy had. And while Thomas too held that enmity, the origin of his own resentment was more deep-seated.

Thomas laughed.

"What's so funny?"

This is it. This is all he's got, he thought. It's so clear to me now. That lack of ambition. He couldn't be Rothwell Glen. He didn't have the balls. Too scared to leave his pathetic little patch of land, his shrunken fiefdom. Lash out now, you old cunt, I fucking dare you. I'll bury your face in the salt water shallows and let the crabs dine on your vinegary skin. And I'll keep laughing.

"Why are you telling me all this?"

"I'm going to be dead soon. I just wanted you to know."

"You want me to feel sorry for you?" smirked Thomas.

"You? Feel sorry for me?" Leonard replied. "At least it's only my body that's fucked, boy."

The ferocity of his father's comment triggered in Thomas a derisive snort which was accompanied by an involuntary bubble of snot out of his nostril.

"That reminds me. How are you getting on with the shrinks these days?" spat Leven.

Keep it coming.

"Your mother was weak and you are weak. She may not have birthed you but by fuck, in her image you most certainly were created. How's your God treating you these days?"

My God is a vengeful God.

"Thomas. Where are you going?"

"I'm away now."

"You can't leave me here…" shouted Leonard. As he tried to stand, the back wheel of his chair sunk into a patch of damp sand. Slowly toppling, he threw his stick at his son.

"See you around, Dad."

"I'm not your fucking Dad."

Fine.

Man up, Leonard.

Chapter 13 - Racing Green

Even a wisp of straw, hewn from the side of a riverbank will provide succour to a drowning man. But at what point does the man realise that he is drowning? Whether conscious or instinctive, the tightness of the hold is harder to define. Standing at the door of the Adelphi Hotel on that icy morning in January, Mark Sheridan did not know. The first reviews were in but they weren't as favourable as he'd hoped, not that they were uniformly negative. He realised that it was unlikely that Gay Paree, a broad musical burlesque depicting the relationship between Napoleon and his Josephine, would tempt theatre goers out during such a cold snap and certainly not in the numbers required to make a dent in the four-figure sum he'd personally invested. Over eggs and bacon, Ethel didn't say a word. They both knew. She had always been a brick. Even when their boys were off fighting for King and country, Ethel held it together for both of them. But she'd always been dead against Glasgow in the winter. Do what Napoleon didn't, she suggested. Sound the retreat. What about Sunderland? Your hometown. They love Good old Mark there. Or The Palace Theatre, Southampton? More temperate and closer to London. Let your forty strong Grande Armée regroup on familiar ground. Our boys will find us there.

'Do you need a carriage, Mr Sheridan?' asked the doorman of the Grand Hotel.

'I think I'll walk a while,' he replied.

'Careful out there, Sir. Very cold last night. Conditions are quite treacherous underfoot.'

Treacherous, eh? Again, he thought of his sons. How cold they must be, on the pockmarked fields of Polderhoek Spur or on the unforgiving crests of the Southern Baltic. That's where the real danger lay, not the thin panes of ice, cracking under his heels. The infrequent letters they'd sent from the corridors of combat were brief but welcome. The last, from his youngest boy, he kept close to his heart.

Mark Sheridan was expected at the Coliseum at midday. The issues they'd faced in Liverpool before Christmas had come to the fore again. Voices were raised. Ethel said she'd nip that in the bud. A sudden cloudburst mottled the ice, giving way to a flurry of snow. At the entrance to Kelvingrove Park, a pack of school children was being herded by their school matron. A lone child stood and stared at the sky above her head. She closed her eyes and lost in the moment, reached out her bare hands, smiling as the feathery droplets kissed her cold, rosy cheeks.

'Hurry up Elspeth,' barked the matron. 'And for the last time, put your mittens on.'

The command was ignored.

'Elspeth,' she yelled again.

Spell broken, the child opened her eyes and returned to the fold.

On the western side of the River Kelvin, as the snow became more than a light dusting, Mark Sheridan took a seat on a recently vacated bench. He pulled the collar of his woollen overcoat over his scarf and removed his hat.

'You'll catch yer death there, my friend.'

Mark Sheridan nodded in silent acknowledgement.

There's always the Tivoli. Ethel loved Liverpool.

He looked up to the heavens and closed his eyes. Just as the child had done minutes earlier, Mark Sheridan smiled.

Thank you Lord, for blessing me with so much love and joy. Please extend your mercy to my family.

Mark Sheridan removed a Browning pistol from his pocket and placed its cold barrel to his temple.

No Ethel, it has to be Glasgow.

****

Thomas woke with a start.

"Might have to borrow this once you're done," said Kaitlin from the seat opposite. Thumbing through the book Thomas had been reading, she added, "I had no idea that Adrian Marcato was born in Glasgow?"

"Adrian who?" replied Thomas with a deep yawn.

"Maybe we should resume this conversation when you're properly awake." Kaitlin snapped the book shut and tossed it back towards its slumberous owner.

Somewhere between Paisley and Glasgow, Thomas had succumbed to the more potent of the pills he'd taken from his father's kitchen. Barely conscious, he stretched out, rubbed his eyes and saw that the train was now empty and berthed at Central Station.

"How did you know where to find me?"

"You're hardly a mystery, Thomas Leven. You get comfortable, you fall asleep, then you miss what you need to see."

"Like a train pulling onto a platform."

"Like you did last night."

"Yeah about that…"

"Forget it. We need to get to Charing Cross before half three."

Before Thomas had a chance to reply, she grabbed hold of his hand and pulled him up.

"Do you still have access to a car?"

****

As every resident of this sandstone metropolis knows, taking a taxi from the official rank outside of one of the main stations is an arseache of unimaginable proportions. At night, flashpoint drama tends to flare in and around the queue but during the day, swathes of unsuspecting visitors, untrained and unwilling to comprehend the complexities of Strathclyde's deregulated bus system, wait in turn to open the reverse hung doors to a grim, uncomfortable charcoal coloured portal of cracked vinyl, restrictive regulations and unwanted opinions dispensed by one of the city's crowded pool of licence-bearing misanthropes. For many, this taste of the unexpected is their first experience of a city they'd been mistakenly assured was uniformly friendly.

"Where to, pal?" asked the driver.

The key question. If your destination was within walking distance of the station, the cabbie's hour-long wait to get into the prime position was now worthless. At best, one would be bluntly cursed in an unfamiliar tongue and sent packing. The less honourable ones would take their *pickups* for a twenty pound sightseeing trip around the city centre before dropping them off fifty metres from where they started.

"Hyndland, corner of Airlie Street and Hayburn Park."

Tough one for the driver. Not too close but not as far as he'd like. Roadworks on St Vincent Street so, perhaps a wee detour? Drawbacks. His passenger was Scottish. And a big lad. Damn. Local accent too. Quandary. Damn.

"I'll go down along Waterloo Street, pal. Bath Street and the Expressway are murder the day."

"As long as we're there by three."

Oh, you will be.

****

"Just drop us at the corner," said Thomas.

"Let me turn around," said the driver.

"No, here is ideal."

Thomas tapped his card on the reader. £18.40. Been a

while, he thought. Was it always so expensive?

"Yes, I'd like a receipt, please."

The old habits were returning. Receipts. Claim. Bus. Claim. Taxi, claim. Lunch, claim. New suit, claim.

Claim.

The driver didn't turn to acknowledge Thomas as he passed the scrawled card back and through the gap. The engagement side of the arrangement was over and he was now eager, impatient even, to have the large black six-seated cockroach assigned to his licence, magnetically sucked back in the direction of the city of gold. This time, he'd go via Kelvingrove and snake around the streets, looking for some bewildered tourists, lost and dehydrated, or a concupiscent pair of swipers hoping to get back to her house and gone before her husband's shift ends.

Thomas closed the door and as the taxi circled back around the park, Kaitlin looked back down the street at the infinite number of car fins, jutting out from either side like colourful herringbones.

"Which one's yours?"

Thomas shook his head.

"Down here," he said, heading along the gravel path, situated behind the terraced townhouse he once shared with Milene. "I still don't understand why we couldn't have just taken the cab straight to Charing Cross."

"Do you trust me?" asked Kaitlin, rhetorically.

Given the weather, it was no surprise to Thomas to see Hayburn Park filled to the brim with barelegged locals supping wine from bottle necks while their offspring, similarly uninhibited, hung from the lower rungs of the climbing frame, like a collection of undernourished little Bretons. Unlike other parts of the city though, the alcohol that was being consumed from the benches of this picturesque square was not being closely monitored by one of Campbell Ames's anti-social task forces. Different schools. Different rules. The children of Hayburn Park may have been rowdy, but scheme kids, they were not. Precociousness might be mocked elsewhere but here, amidst the bountiful pergolas and the lovingly maintained book exchange it was not only permitted but encouraged. Other than the occasional wayward basketball, the indulged progeny of professionals offered no threat. The animals they brought with them, sheltered in peace in the shade.

On the tree lined far side of the park, ran the soft narrow L-shaped path of Banavie Lane, its unappealing myriad of crumbling brickwork hidden from view by some anaemic foliage, and a length of paint peeled wrought iron fencing.

Kaitlin's wrinkled brow suggested that her first impressions of the lane weren't positive. It was hardly a city's ripped backside, Thomas thought. On familiar ground again, his mind returned to more settled times.

Before the crash, a friend of the old man had required some assistance to help him navigate his way through a legal minefield caused by the tenants of one of the many houses he owned. As he lived in the adjoining terrace, it wasn't too much of a stretch for Thomas to offer some guidance. His swift untangling of the legal knot earned him not only the old man's gratitude but his neighbour's trust. And every month, while they still lived on the main Banavie Road, Thomas and Milene would receive a bottle of wine, or sometimes a small hamper of fresh produce as a token of appreciation from the grateful neighbour. Equally generous though was the offer to store Thomas' sporty car in the garage he wasn't using on the lane at the back of the property. When the neighbour died suddenly, as a favour to his now almost senile widow, Rothwell Glen selflessly snapped up his house as well as much of his property portfolio.

"When does your ban expire?"

"Still got another few months. I suppose you can drive it?"

"Is it manual?"

"Yes."

"Sorry. I thought that you knew that I'm a strictly automatic girl."

Her words and the way in which she delivered them caused Thomas' penis to uncoil.

"This is it."

They stopped beside a graffiti tagged door. The chrome handle was discoloured and the lock mechanism looked as if rust had bitten into it.

"Twist to the left then a flick to the right," said Thomas, reminding himself. It didn't work. The lock remained stiff.

Damn.

Kaitlin asked if there was a key somewhere but as it was buried among the boxes in the flat like the lost Ark of the Covenant, it was almost irrelevant. Thomas tried again but still the lock wouldn't budge.

He kicked at the thin metal door, the echo of which didn't make it as far as the sun worshippers fifty metres away. Thomas put his hands to his head and turned away in frustration. He stared at the happy groups in the park. For a moment, he envied their simple contentment. Beyond that, there was nothing. Only this one moment.

"It's the weekend so why don't we just grab a bottle and join them?" he offered. "There's a shop just around the corner, you grab a bench and I'll be back…"

"No," said Kaitlin, softly but firmly. "We need to speak to Innes Guthrie and it needs to be today."

"We can do it on Monday," he whined.

"What has happened to you? I used to look up to you. All of the interns did. Thomas Leven. You were like a fucking superhero to us."

"Superheroes don't kill children."

"Snap out of it," said Kailin, grabbing onto his upper arm. "Look at me."

Thomas couldn't.

"Look at me, Thomas Leven. You're not the man you think you are."

Kaitlin pulled Thomas close. Against his cheek, her face felt soft and warm. As she cradled his head in her hands, the side of her lips brushed against his.

"You've got this."

Lost in her eyes, her sweet breath coupling with his in the shade of the foliage, Thomas felt giddy. A rangy teenage boy, retrieving a ball wedged between the dip of the verge and the fence, stopped and momentarily watched. And as Kaitlin placed her hand over his abdomen, Thomas' skittish state changed to something more primal. Inside and out, he felt it. Mortified by a show of affection more explicit than he was used to, the boy curled his foot to claw the errant football out of the thicket and scampered back to his friends.

"Now let's open that fucking door," whispered Kaitlin.

Beside the fence, among the weeds, sat a collection of discarded bottles, twigs and odd stones. Using a dry branch, Thomas dislodged a diamond shaped rock from the earth. He ordered Kaitlin to keep a look out.

Thomas glanced the stone down at an angle but this time the echo from the metallic door drew the attention of a breastfeeding mother at a nearby bench.

"The best way to disable something is to hit it dead centre. Keep that stone but we need something sharp," said Kaitlin.

"You've got experience in disabling things?"

"You want to find out?" she replied, pointedly.

By the black plastic refuse bin was an abandoned umbrella, temporarily rendered obsolete by the weather. Clasping the handle, Kaitlin stood on the fabric end of the brolly and gave it a sharp twist. Snapping like dry twigs in the spinney, she handed the sheared, thin aluminium shaft to Thomas.

"Sharp end to the lock," she said.

Thomas cracked the side of the flat stone against the plastic handle of the umbrella and there was a pop. He tried the lock again. There was movement but not enough. In the park, the merriment continued. The sound of a bottle smashing triggered no wilder emotion than a collective whoop.

"One more time," urged Kaitlin.

Again, Thomas lined up the stone and the shaft. A slight buckle meant that the latter wasn't true but his strike was. Thomas wrenched the handle round and the mechanism released. Well oiled it may have been, but the door was weightier than he'd remembered. Thomas held it up just enough for Kaitlin to scurry under. He followed, gently easing it back to the ground.

Thomas hit the switch and the strip light crackled. The garage may have looked nondescript from the outside but from within, it appeared larger than the space Thomas once used. At the far end, a barred window with a wooden shutter closing out the light took up most of the wall. On the other side of the door was a tall, functional metal cabinet, slightly ajar. To the left of the room, under an old fashioned pulley, ran a long sink with an industrial style spray tap and drying rack. Opposite, stood a sturdy looking workbench. Dotted around the covered car in the centre of the room, were stacks of chairs, similarly concealed.

As the room became marginally more familiar, something about the configuration of the chairs left Thomas feeling unsettled. Something odd. Pushing the stacks away, he lifted the edge of the canvas and an old familiar body instantly suppressed his apprehension.

"Not bad, eh?"

Impressed as she may have been by the dark green coupé, the breeze which caused the dust covers to ripple, only added to Kaitlin's unease.

Thomas opened the car door and climbed in. He placed his hands on the thin but durable wheel. It had been some time since he'd been in the driver's seat of any car. It felt both alien and natural. There were dirt marks above the door and the leather interior was more cracked than he'd remembered, but it felt good. For a brief moment, Thomas imagined himself leaving all of this behind, with Kaitlin by his side. Maybe after MacMillan. Once he'd allowed the scent of the vehicle to fill his nostrils, Thomas felt around the ignition mechanism for the key. Nothing there. OK, now the cubby next to his right knee. An expired parking permit and a musty packet of mints was all he found.

"Take a look in that cabinet. The key must be in there," he said.

As the breeze continued to blow, and the dust sheets swelled, Kaitlin walked towards the cabinet with a nervous reluctance. "What is this place?"

"It's called a garage," replied Thomas, flitting between glib and sarcastic. "They're quite handy, actually. You can keep tins of paint, car parts and tools."

"Like these?"

From a double headed clip on the outside of the cabinet door, Kaitlin removed a pair of curved blades.

"Pretty hard to change a plug with this," she replied.

They each took a handle and opened the cabinet wide. Between the doors and the panels, hung close to fifty implements of which only a handful were easily identifiable.

"Holy shit."

"Your neighbour wasn't Torquemada, was he?"

Ignoring the comment, Thomas instructed Kaitlin to start checking the drawers.

Kaitlin opened one and recoiled. "I don't like this. I want to go."

In the top drawer on a dark velvet cushion, sat a collection of teeth and small bones, displayed as if arranged by a meticulous jeweller.

"Now," she said insistently.

"Wait for me in the car," said Thomas, curious to see what the other drawers had to offer.

In the deeper drawer underneath was an almost complete set of surgical lancets and scalpels, the handles of which shared the same double knurled pattern. For reasons best known to himself, Thomas felt compelled to touch the tip of the one blade that was not fixed in position. Before he'd realised what he'd done, a bubble of blood formed on the tip of his index finger and dripped into the wooden case.

Damn.

"Shhh…" urged Kaitlin. "Listen."

The deep, menacing growl of a dog. But not from the direction of the lane. A strong and steady footprint.

It's not from the park, Thomas realised. It's coming from the direction of the house. His attempt to mop up the droplet with his middle finger was futile but the impending arrival of the visitors sharpened his focus.

"Try behind the visor."

Kaitlin pulled down the shade and the keys dropped into her lap.

"Quick!"

Dashing towards the car, Thomas didn't see the dark, canvas bag on the floor. The top of his left foot took the brunt of the collision.

"Bastard," he muttered through gritted teeth as the pain shot through his sensors. What was in that, Thomas wondered as he hobbled towards Kaitlin. Bricks?

As she shuffled across into the passenger seat, Thomas lifted up the garage door. The sun, now directly ahead, was blinding.

With his eyes straining against the light, Thomas turned and saw, standing in the doorframe, the silhouette of a man with a large dog, pulled up on its hind quarters, growling with barely restrained menace. Before he could focus, the dog was released and within seconds, it was by his side. Frozen by fear, and backed up against the open door of the car, Thomas felt Kaitlin's hand grabbing at his waistband, pulling him down and onto the seat.

As the animal's mucus filled nose edged towards Thomas' face, he looked into its clear blue eyes and said the first thing that came to mind;

"Is MacMillan your master?"

Instantaneously, the dog's mood changed. Its ears softened and its teeth retreated behind the fold of its lip. While it sniffed around Thomas' face, the silhouetted figure remained impassive by the door.

The dog has MacMillan's eyes.
Fucking hell.
The dog has MacMillan's eyes.

Despite the knowledge this was a ludicrous assertion, one based on nothing but the instincts of a confused and tired mind, Thomas felt emboldened.

He brought his face up to that of the beast and looked into its eyes.

Beyond the blue.

The ochre.

The blue again.

A room of blue and black.

"You are the birdman," the dog said.

"I am," replied Thomas.

Thomas extended his hand and asked another question of the dog.

"Am *I* your master?"

The dog shook its head. "My master brought you here. What do you have for me?"

Intuitively, Thomas squeezed at his recently sliced finger. Thick beads of blood stemmed from the fleshy pad. As the creature enthusiastically accepted the offer of Thomas' vital fluids, Kaitlin's concern had become more pronounced.

"What are you doing, Thomas?" she said, quietly. "Get in the car."

"That is not enough," said the dog as Thomas returned through the ochre to the plain blue.

Slowly, he moved his legs into the footwell then sharply pulled the door shut, an action which the dog took as a more hostile act than the last. Enraged, it climbed up on the door, its long claws scratching deep into the car's paintwork. The dog growled and snarled from behind the window, a mouthful of teeth on full display in its powerful jaw. More and more, without concern, the now frenzied beast began to bang its head against the side window. Knowing that it was being denied, the dog pulled itself up onto its muscular hindquarters and with its clawed forefeet and teeth, started to tear at the black roof fabric. As the growls and the moans became deeper, more ancient, Kaitlin's one word request grew louder.

"Drive," she said. "Drive."

Drive!

Thomas dropped the hand brake and sped out onto the lane. In his haste to escape, he saw neither the box of unwanted toys that he crushed nor the recycling bin that he winged, sending bottles flying in all directions. Thomas' focus was entirely on the rear view and the fast approaching hound.

As it neared, he heard a shrill whistle and the dog gave up the chase. The animal obediently returned to its owner, standing in the middle of the lane.

"What if he calls the police?"

"He won't," said Thomas, breathing heavily.

"What makes you so sure?"

"Because he knows that I can have him fired."

Chapter 14 - Bealltainn

Like the neighbouring Charing Cross Mansions, its similarly impressive twin, the St George's building at the corner of Woodlands Road, remains a significant remnant of Glasgow's Victorian splendour. The nearby and much-loved Grand Hotel though wasn't so fortunate. Hacked down in the sixties as part of the area's savage redevelopment and replaced by a now decanted exercise in post-modern brutalist brick, the demise of The Grand Hotel is considered by many a criminal loss to the aesthetic of a city, irreparably scarred by modernity.

"Very good of him to see us at such short notice," said Thomas breaking into a light jog to catch the main door being held for them by a mannerly but security incontinent tenant.

Beyond the dull, shaded close, bursts of sunshine captured by the tall rear windows flooded in, illuminating the wide, mustard tiled staircase. On the second floor, there were two sets of doors. The left flat's heavy outer doors were firmly closed. The name on the small brass plate above the letterbox didn't correspond with the one they were looking for. In the doorway opposite, there was neither a bell nor a name.

"Are you sure this is the right place?" asked Thomas.

"Pretty certain," replied Kaitlin. Leant against the frame of the inner door was a carved wooden cane. She picked it up and gently rapped at the lead lined glass.

Before Thomas had the chance to respond, an elderly man opened the door just wide enough for his long, pointed nose to peer out.

"Can I help you?" he asked, his eyes straining through his glasses.

Even stooped, the man stood taller than Thomas.

"Mr Guthrie?"

"It's Professor Guthrie," he said, "and I'm not interested."

"You don't know what we're here for."

"I'm not buying."

"That's fine because we're not selling, professor. It's about your work."

The professor paused, his interest aroused. "I'm afraid you've caught me at a bad time. I'm just about to head off."

"Can we walk and talk?"

"All the way to Stirling?"

"Stirling?"

"Yes, I'll be reading from one of my books for The Festival of the Bealltainn tonight."

"What a coincidence. That's exactly what I want to talk to you about," replied Thomas with a grin, "one of your books."

"I have to say that I generally find pushiness to be a rather unattractive feature," said the professor, before his face cracked into a smile, "but in your case, I'll make an exception."

As Guthrie retreated into his lobby, Kaitlin whispered, "I think I might be cramping your style here."

Ignoring her jibe, Thomas continued, "I really appreciate your time, Professor Guthrie."

"Innes, please," he said, sliding a notebook down the zipped side of his case. "Which of my books was it you wanted to speak with me about?"

"Westerwick - The Unholy Isle," said Thomas.

Guthrie stopped. "Really?"

"Yes.

"Since I started to dip into commercial writing, I've had ten…no, eleven books published. Some by the more established houses in Edinburgh, but a few more recent works have been self-published. Contrary to the opinions of some of my former colleagues, I see no shame in going down that road when the traditional routes close. If one maintains a loyal, appreciative audience, a self-published title, coupled with regular invitations to the festivals can keep the wolves from the door."

"I can imagine," replied Thomas.

"But none of those eleven books has brought me as much curiosity as 'Westerwick' has."

"I tried to find it but it doesn't appear to be available."

"Unfortunately, that's correct."

Thomas pressed him as to why.

"Around the turn of the century, I'd been carrying out research on the island and on its complex history, when I was approached by a new publishing house. They'd gotten wind of my work and we opened a dialogue. Like many publishers, especially the newer imprints, they promised the world. Although flattered, I remained reluctant to commit, especially as they had no obvious track record and more importantly, I hadn't yet completed an initial draft of the work. Not only did this not dissuade them, it made them more eager to snap up the book. I gave them a sample chapter and within a couple of days, they'd offered me a hefty fee to secure the first option on the book."

"Is this normal practice?"

"Hardly. I mean, if one is a household name or a television personality, it's not unknown to receive a generous advance but as a lecturer whose books tend to gather dust on the shelves of the University Library, it's considerably less common than you'd think."

"What was it about the book that made it so desirable to them?"

"That was obvious," Guthrie laughed. "The television dramatisation of the MacMillan case was in production so I'd imagine that they thought the book could capitalise on the groundswell of interest that was forming."

"Is that how they angled their approach?"

"Not particularly but my feeling at the time was they were looking for some unique insight into why he did what they say he did."

"Was MacMillan himself part of your study?"

Guthrie shook his head. "I had no interest in him personally. But I did expect that his return might revive interest in my book."

"And has it?"

"Well, let me put it this way, you're not the first party to contact me about it this week."

"Really?"

Guthrie looked at his wristwatch. "I'd love to stay and talk but I need to be in Stirling by half past four."

Conscious of the importance of the professor's insight, Kaitlin urged Thomas to continue.

"I really appreciate your time," he persisted. "Can I help you to your car?"

"I need to take the stairs slowly. Two flights aren't great on the old knees."

"Let me take your bag," said Thomas.

"Very kind. You never told me why my unpublished book is of such interest to you?"

He hadn't expected that question. The wide eyed look from Kaitlin told him that he probably should have. Think on your feet, Thomas.

"We're hoping to make a film about the island and its inhabitants," he improvised. "And as we've already spoken to MacMillan..."

"In person?" Guthrie interrupted.

Thomas nodded.

"Fascinating," replied the professor.

"It is. However, most of the works which feature the island are either too dry or overly salacious. From what we can gather, your previous books are respected by your peers and regarded as exhaustive. That's why, when it comes to Westerwick, we're very keen to pick your brain, as it were.

You wouldn't happen to have a spare copy, would you?"

"I'm afraid that the terms of the contract forbid me from using or sharing any section from that particular work," said the professor, double locking the outer door.

"Not to worry," said Thomas. "Tell me, were you teaching at the University when MacMillan was a student?"

"I was, yes."

"Did you know him?"

"I can't say that I did. He might have taken a few of my lectures but I have no recollection of ever meeting him, though I was there that awful morning…"

"Eilidh Broome?"

"Yes, a terrible thing. Her brother had been one of my students. Tragic family." Guthrie stopped on the first stair and turned back. "Give me two seconds. I need to let Gwen and Rhys know that I'm leaving. They're good neighbours."

I should introduce him to mine, thought Thomas. The bold Derek and his fucking otters. That situation will need to be resolved quickly.

Guthrie rang the bell.

"They've lived in the flat across the landing for nearly twenty years now. They always look in on Crowley when I'm off on my travels. His eyes are going, which given his age, is no surprise. And he isn't as limber as he used to be but they love him as much as I do. When I'm away, they bring him treats and sit with him so that he doesn't get too lonely. They even trim his whiskers," exclaimed Guthrie with a chuckle. "Sometimes I think he prefers them to me."

"Cats can be like that though," said Thomas.

"Cats?" he scoffed. "Crowley's my husband."

Thomas felt his face redden as Guthrie's neighbour opened the door.

Kaitlin stifled a laugh by looking at the ground. "I'll wait for you downstairs…"

At the foot of the stairs, the professor took a moment to straighten himself out. Thomas passed him his rucksack.

"I can take it from here," he said.

"It's no bother, really," said Thomas. "Where are you parked?"

"In the one disabled space the bloody council deem the building worthy of having."

"I'm afraid you might have a more pressing issue than the parking bay, professor."

In the rim, a screwdriver had been pushed in so hard that its handle had bent. Pressing her toe against the flat front tyre stood a coy looking Kaitlin.

"That's vandalism," roared the enraged professor. He turned away from the street and shouted towards his block. "I know who did this. And I'll be calling the police."

"And miss the Festival of the Bealltainn? Firstly, do you have a spare?"

The old man sighed and shook his head.

"Remind me. What time do you need to be in Stirling?"

****

"Esoteric philosophy, to be precise," said Guthrie, passing

his cane back towards Kaitlin already squashed up on the back seat.

"Huge interest in the subject these days. Not just the cults, but the history of belief, paganism and the occult on these isles. Do you mind if I push this back a little?" he asked without waiting for a reply. Throwing his hat behind him, the professor slid the passenger seat fully up to where Kaitlin's legs had been a split second earlier.

"We all good?"

"So, tell me more about this film you're making," asked the professor, yanking at his seatbelt.

Kaitlin's shrug in the rear view mirror suggested that he'd have to wing it.

"We'd been wanting to do a feature on the myths, the legends and the songs of the Isles for a while and as I mentioned, the return of Angus MacMillan, has shone quite a bit of light on our project. Obviously, your position as a senior lecturer at the University of Glasgow puts you high on our to speak-to list."

"Former senior lecturer," Guthrie said ruefully.

"Glasgow's loss is your reader's gain. Still, you remain a respected authority on a number of matters."

"Respected authority?" warming to the flattery, the professor smiled. "Can I keep you all to myself?"

"We were hoping to speak with you, in more detail obviously, about the beliefs of the rural cultures and how they integrated into everyday island life and beyond."

"With respect, I can't imagine that your film is going to have them queuing around the block at the multiplexes."

"You'd be surprised, professor…sorry, Innes."

"Very well then. What would you like to know?"

"Why is it considered so important?"

"Of all the islands around this land of ours, Westerwick is the one most shrouded in secrecy and myth. Sure, you have ghosts and legends behind every rock from Tiree to Toberemory but there is something about that one inhospitable mass that so captures one's imagination."

Guthrie continued. "It is believed that the first settlement on the island was in the village now known as Bocquarran around 700 BC. Early Pictish communities formed but only the most hardy stayed. You see, the soil was light and quite heavy in alkaline which meant that not all attempts at agricultural farming were sustainable. A settlement, mainly of seafarers, was established on the West Cove around the ninth century."

"Is it true that there are no trees on Westerwick?"

"Not quite. On the southern edge of the western peninsula, there is a cluster which overhangs the drop to the coast. Among the junipers, there stands a handful of white cedars. You might have seen them in tourist pictures of the area. Quite unusual. I will come back to this though as it does have certain relevance as to the island's reputation. Now, during the Reformation…"

Guthrie paused and pointed.

"M80, my dear."

"Excuse me?"

"I'd advise heading across the M80 towards Stirling. Much quicker."

Before he'd finished, Thomas had cut across three lanes of traffic. The professor clutched the handle above his door, his knuckles tightening as the small car swerved around the hooting vans and trucks.

Kaitlin leant forward and spoke softly. "See those sticky out things, behind your steering wheel?"

"Huh?"

"The wee indicatory things. You might want to use them next time. You know, just to let the other vehicles know what you're up to. Just a thought."

Again, Thomas didn't respond to her jibe. He understood that her slight was playful, an affectionate deflection. His thoughts were consumed not by motorway courtesies but by the subtle scent of her perfume. And her unpierced earlobes. Narrow and lacking in flesh, they moved ever so slightly when she spoke. Thomas wanted to reach back and twist that fallen curl behind her ear then gently caress the lower part of her lobule in his fingers, the way that Milene liked.

Milene.

Milene was gone. Kaitlin is here.

Out of sight, Kaitlin placed her hand on Thomas' shoulder and gently squeezed. Instinctively, she knew that he wanted to touch her.

"Where were we?" asked Professor Guthrie.

"The M80?" said Thomas pulling the car into the empty, nearside lane. As much as he wanted to unload his cargo and be alone with Kaitlin, he knew that the more time spent in the company of Innes Guthrie, the greater his understanding of Westerwick, and Angus John MacMillan, would be.

"'The Reformation," whispered Kaitlin.

"Of course, The Reformation. Right, let's divide that disaster into palatable chunks. Once the Catholics had stopped torturing the heretics, there was about forty five minutes of peace before they themselves were hunted by the Protestants. But during the unrest, the island itself was largely ignored by the warring mainland factions and as such, it gained a reputation as somewhat of a haven of tolerance and understanding."

"So what changed?"

"By the time the new world was being exploited for financial gain, hundreds of ships would leave British ports every week for the fraught journey across the Atlantic. In the milder seasons, some would go around the Fastnet Rock and straight across to New York, Philadelphia and to Chesapeake Bay. However, in the less clement months, a daytime stop on the southernmost peninsula of the island was the final stopping point for many vessels before they spent a torrid six weeks or more in the North Atlantic. And as we've seen with your driving, timing was key."

Kaitlin sniggered.

"How so?" asked Thomas.

"Navigation in the dark, primarily. Before the advent of the lighthouse, the route up through the islands and across the North Atlantic, risky as it was, could shave up to a week off the travel time. British ships tended to leave Southampton and Liverpool in clusters."

"Safety in numbers."

"Yes, especially on a three thousand mile expanse of

unforgiving ocean. However, should finances dictate, and they often did, a ship's manifest might determine one final stop in Glasgow or Belfast. As trade had increased tenfold in the ten years before 1800, a decision maker in a London counting house rarely took the wellbeing of a ship's crew into account. With certain lines leaving British ports at the same time, a more ambitious director might have wanted to introduce his wares earlier, stealing a march on competitors. The sailors themselves were reluctant but the directors would leave it to a captain to quell any rebellion. A few shillings up front could secure the last warm bosom a sailor might find in months but often a captain would have to threaten the cat o' nine tails to freshly sober charges in order to push through. After that, the wild Atlantic would be like a half hour on a Queens Park pedalo. During the winter months, when the western sheriffs received word of passage, they would instruct the farmers to light fires along the coast, in lieu of lighthouses, keeping the ships away from the rocks. However, by the early nineteenth century, there was a schism and this is where it gets interesting."

Guthrie continued.

"A sect of radicals calling themselves The True Cross had started to dominate the southern tip of Westerwick, much to the annoyance of religious leaders not just in Edinburgh but also in Rome. An offshoot of the Swedenborgian New Church, they took their name from the cedars believed to have been brought to the island from the Holy Land by the followers of Saint Augustine around 850 AD. Critics quickly realised that their adherence to traditional Christian tenets was quite fluid. Steadfastly refusing attempts at integration with the wider Kirk, The True Cross became increasingly marginalised by the island council and subjected to heavier levies and taxes than the other Christian denominations. By the start of the winter of 1817, matters had come to a head. After the poorest harvest in living memory, the other religious communities on the island, with the blessing of their leaders, blocked the movement of much needed provisions to the areas under The True Cross' jurisdiction."

"Not very Christian of them."

"It seemed that the parameters of Godly worship on the island barely extended beyond the weaponisation of hunger. As a result, a significant number of men, women and children starved."

"How did the sect react?"

"In a number of ways. Raiding was the obvious one but when the two youngest children of a farmer named Fyvie disappeared, things turned ugly. Accusations of kidnapping and rituals were levelled at The True Cross community and when bands of angry islanders forced their way onto their land, bloodshed was inevitable. Starved, then beaten and diminished, one young parishioner named McCandlish recorded witnessing the Pastor making an unholy pact. The lights which helped provide safe passage for the sailors were extinguished and if the myth is to be believed, in pitch dark conditions on the evening of the feast of All Saints 1817, the SS Anthony Silver, carrying a crew of fifteen and an official cargo of machinery parts and silks from the east, ran aground on the rocks beneath the Augustine cedars. Though word of the wreck reached the mainland quite quickly, sadly those were days before a national rescue service. When the authorities did arrive, they found little of the Silver.

"I take it that everyone on board perished?"

"That was the initial thought until Spencer Colville and Douglas Simpson got involved."

"And they were?"

"Prominent businessmen would be the polite term. In actuality, they were traders in human flesh. Leaning heavily on their civic contacts, Colville and Simpson, both of whom had a stake in the Silver, were very keen to assess the site before the authorities arrived and for good reason. Though the official record showed the Silver was a ship laden with fine quality goods and machine parts, the hidden inventory which washed up on the island's northern shore four days later disclosed the real reason the pair were so keen to investigate for themselves. Aside from silks and machinery, the true records showed that the vessel had left Liverpool with a cargo of forty three slaves taken from the Ashanti Kingdom in West Africa."

"Hadn't slavery been abolished in Britain by then?"

"Technically yes, but though Wilberforce's act ten years previously had officially abolished the trafficking of human beings in the British Empire, it wasn't until much later that the actual abolition of the trade took effect. Men like Colville and Simpson had little time for legislation which neither suited them nor the people they were trading with."

"That would be why they wanted to investigate the scene first."

'Precisely. A cargo as precious as this was one thing but any trace of enslaved peoples would shine unwanted light on them and others involved in similar nefarious trading. So utilising a small but adept private militia, Colville and Simpson pretty much invaded the land controlled by The True Cross and took over."

"What did they find?"

"Officially, very little,"

"Unofficially?"

"Human remains. And plenty of them."

Thomas caught Kaitlin's reflection in the rear view mirror and exhaled.

"Every croft in the area was searched; bunkers, sheds, everywhere. Once they reached the Pastor's house, what they found shocked even the most battle-hardened of men. After breaking through the doors of the manse, the first person they encountered was the Pastor's maid, Agnes Lorimer. Naked and babbling, Lorimer was on her knees scraping her already bloodied hands against the parlour's stone floor. The men carried on to the long room where they found, suspended from the cross beams three brutalised bodies; one male slave and one expectant female captive, together with a young boy believed to have been a member of the ship's company. All three were missing sections of their skin and though the latter two were alive albeit barely, the former had already bled out. The ropes which trussed him, crushing his rib cage, were saturated with blood, the same blood with which the Pastor had coated the room an infernal red."

"Jesus," whispered Thomas.

"Naturally, they detained him and under questioning, he insisted that God was dead and that any prayers his people offered up had been answered by this strange harvest. Magic had healed and magic had provided. Who were they, he'd asked, to turn down such a bountiful gift? Next turn on the left."

Thomas hit the indicator and slowed the car down to make a sharp turn. "So, what happened?"

"Conscious of what would occur should word reach the mainland, Colville and Simpson ordered that every house loyal to The True Cross be razed to the ground."

"And the Pastor?"

"The parish recorded that he died in a house fire. The truth though, was something different. First he was tortured by the militia, then refusing to repent, was strangled using an improvised garrote. Still defiant, they tied him to a horse and dragged his body to the cliff at Scharr Point. Given one final chance to atone, the Pastor laughed in the faces of Colville and Simpson, cursing their families for eternity. Enraged, Colville himself drew a dagger and drove it into the pastor's throat. His body was thrown into the water. Without its figurehead, the first incarnation of the church of The True Cross no more."

"Are you suggesting there were subsequent incarnations?"

"Almost certainly," replied Professor Guthrie.

"What about Colville and Simpson?"

"When abolition was made final, both Coville and Simpson, like most slavers, were compensated for their business losses. Simpson himself donated a considerable sum towards the erection of the Scharr Point lighthouse before dying of the palsy."

"And Colville?"

"Four years to the day from the events at Scharr Point, Colville was standing behind a horse when it kicked out. Its hoof cracked Colville's skull like a watermelon. Despite considerable attempts to save him, he succumbed to his agonising injuries two days later."

"The Pastor's curse?"

Guthrie chuckled. "Who's to say?"

"I had no idea…"

"The history of cults is a particular passion. Most people don't have the inclination to carry out even the most basic of research beyond the headlines. As a result, their understanding will always be lacking. In this instance though, my knowledge of the subject has more to do with luck than design, to be honest."

"How so?"

"Occasionally, as part of my duties as professor, I'd be asked to cast my eye over certain collections offered to the University's library. In one such lot, buried among the usual antiquities were the journals of one James McCandlish, formerly of the parish of South Fintan, Westerwick. Despite my protestations, the university chose to rebuff the journals as the veracity of McCandlish's claims couldn't be established. Unsurprising really as the faculty has been distancing itself from anything to do with Westerwick since the MacMillan affair. Before they went to auction, I made a proposal to the estate for that part of the collection and they were mine. Without the testimony of McCandlish, my work would have contained far less colour."

"And we'd know little about The True Cross."

"Precisely."

"Are the journals still in your possession?"

Guthrie's slow, deliberate nod confirmed that they were.

Following the professor's directions, Thomas turned onto a road which quickly narrowed to a point where the slightest movement either side would mean a trip to the garage. Sensing the driver's concern, the professor calmed Thomas with some words of reassurance.

"You know you can't go back," said Guthrie with the serenity of a saint. "Concentrate and you'll be fine."

Slowly, Thomas edged the car beyond the wall, its wing mirrors missing contact by the length of a final shave. As the road widened, in the rear view, Thomas could see Kaitlin's limbs unravel.

"Anywhere by the gate would be just fine," said Professor Guthrie, reaching for his hat. Thomas, determined that their brief but illuminating encounter wasn't at an end, wasn't done. He deployed the hand brake and unbuckled his belt.

"Will you be reading 'The Diel Walks on Westerwick' tonight? To hear that in person, I mean…"

Thomas took a stab at the poem's ending…

"With everything that he does see, the diel waits, the diel waits for me. Wonderfully powerful stuff."

"Nearly," clapped the professor, impressed, "but bravo, Thomas. Did you know that Manus' spellbound piece of work predates Robert Johnson's blues by more than a hundred years?"

Thomas shook his head.

"Like the late musician, perhaps Manus was warning the listener to keep on moving, lest the hounds of hell catch up with him? And on that note…"

In front of a three bar gate, and under the shade of an

oversized yellow marquee, two young men sat at a flimsy looking table. Upon seeing the professor helped from the car, their demeanour changed from forlornly bored to excited.

"Thank you for the lift. And the chat," said Innes Guthrie. "I'm reassured to know that there are still people out there with just enough curiosity to make things happen."

As the smaller of the young men scurried towards the car then stopped, without a word, the professor handed over his bag.

"One final thing," asked Thomas. "Do you believe that Angus John MacMillan could be involved in a modern incarnation of The True Cross?"

The professor smiled ruefully and spread the palms of his hands.

Recognising that he'd received more insight about Westerwick in one short drive than what he'd gleaned from weeks of dusty papers and the arcane anecdotes of a convicted madman, Thomas continued. "Those journals. I would love to take a look at them, if that's not too much of an imposition."

Sheltering from the sun under the wide brim of his Fedora, Innes Guthrie turned to Thomas and said, "Enjoy the Bealltainn."

"Shall we follow him?" Thomas asked Kaitlin.

She reached up, stretching into the sky as would a cat after a long sleep. "We should do what the man said we should do."

An hour ago, Kaitlin wouldn't have needed to ask him twice. Keen to continue the illuminating dialogue, Thomas approached the remaining young man under the marquee.

"Invitation only, Sir."

Sensing that the patronising smile which accompanied the young man's denial had annoyed Thomas, Kaitlin looped her arm around his and led him away from the scene he was about to cause. "We'll make our own fun."

In a clearing by the back of the house, Kaitlin sat down. She reached her hand over and Thomas took it. Under the cloudless sky they lay in silence and surrendered to the blue. As Thomas' thoughts became hers, Kaitlin's became his. Hours passed in moments.

Heading back to the car as the sun crept away, a deep hunger had taken hold. Conspicuous and unambiguous.

She bit his lip.

He pushed her back against the rocks and pulled up her skirt.

She dug her nails into his sides.

He climaxed quickly.

Chapter 15 - The Devil's Pulpit

There was little traffic on the narrow road from Gilmour's Linn. The failing light had given way to an interminable darkness, broken only by the scintillant glow from the occasional farmhouse. The cool night air whistled through the half-open window, whispering melodies in Thomas's ear. Behind them, there was nothing. There was much to say but again, neither felt the need to speak. Some silences are less awkward than others. Thomas wanted to close his eyes and give himself up to the possibilities of the night but that would have to wait. He didn't know where they were headed but Kaitlin did. She reached for the indicator. The sound of its rhythmic pulse saved Thomas from an untimely slumber.

"We're here."

As the car turned slowly onto the drive, gravel crackled beneath the weight of the tyres. Ahead, a fox, transfixed by the headlights, stood motionless, its eyes reflecting back towards the car. Thomas dipped his light and the small creature darted into the hedgerow.

"Haven't seen a fox in years," said Thomas.

"There's a family of them that hang around. I'm often told off for leaving them scraps but they've got to eat too, don't they?"

Thomas made a mental note to sketch a fox.

"This is your folk's place?"

Kaitlin nodded. "Normally they're here every weekend but they're out of the country at the moment. It's only you and me."

"And Mr Fox," replied Thomas, turning the engine off in front of the single story, white washed cottage.

"Is that water I hear? We're not that close to the loch are we?"

"No," replied Kaitlin. "There's a waterfall nearby. It's called The Devil's Pulpit."

"Sounds ominous."

"If that sounds ominous, are you sure you want to enter the dark and mysterious world of Venning Cottage?"

Thomas chuckled, "Of my own free will."

Kaitlin turned the handle and opened the door.

"It's not locked?"

"There's a key under the blue plant pot but to be honest, we've never felt the need to."

Thomas took the small step down into the living room.

"As you can see," said Kaitlin, following him, "it's a very modern haunted house."

"Hammer House of Habitat, eh?"

Kaitlin didn't get the reference.

"So, the professor," said Thomas. "Thoughts?"

"I think he was lovely. Just wanted to give him a cuddle."

"No, about what he was saying."

"It was interesting and all that but…"

"But?"

"I'm not sure that I buy it."

"How so?"

"Firstly, I think it's living creatures who are disturbed not buildings, or houses."

"Or islands?"

"Exactly. I find it hard to believe that an inanimate object can be possessed by a demonic power."

"Fair point but what about this cushion cover?" Thomas asked with a shudder.

Kaitlin continued, "Playing devil's advocate for one minute, the torture, the cannibalism. I don't know. Maybe the University was right about McCandlish's journals?"

Knowing what he did about MacMillan's 'Red Room', Thomas changed the subject. "How long have you had this place for?"

"Must be ten, eleven years now. My stepfather bought it from the estate of this actor who believed in a lot of the same things that Professor Guthrie does."

"Seriously?"

"Yep."

"It wasn't the guy from …?"

Kaitlin rolled her eyes, confirming to Thomas that it was.

"Seemingly he and his idiot pals believed that this area was prime devil worshipping territory. Naturally, they bought into the whole thing," she said. "Though to be fair, there was one bad experience."

"Occult related?"

"A drug overdose but his publicists thought that the more sinister angle would scan better for his fans. The actor quickly headed back to the States and once the police had done their thing, they pinned the blame on one of the expendable weirdos that hung around. Sneaky but not unheard of."

Recalling the details of his own crash, Thomas again moved the conversation on. "So he sold up to your step dad?"

"Not quite. A couple of regrettable film choices and the offers soon dried up. His lifestyle eventually caught up with him and the executors of his estate, led by his estranged widow, wanted to cash in on anything she could to keep his creditors at bay. One of Daddy dearest's recurring boasts was how he'd managed to take Jimmy Hollywood for thousands in a golf match at Gleneagles or St Andrews or somewhere. Anyway, when he died, Dad bought the whole thing, contents and all. Devious fuck that he is, he made most of his outlay back by selling guitars, scrips and artworks to collectors but a few things he kept as he found them. Including this."

Kaitlin undid a rope that had been tied to a fixing on the wall by the door. Slowly, she lowered the large metal wheel from the ceiling.

"Here, hold this," she said.

"Jesus," said Thomas as Kaitlin passed the rope to him. "It weighs a ton."

"Hold it steady." She picked up a lighter from a bowl on the wooden table and lit the seven candles. Kaitlin then took the rope from Thomas and tied it around the swag handle on the wall.

"Now turn off the light."

Thomas reached round and hit the switch.

As the chandelier stopped moving, the light from the candles cut through the darkness. On the ceiling, the shape of a pentagram.

"Dad thought that was worth keeping. Pretty cool eh?"

"I can see why the demons would feel at home here. It's roasting."

"Yeah, the cottage does keep the heat."

Thomas pulled back the curtain. "You wouldn't mind if I opened a window, would you?"

Kaitlin stopped. "Probably best not to," she said, apologetically. "The animals are funny around these parts, especially at night. If you so much as leave a door ajar, they'll come straight into the house, as brazen as you like. Even a window cracked open and they're on the scent. They'll be scraping at the door all night and that can be quite off putting."

"Speaking from experience?"

Kaitlin stood toe to toe with Thomas. He wanted to touch her again.

"If you're getting too hot," she whispered, "take a cold shower."

Maybe not, thought Thomas.

"Suit yourself," smirked Kaitlin. "There's a fan by the door to the kitchen. Drinks are in the cupboard. I'm going to get changed."

"And then?" asked Thomas.

"We're going to put some spooky old records on and get fucked up."

Chapter 16 - Abstract

God is alive and magic is afoot.

Thomas woke with the refrain in his head and a terrible thirst. His palate was bone dry. He forced his mouth open and chewed at nothing. Each eyelid, like his lips, felt glued to its partner. But for a few scores of light which crept up and over the seams of the heavy curtains, and the not too distant sound of stone and earth being cut and moved, the room was dark and silent. Weighing up the lack of hydration against his comfort, Thomas turned and buried his face into the unfamiliar pillow he'd been resting on. Its scent helped with the spread of recognition. This was Kaitlin's bed.

Slowly, Thomas reached over to the other side but no one was there. He raised his head just enough to bunch the dense but now flattened pillow. Kaitlin. At the end of one day and the start of another. He could still taste her tongue in his mouth, not long but determined. The thought of her returning momentarily and slipping back into bed, filled Thomas not only with a rush of excitement but more, a semblance of contentment, something he hadn't experienced in quite some time. He had fully given in to her as she had to him. His bruised glans recognised this too. He placed his hand on it. Still tacky, Thomas gently pulled it away from the skin at the top of his thigh, and stretched his frame towards the opposite side of the bed. As he did, he recoiled as his right knee touched a slightly damp patch on the cool cotton bed sheet. Thomas turned his wet knee and rubbed it against a less moist section of the sheet. He squinted at the clock on the bedside table but he couldn't focus on the bright blue display. It didn't matter. Today was God's day, and unlike Sundays of days past, nothing was planned. Truly a day of rest, he reckoned as his semi-conscious thoughts comprised entirely of Kaitlin. The odd wee girl with piercings. Four, she'd said but he hadn't realised just how perfect they were. Thomas believed that he could spend an eternity musing on the intimate detail of each of them. The tattoos, in varying shades of azure, teal and black, he couldn't cover with both hands. The most beautiful birds, inked onto her flawlessly smooth skin. Her entire back was a vivid encyclopaedia of pleasure. He closed his eyes and pushed his almost erect penis under his body, as if punishing it for its impertinence.

God is alive and magic is afoot. God is alive and magic is afoot. Need to think of another song…where is she?

Thomas drifted off again.

He had no idea how long he'd been sleeping when he noticed the return of that sound. Beyond the soft tremolo of the birdsong. That odd sound.

What is that?

Thomas had been waking to the sound of pointing and

drilling and blasting for the past few months, but this was different.

Like scraping. Three scrapes then some dull implement striking wood. No, not wood. Soil? Are we near a farm? Is *this* a farm? I can't remember. What the fuck is Kaitlin doing? Do farmers even work on Sundays?

God is alive and magic is afoot. That fucking refrain. The weirdest thing.

This time, however, it was closer than before and coming from somewhere to the left of the curtained window.

Thomas's eyes were now fully open. He pulled himself onto his elbows, lifting his head and shoulders from the pillow. The room remained dark but narrowing his focus, he could just about make out the high backed, peacock chair beside the door and to its right, a dressing table with a triple mirror. As he pushed back his hair, still damp with sweat, he winced.

"What the fuck?"

His skull ached. He pressed his fingers on the most tender part and recoiled again.

Definitely a wound, he thought. Not one from the crash though. No, those were long healed and anyway, this was closer to his right ear than to the top of his scalp. A new, fresh cut.

Did I crack my head during the night, he wondered.

Thomas slowly spun his legs around, draping them over the edge of the bed. His gaze shifted to the artwork on the wall opposite.

Is that an abstract?

He had no recollection of seeing it last night but the truth was that he couldn't actually remember getting into this room, never mind Kaitlin's bed. But here he was. And that song, with that refrain…

God is alive and magic is afoot.

There were definitely candles. That's it, he thought.

Thomas yawned then stretched out, instantly feeling a painful twinge. He clutched at his right shoulder. That too was tender. Unlike the one on his head, the marks on his shoulder he could see. Gently, he dabbed the flesh wound and started to wonder what kind of night they must have had.

The refrain persisted, as did the dull scraping.

Though Thomas had begun to piece together the sonic blocks which comprised the sound, he still couldn't articulate it. He attempted to stand but the effects of the previous night's excesses hampered his balance, pulling him to the left and sending him immediately back to the edge of the bed. Thomas squeezed at his temples. His head throbbed both inside and out. I'm never drinking again, he told himself. Placing one hand on the sharp edge of the marble topped bedside table, Thomas slowly tried again. More so than normal, his thighs and calves ached, in the way they used to burn after a satisfying run on unforgiving ground or when he lifted Milene against a tree, her legs wrapped tight around his waist. Milene. The thought of her and her name no longer stoked the embers of his desire.

I want Kaitlin.

More than anything. More than this job, more than my father sinking into the sands at Skelmorlie, more than life itself. I need her to be here, right now. To continue where we left off. To taste the tang of sweat from the cleft between her breasts. The sweat I created. Her morning mouth, bitter as a walnut.

Thomas cursed his head. Where is she?

God is alive and magic is afoot.

As that one repetitive lyric played in his head, over and over again, digging and burrowing, Thomas scoured the floor for his bag and his discarded clothing. The need for a capsule was greater than that for his trousers but at this juncture, either would suffice. Even a couple of run-of-the-mill, bathroom cupboard tablets would help with the pain. He pulled apart the heavy drapes and sunlight exploded into the room.

Slowly, his eyes adjusted. Thomas looked across his shoulder, a bite mark fresh and visible.

There was no frame around the abstract on the wall. Odd.

Thomas stretched again and yawned. Putting his hand over his mouth, he could feel some tenderness on the left side of his cheek. He picked the coarse woollen blanket from the floor, wrapped it around his waist and yawned again. With the balls of his hands he rubbed his eyes, clearing his vision. Thomas looked down at his torso. Like his shoulder, that too was covered in marks. From the corner of his eye, he saw some movement from just outside the window. Must be Kaitlin. He undid the latch and peered out.

"Looking for someone?" The low, deep rasp from behind was chillingly familiar.

"Collins?" asked Thomas. "What are you doing here?"

Leaning against the frame of the bedroom door, the Kunis Clement driver didn't respond. In attire more suited to manual labour than to that of a corporate chauffeur, the older man wore an aged, loose fitting polo shirt over some oil stained denim. Curiously, he appeared more imposing than Thomas had been used to.

The man who'd been ferrying Thomas to Kirkmalcolm lit a cigarette. "This is becoming a bit of a habit with you, isn't it?"

"Where's Kaitlin?" asked Thomas, straining not to give in to panic.

Collins continued to wipe his hands with a dark hand towel. "Who's Kaitlin?"

"Kaitlin. The paralegal. My paralegal."

"She's not here."

"She lives here. Her parents live here."

"I think you're mistaken."

Thomas' fear gave way to rage. He propelled himself towards Collins who nimbly stepped forward and inside. He spun Thomas around, slamming his larger, but now naked frame against the cold, damp brick wall.

Collins' pupils dilated as his rough left hand gripped Thomas's throat. The more Thomas struggled, the more Collins laughed and the tighter he squeezed. Thomas looked into the face of his assailant. Blood at the corner of his mouth. The driver's eyes, unblinking but manic. Beads of sweat ran into his narrow, greying eyebrows. His teeth were missing. At least four of them but the incisors remained and they were bared and viciously sharp. The eyes, however, remained locked on.

"What have you done with her?"

"Maybe the question you should be asking yourself, Thomas, is what have you done with her?" he whispered, nuzzling his nose against the scar on Thomas's cheek.

Like a ventriloquist controlling his doll, Collins angled Thomas's head away and towards the wall. The pattern which had earlier intrigued him was in fact, no abstract piece of art. Now close enough to touch, Thomas could see that this was flesh and blood, hair and membrane, crudely plastered over the painted brickwork. A large splatter, its circumference the size of a bin lid, trailing like the stem of a flower to the skirting and through the cracks in the floorboards. Markings, the likes of which he'd seen before; letters coarsely daubed. Thomas felt his stomach tighten and his legs go. Every permutation, each more nauseating than the last, punctuated by the same mark. Kaitlin. Kaitlin.

"Bastard," Thomas spat.

With his fingertips, Collins wiped the saliva from around his nose and cheek and, smiling, dabbed the residue onto his tongue and smiled, "Is this what Kaitlin tastes like?"

His grip, like a vice, turned and tightened underneath Thomas's jaw, tilting his chin upwards, cutting off the younger man's air supply. Conversely, despite slamming his fists into the older man's rib cage, it was Thomas who weakened with each act of resistance. He looked again into Collins' eyes. They remained fixed, firm. This was a struggle that he could not win. Thomas recognised his survival instinct had once again deserted him. He closed his eyes and as he had as a child, prepared to sink to the bottom of the pool. At that moment, Collins released his grip and Thomas dropped to the floor. As the particles of dust danced around in the bright morning light, he lay on his side with his chin pushing down on his chest, gratefully watching it expand and contract.

Breathe, he told himself.

Thomas raised his fingers to his neck. His skin was raw and unbearably tender as if a noose had tightened and scored his skin. He felt the phantom grip of his assailant as if he still had him at his mercy.

Breathe.

Damaged from the struggle, his hands were as dry as his mouth. He needed water. Thomas looked at his fingers. The tips were covered in dried blood. "Where is she?"

Collins stared down at Thomas and kicked the blanket towards him.

"Cover yourself up," he said contemptuously, "and come with me."

Thomas stood and followed Collins into the living room. Cushions were strewn across the floor, fresh candle wax dried on the cart wheel. There was broken glass on the table. The tip of one larger shard had a thin coating of blood upon it.

"Sit down," said Collins.

Thomas did as he was told. Collins threw him some clothing and said, "Put these on."

"Where are my clothes?"

"Your clothes were a mess."

"My wallet…"

"Don't worry about that. Just get dressed."

Thomas pulled on the t-shirt and cords. They were shabby and musty. "And my shoes?"

Collins stopped by the door to the cottage and dropped the holdall he was carrying.

"Wait here."

With no idea what was coming next, Thomas knew that it was prudent to presume that he remained in some kind of danger. As Collins was clearly capable of halting a larger, younger man, albeit one with a diminished physical presence, Thomas visually scanned the room for something he could use to even any return contest.

H.A.C.

The initials on the heavy canvas holdall, faded but neatly stencilled.

If anything the bag was even older and fustier than the clothes. Thomas was sure that he'd seen it before, in the boot of the company car. That's right, he told himself. When Collins first carried the boxes to his flat. The driver's old bowling bag.

H.A.C.

No, wait a minute.

It was in the garage. The one I kicked. H.A.C. I'm sure of it. Maybe, just maybe there's a tool it? Or a knife. Or a scalpel. Double knurled handle. Yes. *That's* where I'd seen it.

Thomas gripped the arm of the sofa and went to stand.

Don't be fucking stupid. Why would anyone carry a scalpel to a bowling green? A heavily weighted ball though...hide behind the door and bring it down on his head. Risky but at this stage, my options are almost gone.

Despite the present danger of his assailant's imminent return, Thomas lunged for the bag and lifted it by its handles. Not knowing the heft of a single bowling ball, he still knew that the bag felt lighter than it should've. In less fraught circumstances, this would've been the first indication to an alert mind that something wasn't right but as Thomas had woken from a drunken slumber, in a pool of blood and covered in cuts to find a paramour gone and a driver in a malevolent mood, his naturally inquisitive edge had been somewhat blunted.

He tugged the zipper ring and separated the teeth, the bag opening like a silent, baneful roar. Thomas had expected something, just not the revelation of a partially skinned skull with strands of blood matted hair. Its eye sockets, barely covered by rotting flesh, stared back at him.

Stunned, Thomas stumbled astern against the counter top, its jagged edge catching him on a delicate section of his side. He turned suddenly, instinctively, clutching his scraped muscle, knocking over one of the tall, brass tealight holders that was on the table. The short stack of magazines prevented the hollow brass from making a sound.

Panic was spreading.

Kaitlin.

Logic was telling him that it wasn't her. It couldn't have been her. Thomas knew that logic was the all-seeing parent of panic. He didn't have to tell himself that. Its truth was detonating like charges through each nerve end.

His eyes fixed on the table and the fallen candle holder but his processes lagged a step behind his gaze. Once they'd caught up, he grabbed the candle holder, jamming it awkwardly, top first, into the deep pockets of the old corduroy trousers. He pulled down the t-shirt in an attempt to cover the holder's wider base.

When Collins returned, carrying a pair of gumboots, Thomas had just made it back to the sofa. Covering the badly hidden implement, he folded his hand over his elbow.

"Put those on and follow me."

Thomas pulled his bare feet into the boots. They were ragged and even more dusty than the clothing and his captor. Though too tight to be comfortable, he thought against further risking his driver's ire. Pulling at the fabric of the t-shirt, Thomas complied with the order.

From the back door of the cottage, there was a narrow but twisted path bordered by well maintained, head height bushes. Overhead an arched arbour, veiled with thin, interlocked branches, provided partial shelter from the blazing sun.

"Straight on," Collins said, insisting that Thomas go first. Despite the discomfort, Thomas made sure that he kept clear of his captor's reach.

"Over there."

Directly ahead lay a twenty foot square patch of freshly turned earth, a stone's throw from the property's garage.

Need to divert his attention somehow, Thomas thought.

"Pick up the shovel," Collins ordered.

"Fuck you," replied Thomas. "You pick it up. Don't forget, you work for me."

With his gaze fixed on Thomas, Collins laughed as he reached down for the shovel. "They did say that you were a bit touched but you know what? I've grown quite fond of it."

The driver handed the shovel to Thomas.

Clutching the shaft, Thomas forced the tip of the blade into the earth, then running his fingertips over the top of the handle, he said defiantly, "Didn't you hear me the first time?"

With his heart racing, he pushed the shovel over, adding a further, "Fuck you."

"You're starting to test my patience, boy."

As Collins again reached for the shovel, Thomas brought the wide end of the candle holder down against the side of the driver's skull.

He staggered forward. His right leg bent awkwardly causing him to lose his footing on a mound of loose, dry earth. Pulling himself up and onto one knee, Collins moaned then turned towards the sun.

"Be careful now…"

"Last time," said Thomas. "Where is she?"

"Lest the Gods curse ye."

Thomas Leven didn't wait for clarification. A second blow, to the same now swollen area of Collins' head, split his skin and drove his face into the dirt. The driver raised his head and tried to push up on his elbows. Bile filled Thomas' mouth and nostrils. He needed to cough it up but not before delivering a third, telling blow.

Thomas hacked then retched into the dirt. Using his feet, he covered it up. Collins was perfectly still. He placed the sole of his ill-fitting boot on the backside of the driver and shook him.

Safe now.

Despite every instinct telling him to run, Thomas returned to the cottage. There was still too much to consider.

Collins will be found. Maybe not today but soon and they'll open an investigation. There's blood everywhere, some of it might be mine, he thought. And fingerprints over everything from the toilet seat to big fucking brass candle holder. His body is still warm and there are already too many questions.

Wouldn't it be ironic, even fitting, Thomas reflected, after the crash to be dragged into something that he actually wasn't responsible for.

Like MacMillan, I suppose. He too claims to have been the victim. And who believes such a person? No one. No, I need to clear this mess.

As reluctant as he was to revisit the contents of the holdall, Thomas knew that he had to confirm for certain that the head inside didn't belong to Kaitlin. By the door, he took a deep breath and opened the bag. Other than a beer towel, the bag was empty. Just then, to his right, he heard a noise. Not like the earlier one from outside. This was from down the hall.

In the room.

He wanted to run.

Collins' car must be nearby. He won't be needing that again. Find your bag, your phone, your clothes, the driver's keys and get going.

But that noise.

A moan.

Definitely human.

It could be Kaitlin. It must be her. She might be trapped or injured and in need of my help. And at this point, I may be the only one who can save her. Then she would love me forever and ever.

Quietly, Thomas called out her name.

There was no response. Only silence, then the moan again. Faint but distinct.

Just run, Thomas. Go. You don't owe anyone anything.

He knew he couldn't.

Fingerprints.

Burn the place to the ground.

Step by step, Thomas moved closer to the room, the room he'd slept in. The room where Collins emasculated him. And now he was wearing his clothes.

Thomas called her name again, this time a little louder. With caution in mind, he entered the room. The scent of Collins, his cologne, and tobacco was all that remained of him. Thomas felt an inexplicable yet overwhelming urge to lie down. Like a tired animal resting on a spot warmed by the sun. In the light of day, he could see how much damage was done the night before. Bottles on the floor.

Under the bed.

The noise is coming from under the bed.

As he crouched down to take a look, Thomas gripped the now damaged candle holder as he whispered Kaitlin's name.

Under the bed.

With its back to Thomas, lay a dog. Taking shallow but rapid breaths, the animal convulsed as its circuits were being cut, one by one. From behind the animal, a small hand appeared and rested on its neck. Though dark, Thomas could see the crown of a child's head, jerking. The moaning stopped.

"He said you would come."

As Thomas recoiled in terror, the child started to crawl towards him, over the animal's lifeless remains. With its teeth bared and stained by blood, it said, "Who are we to turn down such a bountiful gift?"

Thomas shook so hard that he dropped the candle holder.

The sound…outside.

A motor.

The car? Kaitlin?

Thomas ran down the hall and out of the house.

From the pathway, where he'd parked the car the night before, a cloud of dust blew out onto the road.

He knew that he had to leave this place immediately.

Chapter 17 - Twinty

Seven miles. The early pace with which Thomas had left the cottage now gave way to a pained lollop. The tight rubber boots Collins had forced him to wear not only cut into his calves but were restricting the blood flow to his toes. Thomas sat on a style and removed them. He knew he might need them the closer he got to civilization. Or Balloch, whichever arrived first. Seven miles. It might be less, he didn't know.

Have I killed a man? Maybe I'm just like MacMillan, he thought. No. I was defending myself and Kaitlin. I am no monster. Kaitlin will know that and that's all that matters. Kaitlin wasn't at the cottage. Maybe she left earlier. Or maybe that was her who drove away in the car? No, she was the automatic girl, remember?

The sense of queasiness returned to the pit of Thomas' empty stomach.

What if it was Collins who drove away? Need to get back to the city, to my flat. To *their* flat. With no phone, no wallet and no keys. Damn. Collins stole my phone, my wallet and my keys. That's it. But why? Jealousy? I'll figure something out and explain it to Mira. She might not fully understand, hell I don't, but she will understand, right? And her loyalties lie with me. Obviously. And the company, of course. The company. And Milene. They would make things right. As Rothwell Glen said after the crash, men like us don't go to jail. Seven miles. Must be close to five, maybe four now.

As the April sun beamed down on the bright, rain starved green fields, a steady stream of vehicles slowed to pass what appeared to be a carefree traveller, walking barefoot on the road's verdant apron. Like the meadows behind the wire, Thomas was parched like never before. He'd pray for a downpour and the solace of some fresh water but the realisation that he may need those prayers for something more appropriate, drove him on along the Old Military Road. Thomas knew that there was a bird sanctuary nearby. Somewhere to slake that thirst and check on feet which were now as torn as his body.

"You alright there, pal?" called out a voice.

"Aye, I'm fine."

"Some day for a walk. Especially with no shoes on."

"It is that," smiled Thomas ruefully.

"You a wee bit lost?"

"Something like that."

"I'm going to the shops in Balloch if you want a lift?"

At this stage, Thomas would've accepted a lift from Collins himself. He pulled on his boots and climbed into the passenger seat of the white van.

"Rough night last night, big man?"

Thomas nodded. On the dashboard was a half full glass

bottle of soft drink lying on its side.

"Sorry to be a nuisance, but would you mind…"

"It's been there since Friday," winced the driver, noticing the dry cracks around Thomas' mouth. He passed the bottle to his passenger who gratefully gulped down the warm, sugary brew as if it was the water of life itself.

"Peter," said the driver.

Thomas took the offer of the driver's hand, "Simon."

Occupying the southernmost shores of Loch Lomond, the picturesque town of Balloch is one of the country's go-to locations for thousands of the west coast's day revellers. On this cloudless Sunday, with temperatures rising to summer level heights, the town had found itself overrun by a multitude of people willing to overlook being gnawed at by the midges in order to spend a relaxing time by its calm waters. Even a heat bowed stretch of railway track didn't stop the invading, sun worshipping hordes from descending on the town like sportswear clad barbarians.

The journey from Wemyss Bay the previous day was the first time that Thomas had been on a train in years, so approaching the station, he'd anticipated something similar.

"No trains, Sir," said the smiling young man in a blue visibility vest.

"How can I get back to Glasgow?"

"Show your ticket to the driver…you do have a ticket?"

"Of course," he lied.

"Then you're good to go. Replacement bus, in the car park. All stops to Glasgow. Leaves at quarter past."

Thomas followed his instructions and joined the back of

the small queue of people boarding the double decker bus.

Ahead, the passengers held up their tickets to the muscular driver for inspection. Wearing sunglasses and a short-sleeved shirt that was so tight, if he turned around to actually check the tickets, his buttons would have sprayed like bullets all over his cabin, the driver looked as if he'd rather be stripped down to his shorts in the loch than on the road back to the airless city. Holding up a ticketless hand, the disinterested driver waved Thomas on. Taking a seat two rows from the back of the bus, Thomas awaited departure. Tucked down the side of the seat was a folded Sunday tabloid and a discarded bottle of water. Still thirsty, he picked up the bottle and wrapped it in the journal. For the road, he reasoned. As he did, his eyes were drawn to the newspapers' garish headline. He unwrapped it.

The Clyde is High!

Under a picture of a grinning couple, the article said that thirty eight arrests were made at the Riverside Garden Festival, mainly for drug related offences. That'll keep the juniors busy, Thomas thought. At the top right corner of the page, sat a pair of grim straplines. No Breakthrough in Kelvingrove Death Probe and Tragedy at Beast Prison. Pages 12 and 13. Thomas flicked through the newspaper, to be met by a large image of Angus John MacMillan's mugshot behind what can only be described as an artist's impression of cell bars. What both articles lacked in substance and fact, was more than made up for with salacious innuendo and supposition.

Instinctively, Thomas reached for his phone, momentarily forgetting that he'd left it at Kaitlin's cottage.

Damn.

He looked at his bare wrist. I don't even know the time, he thought. Just then, the rail worker came aboard the bus with a clipboard and cheerily asked the driver how many passengers were on board.

"Twinty," growled the driver, printing off a ticket.

The rail worker leant to his side and looked along the aisle of the lower deck. Unless there were fourteen people upstairs, the driver's estimate was more generous than accurate. The rail worker sighed and tore off the ticket, clipping it to his board. As he did, a small, ruddy faced older woman wearing a blue vest emerged from the top deck. In her hands was a refuse sack and a litter picker. Neither the driver nor the rail worker acknowledged her. She started to pick at hollowed out crisp tubes and sweet wrappers strewn across the floor around the first few rows of the bottom deck, stopping only when she arrived at the seat Thomas had taken. As their eyes met, a look of dread terror filled her face and the colour vanished from her cheeks. Dropping her bag and picker, the woman slowly raised her arms, pointing at Thomas with the index fingers on each hand overlapping. As she breathed, she moaned.

Behind him, a young couple seated in the back row giggled at something they were watching on a mobile device, blissfully unaware. Thomas stood and hurriedly shuffled past the cleaner. As another passenger reached down to help her with her litter picker, she turned and mouthed something indecipherable Thomas' way. He took the steps two at a time and slumped longways in a seat at the front of the empty top deck. As a child, this was where he always wanted to sit when his mother took him on trips to the city. Like the captain of a ship, heading for places as yet unknown, but now all Thomas wanted to see was who or what was coming onto the bus.

A burst of compressed air from the closing door kept Thomas' nerves on edge and as the bus turned slowly out of the car park, he could see the smiling rail worker speak with the now distressed cleaner. As he comforted her, she unscrewed the handle from her litter picker and with force, thrust it into his throat. As she had moments earlier, the cleaner turned and raised her hands, her fingers overlapping as again they pointed in the direction of Thomas.

Perturbed, he immediately turned away and, covering his eyes from the sun, tightly squeezed the skin around his temples.

I need my medication.

Chapter 18 - Drouth

"Thanks driver," said each of the four people who disembarked the bus at Partick train station ahead of Thomas.

Stepping into the afternoon sunshine, he drained the last drops from the bottle he'd been nursing since leaving Balloch. Judging by the amount of teenagers bouncing around the station, the previous day's arrests had little impact on the draw of what appeared on paper at least, to be a rather conservative annual gathering. If anything, Thomas thought, the reporting had probably encouraged them to head there in search of a wilder time.

All he wanted to do at this point however, was to get back to the flat, medicate and tend to his body. Only then could he start the process of piecing together the catalogue of chaos that had engulfed his life since he left Kirkmalcolm on Friday.

Realising that by wearing an old, soiled t-shirt and ill-fitting footwear meant he blended in more easily around these parts than he would've in his own attire, Thomas allowed himself a chuckle. On the less busy, shaded side of the thoroughfare, Thomas headed past the library and Gardner Street - far too steep to attempt wearing gum boots - before turning left at the Quarter Gill pub.

"Mr Jamieson!"

Again, a familiar voice shouted out the name of one of Thomas' pseudonyms.

Crossing from the deli on the sunny side was Stacey from the Good Health Pharmacy. Heavily made up and wearing a short cream dress with a lace trim, she looked unrecognisable from when Thomas had encountered her a few days previously. A yard or so behind, but still holding the tips of her fingers was a robust man with short red hair and badly sunburned cheeks. He was wearing a tight fitting three piece suit and a shirt which struggled to contain the entirety of his neck.

"How are you doing?" she said, her excitement tailing off by the state of Thomas' appearance. "You been out gardening today?"

"Something like that."

There was an awkward pause.

"This is my Davie. You remember me telling you about him?"

"Yeah, hi," said Thomas, half heartedly offering his grubby hand. Davie's handshake was flat and weaker than Thomas expected.

"Where are you off to, all dolled up?"

"First Holy Communion up at the chapel. My sister's youngest. The mass finished hours ago but the after party's been going on since lunchtime. It's a nice do but the food's brutal. That's why we nipped down to the deli. Absolutely starving. Still, there is a free bar so we'll be there all afternoon."

"Sounds great," replied Thomas, without any irony.

"He'll no' be drinking though. He was mad wi' it yesterday, weren't you?"

The big man nodded, apologetically.

"And besides, he's got the van."

By the pub on the corner, Davie was asked for a light by a fellow smoker.

As her partner checked his pockets for a lighter, Stacey whispered to Thomas.

"What's going on? If you don't mind me saying, you look like ten tons of shite in a five ton bag."

"It's been a really rough weekend."

"Looks like it, but we all get them."

As her partner caught up, Stacey's voice rose. "Well, if you're not doing anything later, you should pop down and join us for a drink. Obviously once you've showered and all that."

"Of course. Might just take you up on that. Was nice to meet you, Davie."

Davie nodded.

"Doesn't talk much," said Stacey, "but you should see him on the dance floor. Some mover for a big lad, aren't you darling?" At this, her partner's face turned an even deeper red.

"Maybe see you later…"

Even before he turned onto Partickhill Road, Thomas could hear the high pitched, excitable bark of the Bichon Frisé. Given the position of the unrelenting sun, he suspected that the nurse from the ground floor flat would be present in the minute basement garden with her even more miniscule dog wearing an almost microscopic bikini topping up her year long sun tan. Hidden from onlookers by a well maintained, shoulder high hedge, Thomas had caught a few glimpses of her from his window on the second floor. Reclining, with the faint sound of a grinding beat emanating from her earphones, she was more impervious to the demands of her excitable pet than her neighbours were. Still, while she lounged, Thomas found that she had a tendency to wedge the close door with a brick from the garden, much to the chagrin of their mutual neighbour Derek who had, despite making a point of washing his windows or fostering the lost art of hedge manicure each time she bared her body, recently chided her, albeit mildly, for her lack of inter-close vigilance.

As pearls of sweat and blood swirled between his crushed toes, Thomas approached the flat from the cover of the fence next door. Latching on to his scent, the toy dog moved beyond excited and into the realms of hysteria.

"Fucking shut up, you little cunt," muttered Thomas shuffling towards the pathway.

"Marion sweetheart," came the voice he dreaded. "What have we talked about vis a vis the door situation?"

Motherfucker, thought Thomas turning sharpish. Heading away from the house, he noticed that the close next door was wide open. He figured that if he could get through and over the adjoining fence, he'd be able to walk straight through the back door of *his* close, which was almost never locked, and straight up to the second floor and the hallowed haven that was flat two stroke one.

Thomas cut into the close, the sound of his rubbery feet slapping and echoing in the lobby. As he passed through, he noticed that the tiles in this passageway were dark green, chipped and very grubby, in marked contrast to the pristine oxblood red of his own. Am I becoming Derek, he asked himself.

Shuddering at the thought, Thomas opened the back door. The fence between the flats was only about four foot high, an easy bound when fit, considerably less so in dead man's boots. Nevertheless, he made the attempt. Thomas' sharp ascent ended when the light balsa wood panel creaked under his burden, giving way enough for him to lose his grip. He dropped heavily into one of Derek's crudely fashioned homemade planters, rendering it broken beyond repair. He pulled himself up, scored again by agents of fate, parched and exhausted. Despite the tank of his resolve running as dry as his palate, Thomas knew that the end was within touching distance. On the other side of the door.

Which was locked.

He pulled again.

Locked.

Thomas rested his head against the door. The pain in his stomach was different from that which shot through his body and nowhere near as acute as the tightening around his ears and at the front of his skull. Knowing how close he was to sanctuary had allowed him to suppress the hankering and fight his failing senses but now, with no immediate relief available, Thomas knew that he'd have to face the music and get beyond Derek. Reluctant to concede defeat to that prick, Thomas tried the door one more time and with it, his shoulders sagged. Moving beyond a deep craving for medication, his body was now operating in survival mode. Thomas needed to eat and more importantly, he needed water. Ahead, an urban fox sat on a stack of discarded boxes, like a rusty monarch watching a delphic drama unfold. It approached him and made a call that was more avian than canine.

Wow wow.

In the distance, a bell tolled. Then again.

That's it.

Dipping into reserves he didn't know existed, Thomas followed the tiptoeing fox to the end of the communal back court before continuing down the long, shaded lane to the main road. If his destination had been uphill, he'd never have made it. But from the top of Hyndland Street, it was all Dowanhill.

Thomas made it to the gates of St. Peter's before collapsing.

Chapter 19 - Absolve

"Mammy, is that man Jesus?"

It was the sound of the laughter which followed the child's question that began to bring Thomas around.

"Can someone get him a drink of water?"

"We've got beer, wine, soft drinks…"

"No. A bottle of water, please."

"We've only got Holy Water in here, Stacey."

"Well get me some fucking Holy Water then," she barked. "Can't you see that Mr Jamieson needs all the help he can get? Jesus fuck…"

As the echo from her statement died of shame around the altar, Stacey looked up and whispered her contrition. "Sorry Father."

"I'll go get Bernie," replied the priest. "She's a paramedic."

"Can you hear me Mr Jamieson?" asked Stacey cradling his sweat soaked head on her lap. Bringing a small plastic bottle in the shape of the Virgin Mary to his dry lips, she gently squeezed.

"Davie, take his boots off."

After an incredulous pause, her partner did as he was told, blanching at the sight and smell that emerged from inside the tacky boots.

"Mammy, I'm telling you," insisted the child, "that is Jesus. Look at his hair. And his beard and feet. It's definitely him."

Stacey took a handful of green paper towels and with the water the priest brought, she dampened them. The cool water on his forehead was a tonic in more ways than one.

As Bernie the paramedic arrived to take control, Stacey moved to Thomas' legs and feet.

"How well do you know this guy?"

****

Once Thomas came around, Davie brought him a plate of buffet food. Despite Bernie insisting that he should refrain from alcohol, the chilled bottle of Belgian beer that Stacey's man snuck in didn't technically count. As far as Davie was concerned, beer was hops and hops were grown so it stood to reason that it must be good for you. Stacey instructed Davie to fetch some of the spare sportswear he'd invariably have dotted around the back of his van. The big man's girth may have been sizable but it didn't prevent him partaking in five-a-sides and golf when his work was done. Thomas gratefully accepted the offer of a still tagged pair of jogging trousers, an old pair of astroturf trainers, sized slightly bigger than Thomas's feet but after the gumboots, blissfully comfortable, and an argyle patterned golfing jersey, in yellow.

After badgering the priest to allow him to freshen up, Stacey waited for Thomas to return from the cleric's private quarters.

"Like a different man," she said cheerfully as he emerged. "Davie brought you a fresh one."

"He's a good lad," replied Thomas, gratefully sipping from the cold bottle.

"Got a heid like a breeze block but a good lad he is. I'm lucky to have him."

"I'll get this stuff back to you once I get home."

Stacey shook her head. "So, are you going to tell me what's going on?"

Thomas took another long swig and ran his fingers through his hair.

"I'm not who you think I am."

"Is anyone? I mean, you look at me and you see a big mouthy lassie who swears like fuck. God forgive me. But Davie knows who I am and that's good enough for me, Mr Jamieson. Or can I call you Stuart? You know I was worried about you."

"Seriously?"

"Something about you always struck me as troubled."

"Thanks," replied Thomas sarcastically.

Stacey put her hand on his arm. "You seem very alone."

In that moment, as kindness lifted the burden, his eyes filled.

"My name is Thomas."

****

Stacey returned to Davie and the party but not before letting Thomas use her phone to call a locksmith. Determined not to take up any more of her valuable time, Thomas accepted the kind donation of another cold bottle of beer and a paper plate filled with lukewarm sausage rolls and hard garlic bread. By the church, a number of local teenagers hung around the basketball court. Given the number of balls in play, it appeared that there were two games taking place simultaneously. Like two random thoughts independent of each other, occupying the same mental space. Thomas was exhausted, but knowing that he was only an hour away from regaining access to his flat, he took a seat on the metal bench and relaxed while trying to figure out which side was playing which.

Within minutes, his state of calm was disturbed by the yelping of a toy dog and another sound, equally familiar but even less welcome.

"I know what you did."

Thomas, shielding his eyes from the evening sun, looked in the direction of the voice.

"Just fuck off, Derek," he responded wearily. "I'm not in the mood."

"I don't think you realise," said his neighbour, "that if I was so inclined, I could make things very difficult for you."

"Really?" replied Thomas, stirring. "Do your worst."

"A lawyer, claiming a prescription under someone else's name?"

"I was getting it for a friend."

"You'd have to understand that as a reporter…"

"A reporter," laughed Thomas, coldly. "You're a fucking columnist."

"...working for the Glasgow Citizen, it would be remiss of me not to investigate something that could have an impact on the biggest story of the year. And the scandal that would fall at the feet of your employer for hiring such a criminal, would put an end to your career, would it not?"

As much as Thomas wanted to crack his half empty bottle over Derek's head, he remembered that while he had just accepted a form of absolution, he was now too weary to embark on a successful post-assault getaway.

"Obviously you haven't done it yet so what do you want from me?"

"I'm writing a book."

Thomas groaned. Everyone's writing a fucking book.

"And?"

"I would warmly appreciate your input."

"With what?"

As Derek grinned, the penny dropped.

Chapter 20 - Barricade

Stepping from the shower, it occurred to Thomas that an unexpected benefit of losing one's phone was the advantage of not having a number to share, particularly with those who'd use said phone as an interminable irritant. Still, even for someone as antisocial as he, Thomas realised that if he was to keep Mira happy - and with it, the roof over his head - he was in need of an alternative means of communication.

In the drawer at the bottom of the kitchen cabinet, below the cutlery tray and the one for the takeaway menus, was the place he'd dumped all of his and Milene's outdated devices. Buried beneath a couple of metres of white electrical spaghetti, Thomas found what he was looking for. He plugged the charger into the mains and connected the phone. As it illuminated, the picture on the screen was one from an earlier, less complex period of his life. A swift but necessary check with the present would allow him to wallow in the past, one more time.

****

"How odd," said Mira. "Collins was robbed too."

Thomas' knuckles tightened.

"Shit. Is he alright?"

"You know Collins. Tough as old boots," replied Mira, placing what he thought was undue emphasis on the end of the sentence. "Between the robberies and bodies, it's starting to feel like the eighties again."

Thomas squeezed his temple. Bodies.

"I really need Campbell Ames to start doing what we pay him to do and sort out the crime in this place. It's bad for business. And speaking of business, I hope you don't mind but I took the liberty of sending someone over to give the place a bit of a tidy."

"Sorry Mira, my mind has…"

"Been on weightier things, I know," said Mira. "Been quite a weekend, hasn't it?

What does she know?

"I'm sure you caught the headlines…"

"The Riverside Garden Festival?"

There was silence on the other end of the phone.

"No, another incident at Kirkmalcolm. Don't know the ins and outs, to be honest. Mr Armour will fill you in tomorrow."

"About that, who'll be picking me up?"

"You'll have Piotr tomorrow. Collins is off to collect the old man."

Thomas' relief was almost audible. "So he's finally decided to return?"

"Well, with events at Kirkmalcom, he realised that he can no longer 'phone it in'. Besides, the weather on the Côte has turned…"

****

Mira would have to wait to hear about the new - and costly - lock he'd just had replaced. Still, to be on the safe side, Thomas drew the curtains in the living room then bolted the two outer doors before sliding the dresser up behind both. Just to be safe.

Thomas dropped his towel and looked at his naked body in the bedroom mirror. More aggrieved at the state of his physique than with the numerous cuts and welts he'd accumulated over the weekend, he tensed his stomach and for a brief moment, there was definition. He took a step to the side and fell back onto the bed. The cool of the freshly laundered top sheet against his bare back was the receptor, the shot of calm for which his body ached. Soothing the angst that had been gnawing away at him all day, Thomas closed his eyes and reached under the pillow for Milene's t-shirt. Its absence irked him, though not enough to prevent his thoughts from drifting back to St Peter's and the bare thigh of his unexpected nursemaid.

> *Shall we? We shall.*
> *The speed of the bus.*
> *Shall we? We shall.*
> *Its rhythm.*

Shall we? We shall.
Running alongside, the boy's fist punched
Through the window.

The heavy crack of a firework from a nearby garden shook the window frame, waking Thomas suddenly. Its blast, as close as if detonated within his walls, resonated intensely in his chest. Realising that he hadn't yet broken the night, he sighed bitterly. His body ached and his stomach ached but worse, despite the sleep, his mind remained fatigued.

Thomas stood up and looked around the room for a clean pair of shorts. He ran his hand across the surface of the dresser which had stood empty since he'd moved in. Dust free. Thanks Mira. He opened the top drawer and found his socks and shorts, neatly arranged.

A bit much but…

He opened each in turn, finding t-shirts and jumpers, all clean and folded. After a status check of the door, Thomas returned to the living room. Opening the curtains, he marvelled at the deep purple of the night sky. Like the dresser in the bedroom, the window sill was dust free and clear. As was the table.

My papers…

His eyes darted around the room. He hadn't noticed earlier but his fortress of boxes was gone. The pile of papers on the table, the entirety of his work on MacMillan. Gone. Thomas ran into the kitchen and checked the bin. It was empty. Panic returned and had started to spread. Back into the living room. Under the table was one solitary box. He flipped the lid and placed his hand across his chest in gratitude.

Thank fuck.

Thomas returned to the kitchen to collect a roll of tape and the last of the cheese from the pack he'd opened a week ago. There was nothing in the fridge aside from a few drops of milk and three unloved containers of gourmet broth.

Note to Mira, any chance of the maid doing some shopping for me too? Tell her that I'm good for soup.

Thomas removed the files from the box and put them back on top of the table, separating them into order of date and significance. Using his teeth, he snapped off small strips of tape and fixed some key info to the walls. He knew that the interior of the flat was next to be refurbed so marking the wall wasn't going to impact Mira's chances of making money from the place.

But the old man's on his way back and wants the case sorted promptly, so enough dancing around with this maniac. Stick to the brief. In and out. I'll throw Derek a bone or two, just to keep him off my back. I really need to speak with Innes Guthrie again.

If Kaitlin shows up, we'll nail it this week, Thomas thought as he stretched to attach a picture of MacMillan to his wall. But if she doesn't...

He took a handful of pills, and with a swig from the remainder of his Black Mezcal, he said, "Man up, Thomas."

Chapter 21 - Intuitive Beasts

Put it on.

No.

Put it on.

Canary yellow. With diamonds. Just as I remembered it. Remarkable. It's almost identical. We're almost identical.

No.

Can't you see it? Look closely.

No.

Ask me how I came to own it.

A couple of heavy raps on the storm door was what released Thomas from the grip of his latest semi lucid dream. He quickly realised that if it was a driver with a bone to pick, no prior warning would've been issued. As soon as the mechanism detached from the holding, Derek invited himself in, carrying a peace offering; a small plate with some freshly baked bread.

While his guest's gaze was immediately drawn to the tapestry unfolding on the living room wall, Thomas' remained on the still warm slices in his neighbour's hand. Quickly devouring the contents, the still famished Thomas dispatched Derek back downstairs for a second plate. He returned, with the bread and a notebook. No pictures, Thomas told him. That's a deal breaker. Understood, Derek replied, like a child in a toy store with an empty gift voucher.

Even as Thomas ironed his shirt, the questions from the hallway were unrelenting.

"So, where was he?"

"I don't know."

"Why did he hand himself in?"

"Not got to that yet."

"Did he really kill those people?"

Thomas pretended that he didn't hear that one but it did strike him that in all his time with MacMillan, the key information he was sent to find out, he'd failed to retrieve. Bricked in by those questions, the one Derek didn't broach remained the cornerstone:

Why did he ask for me?

****

"We're here, Mr Leven."

Thomas rubbed his eyes. His customary pre-prison drive had been serving as a much needed resting post, especially on mornings like this and even though only three full days had passed since he was last at Kirkmalcolm, the events of the weekend had made it feel like an age.

Thomas left Piotr by the car and made his way through the familiar checkpoints. As he signed the register, the desk officer advised him that Mr Armour would like to speak with him before he saw the prisoner. Given everything that had seemingly gone on, it wasn't unexpected.

Shaking hands, Thomas noticed that Armour was even more skittish than normal. As he poured tea from the pot, he placed his left hand over his right to stop it from trembling.

"He should be clear for you to see very shortly. We've had to increase the levels of his sedation since the latest incident."

"And why is that?"

"Do you know animals, Mr Leven?"

"Personally? I don't follow."

"Intuitive beasts. Before you know something is wrong, they do. It's quite remarkable. Their senses seem heightened around danger, even more so than ours."

"Mr Armour?"

"My daughter is fifteen years old. Loved horses all her life. Or one in particular."

Armour opened the case on his phone and turned its screen to Thomas. "Here she is. With Jessie. She's been riding Jessie for three years. They're inseparable. We stable Jessie at Kyleakin Farm, just on the outskirts of Strathblane. Do you know it?"

"Can't say I do."

"Anyway, yesterday before she headed off to school, she decided to take advantage of the weather and take Jessie for an early morning ride. My wife dropped her off but within minutes, she was called back by Jim Kyleakin himself to say that the horse had attacked her."

"That's awful, Mr Armour."

"Bit her through to the bone. And not just the once. It could've been much worse had Kyleakin not been on hand. Naturally the horse was put down. So out of character."

"How is your daughter now?"

"She's stable but very shaken. We haven't told her yet that we had to put Jessie down. She's not ready to hear that."

"I can imagine. Without being callous Mr Armour, what has any of this to do with MacMillan?"

"As with breakfast, there is a rotation for prisoners to exercise or pray after they have their evening meal. Mr MacMillan is allocated a supervised fifteen minute spell in the yard beside the hall."

Thomas listened closely.

"On Friday evening, Officers Rodgers and Raymond took the prisoner and released him to the exercise yard. After a minute or two, he lay down on the grass verge. That in itself is not unusual but with MacMillan, all of his behaviour appears beyond the norm. Five minutes became ten then at the end of his allocated time, as the guards went to take him back to his cell, MacMillan was completely unresponsive. Officer Raymond checked to see if the prisoner was breathing. At that stage, he wasn't and the alarm was raised."

"Ok," replied a confused Thomas.

"Earlier that day you will recall the blockage of the road. The birds…"

"Starlings…"

"Quite. Well a considerable number of birds, presumably the same ones which caused the obstruction in the first place, decided to return and en masse, surrounded MacMillan."

"What was his reaction?"

"As if a butterfly floated in his periphery. That's how little he was distracted. As the guards approached, he was seen carving something into the fence post. Some numbers."

"With what?"

Armour took a clear but sealed bag from his drawer and laid it on the table. Inside was a thin blade. Its tip was covered with a familiar double knurled handle.

"Jesus," said Thomas, pressing against his sliced finger.

"Indeed. Naturally, the guard radioed it in and within seconds, all available staff had him surrounded. After what happened last week, we were taking no chances. MacMillan was instructed to put down the weapon but he didn't respond. That's when the first taser was deployed."

"First taser? How many times did you taser him?"

"Three, maybe four. It got a bit messy."

"How so?"

"He muttered something then thrust the implement into the post. When he went down, the guards surrounded him. That's when it happened."

"What?"

"The birds…"

"I don't follow."

"I've no idea how he was able to but he held off three of our biggest men. Rodgers got a few digs in before he…"

"Mr Armour?"

"I've seen prisoners lose their cool, Mr Leven. It happens. Not as often as you'd think but it does happen. When the reality of indefinite incarceration hits home, for some men it can be very destructive on the psyche. Naturally, some prisoners become very frustrated at being cooped up and given the nature of the establishment, almost all of the patients here have a history of violence. It's what we're trained to deal with, to be fair but this?"

He shook his head.

"What did he do?"

"It's too ridiculous for words."

"Please."

"He blinded Officer Wilson."

"Fuck," said Thomas.

"Two fingers, up to the mid knuckle. Then he took the blade from the post and sliced the end of Officer Rodgers' nose. The birds did the rest."

"The birds?"

"I believe that Angus John MacMillan commanded the birds to attack my guard."

Thomas covered his mouth and swallowed hard. His stomach turned as he slumped in the chair.

"It was already a stressful week, Mr Leven, what with my daughter but this…" Armour shook his head. "I don't want him here. The guards are terrified of him. He needs to go."

"He needs to go where?"

"Anywhere."

"Now come on, Mr Armour."

"Restrained, subdued. It doesn't matter."

Tears formed in the eyes of the prison's governor.

"There's something unnatural about him."

"Isn't that why he's meant to be locked up?"

"He can't stay here."

"Mr Armour, forgive me but to suggest that the country's most secure facility is unable to cope with one small, middle aged man is ludicrous, regardless of his supposed past. This is Kirkmalcolm. It was designed precisely to hold people like MacMillan."

"People like MacMillan? Jesus Christ. Don't you get it, man?" Armour raged, close to tears. Teeth grinding, he tapped his temple.

"He's in here."

****

Thomas took a seat opposite Angus John MacMillan and stared. At his face, at his eyes, at his demeanour. Everything. Should he feel endangered being in the presence of such a monster? If he hadn't read the arrest sheets and consulted the few but telling documents Kunis Clement had provided, Thomas would've placed MacMillan into the same category as Derek; self important and irritating. Unlike his neighbour though, Thomas couldn't help but find the prisoner as enigmatic as he was challenging. Aware of the constraints the old man's imminent return was going to bring, Thomas restarted the clock.

"What happened this time, Mr MacMillan?"

"A robin redbreast in a cage, puts all of heaven in a rage," he replied with nonchalance.

Given MacMillan's air of apathy, Thomas decided against asking him to unwrap his latest riddle.

"No Miss Ramsay again today?"

"Eh…no…"

"Been seeing much of her recently?"

Unresponsive, Thomas moved the conversation to more secure ground. "Mr MacMillan, I would like you to start today by telling me where you've been for the last thirty years."

"As opposed to where I'm *going* for the next thirty? No Thomas, I could tell you but what if I need to return there? Though I am aware that dark clouds are gathering overhead, given your obligation to your firm and to the sovereign laws that govern it, you'd be duty-bound to pass that information on. And if my happy place is compromised, I wouldn't be…"

"Happy?"

"Exactly. Anyway, if I told you, you wouldn't believe it."

"Try me."

MacMillan laughed. "I'm afraid not. Too risky. However, I'm rested, I'm well and I'm imbued with a fresh sense of candour, so…"

Despite his earlier miss, Thomas took another swing. "I'd like to know the precise details of the death of Eilidh Broome."

"I think it's time," said MacMillan quietly, lowering his guard. This was not the glib response that Thomas had expected.

"Drugs are incredible things, don't you think? Used correctly, medication can help you walk when your muscles are failing or send to sleep a mind that is careering out of control. As you know yourself, Thomas, the right combination of pharmaceuticals can ease one's physical agonies as little else can. As a stimulant or a relaxant, the number of people on this planet who have had their lives made more tolerable by drugs is legion. However, we both know, nature must have its balance. Eilidh's brother was one of those people whose harmony on stage was never replicated when off. Archie Broome's capacity for invention and all of its wonders was only matched by his own excessive impulses. One must quell the beast or submit to it; an addict will always be an addict. In relation to the Broomes, I was to discover that certain inclinations were indeed familial. I'd been spending more time with Eilidh but for her, the draw of Sand and the Red Room was a constant. Being a genuine true born inhabitant of the island that bore the darkness meant that no door was left unopened to me, nor was any offer ever withdrawn. As obsessed as I'd become, Eilidh was in thrall to Sand in the way that Sand was drawn to me. It was in the late winter of the following year when things started to change."

"In what way?"

"In order to spend more time with Eilidh, I'd been manipulating the edges of our triangle. When Archie disappeared, that's when I started to see our friendship for what it really was."

"And that was?"

"A loose collective of misguided zealots, venal egotists and outright hypocrites displaying cruel, sociopathic traits while pretending to aspire towards some kind of psychotic divinity."

"You've given that some thought."

"It's been on my mind for the last thirty years," smiled MacMillan. "And given Sand's position at the apex of the beast, the displays of displeasure were certainly far from divine. I had a suspicion that if they could, they'd remove me. But that would've been…"

"Too dangerous?"

"My feeling at the time was that Sand considered me more a trophy than anything. Had they been able to place me on display in a glass case, like a prize won or a mascot, the party would have continued. As with the possibility of a crop failure in harvest, so it was in our circle. One of Sand's associates worked in a branch of law enforcement and he'd heard rumblings about an investigation into a young woman being treated in the Western Infirmary with skin trauma consistent with the type regularly seen in the Red Room. A storm was coming."

Thomas drew a circle around a date on his notes. "March 11th 1987?"

"That is correct. In the early hours of that morning, I woke to find myself on the steps of the abandoned church in Dowanhill, alone. I buttoned up my coat and made my way back to my flat, but somewhere along the way, I'd mislaid my key so I had to wake Mrs Telfer to let me in. Though less than amused at being disturbed, the reception I received when I reached the landing was not the ferocious one I'd expected and deserved. Remember that there are better things ahead than anything we leave behind, she told me, peeling off my sodden coat. She helped me to my room and fetched me a warm drink. As I lay on my bed with her dog at my feet, she lit me a fire and talked about the summer. Andrew would be back by then, she said. My boys will keep me company. Neither of us realised at the time that her beloved building was days away from being a smouldering wreck."

"The fire…"

"Another crime conveniently pinned on me."

As intriguing as MacMillan's revelations were, Thomas knew he needed to keep him focused on the matter of Eilidh Broome's death.

"I didn't have the heart to tell her that all I wanted was to take Eilidh and leave the city for good. All I could think of was her. In the morning, with the last of the embers still warm in the hearth, I filled a bag and left before she returned from the shops."

"Where did you go?"

"I'd arranged for Eilidh to meet me at the university library. I told her that I had some information about the whereabouts of her brother."

"And did you?"

"No. I needed to get her away from Sand. She showed up eventually but I could tell there was something amiss. We looked at the copy of Blake's European Prophecy that had just returned from The Karlova in Prague. It belonged to a friend of the writer, a man who'd murdered his sister-in-law, which according to Sand made the piece all the more desirable. As we read the poet's words, Eilidh told me that she had something she wished to share with me but not there. We left the library and walked over to The Cloisters in silence. As the rain fell, I made an attempt to cover her bare shoulders with my coat but she threw it off. Despite the inclement weather, she insisted that we climb the bell tower. As we started our journey up, my eyes were drawn to the university's motto on a plaque overhead. 'Via, Veritas, Vita', the irony of which wasn't lost on me. Once we reached the viewing platform, she informed me that she was carrying Sand's child."

Thomas exhaled.

"I knew that was an impossibility, but I let her continue. It shall be our miracle, she told me. An enchanted child of light and of shade. The magic contained within its bones will protect it and make it most powerful. Our child will command legions, she said, skipping under the struts and onto the railings. With the burden lifted, her mood changed. I followed and asked her why one would wish to command a legion when one could befriend a bird?

'All a bird can do is fly,' she answered. 'Anyone can fly. I can fly. Sand said so…'"

MacMillan fell silent and swallowed heavily.

"And with that, she was gone."

Confused yet moved by the prisoner's recollection, Thomas proceeded with tact. "You have to understand, Mr MacMillan, that the testimony you've just given me differs somewhat from the official account."

MacMillan directed a short burst of bitter amusement across the table. "You might want to quiz your boss on that one."

"You implied that Sand couldn't be the father of Ms Broome's child. Why is that? Aside from yourself and Sand, did she have other sexual partners at the time?"

"No. Sand insisted that our twisted little troika remain exclusive."

"So why couldn't the child have been Sand's?"

MacMillan leant forward, "Because Sand's penis was made of bone."

He could see that the young lawyer was lost for words.

"You do understand what I'm saying here?"

Thomas didn't. He couldn't. "And the child? It died with her?"

Before MacMillan could answer, the door to the interview room opened. Thomas didn't recognise the guard who handed a note to him.

"From your driver," he said.

It read…

Mira called.

We need to return to Glasgow. Immediately.

Make excuses and leave.

Do NOT speak to anyone, especially the prisoner.

Knowing MacMillan was watching him for any sort of clue as to the note's content, Thomas folded it and placed it in his pocket. "I'm afraid that I need to end today's interview. Urgent business in Glasgow, I'm afraid."

As Thomas collected his things, MacMillan, recognising the charade, chose this moment for a revelatory indicator of his own.

"Truly a little miracle child"

"I beg your pardon?"

"Would be in his early thirties by now," he added. "Around the same age as you..."

Though he avoided MacMillan's gaze, his implication was searingly inescapable.

"...my boy."

Chapter 22 - Family Matters

For the first time since he'd been travelling through to Kirkmalcom, Thomas didn't sleep on the return journey. As shocking as the news of Rothwell Glen's unexpected death was, it hadn't unsettled Thomas as much as MacMillan's divulgement had. The intimate details of his boss' demise were still unknown to him. All he knew was that Mira was dealing with the fall out. At the wheel, the old man's personal driver Piotr took the A-road bends at the same steady pace as he would any other day. Aside from catching Thomas' eye in the rear-view, he remained unnervingly detached.

The management of the asset, as Mira would've referred to it, was something else Thomas had no control over. Like the news that Eilidh Broome was carrying a child when she fell to her death, a critical piece of information Thomas was hitherto unaware of. Though there was nothing in the paltry collection of files he still had to suggest that MacMillan's story was verifiably true, his version of events seemed believable and no less so than much of what had happened over the last fortnight. Same age as me? Given up for adoption?

Don't bite Thomas, he told himself. Whether he's a murderer, that's up for debate but there is no mistaking that Angus John MacMillan was a trickster. A man skilled in manipulation. Mira said as much and she was rarely wrong.

Even though doubt had entered Thomas' mind, MacMillan's final words kept tapping away like a dread presence, a raven at the chamber door. When they reached the city, the tall, spiked gates which kept Mira's home detached from the rest of Kelvin Drive were closed.

"It's ok, Piotr," said Thomas, unbuckling. "I'll get out and ring her."

"Stay seated, Mr Leven," he insisted. "We need to remain in the car."

Piotr motioned to his left. With the driver's side window rolled down, seated in a small hatchback was a photographer.

Thomas knew that in a city like Glasgow, very little escaped the attention of the press. Someone, somewhere knew something and when they did, a tidy sum could be procured, dependent on the magnitude of the leak. The news of Rothwell Glen's sudden death might not register more than a distant ping on the radar of the city's ordinary working folk but to the denizens of Hyndland and Kelvinside, opportunities were there to be had. Piotr checked his phone and keyed in a code. Pointing his device towards the sensor at the post, the gates opened and the car drove through and down to the more secluded rear grounds of the property.

As Piotr opened the door for Thomas, a ball ricocheted against the front tyre.

"Pap!" cried a young boy, running then leaping into Thomas' arms. The child's ball was now a secondary concern as gravity took it down the slope towards the back of the garden.

Taken aback by the warmth of the interaction, Thomas closed his eyes and fought back tears. "You've still got to work on that left foot," he said, reluctantly breaking the child's embrace.

"Will you show me?"

At this moment, nothing would have given Thomas more pleasure than to be permitted to renew a relationship with the boy. But he knew that Mira would be waiting.

"Later."

"Promise?"

Thomas took the child in his arms and embraced him in a way no man had ever embraced him.

"Promise."

As Piotr assumed the role of impromptu footballing surrogate, Thomas entered the house, following the trail of unpacked bags and the sound of the television to the kitchen. At the island in the centre of the room stood Campbell Ames, out of uniform and looking lost. Beside him, Jacqueline from the front desk poured coffee from a steel pot.

"She's waiting for you," she said, stirring slowly. "Upstairs."

On the south side of the building, beneath the Juliet balcony, the River Kelvin foamed and twisted. Mira Berglund took a long draw of her cigarette and exhaled. Gently, Thomas embraced her.

"It's going to break."

"The news about the old man?"

"The weather," she replied. "I can feel it. Any day now

We've been very lucky but it can't sustain."

"Mira, I…"

"You'll stay here for a while, with me," she insisted. "I've sent a surveyor to the flat today to start measuring for…"

"My things?"

"They'll be boxed and sent over."

"What about Kirkmalcolm?"

"Our business there is done. There's nothing more we can do. We need to think of the future."

"I really feel that I'm close to a breakthrough with MacMillan."

"It's not up for debate."

"Mira, please."

"I want my family close. And besides, I have other plans for you."

Thomas returned to the kitchen and with Campbell Ames and Jacqueline now onto the hard stuff, they listened to the early afternoon news bulletin. The announcement of the old man's passing was headline number four. A few lines, crammed in before the weather and behind a last minute concert postponement, an unsettled footballer and an accident near the Cathedral was where Rothwell Glen's death was positioned.

Milene had changed the colour of her hair since he'd last seen her. Natural brunette again over the harsh but stylish tint of the bottle. Thomas reckoned it suited her, though it did remind him of someone else; someone he still hadn't heard from in days. As Mira and Ames spent the afternoon keeping the ship from the rocks and Piotr occupied the boy with some old school football drills and tricks, Milene and Thomas took the opportunity to sneak out of the property by the back channel, traipsing down the sleepers and onto the path by the river. Given how exposed she appeared, Thomas hadn't wanted to push Mira on the details but he knew that Milene would volunteer what she knew, without question.

While the move to London hadn't worked out the way she'd hoped, the brief unhappy spell that she and the boy had in Nottingham convinced her that their futures lay further north. Milene was not particularly fond of the old man nor was she keen on the way he conducted business but his death was a sharp reminder that chances of happiness were fleeting and too rare to be spurned.

Despite Mira's prediction, the weather held. At the cafés and bistros on every street and lane branching out from Byres Road, the dining tables that normally wouldn't be dusted off until June were already full. Al fresco breakfasts had long turned into extended lunch breaks which continued into the evening. Just the right amount of noise, is how Milene described her first afternoon back, walking the streets of her adopted home. Even a mass brawl, started by a bare shouldered, sunburnt drunk attempting to roundhouse kick the mirrors of every car parked by the school couldn't diminish her sense of contentment.

On Kelvin Drive, the press photographer had given up and departed, yielding his prime place to the ever vigilant Piotr, who remained on the clock. Milene and Thomas returned to the house by the same means as they'd left, some hours previously. A week's worth of excitement crammed into one day had finally worn out Milene's son. Unaccustomed to the nuances of the business world, the nine year old didn't fully grasp the impact one odd old man's demise had on his beloved grandmother and why, when normally so patient and accommodating, she'd been so short with him. So while Mira made her excuses, it fell to Jacqueline to put down her glass and slur her way through a book about a supernatural schoolboy that had too many plot holes for her liking.

After staying for what turned out to be an awkward dinner to which no invitation was offered, Campbell Ames and Jacqueline finally left, together. Piotr's final task of the day was to make sure each party got home with the minimum of mess.

"Leave the table until the morning," Milene said.

"My head hurts," said Thomas.

"I know baby, I know."

As they made love on the couch, Thomas couldn't escape two mutually exclusive thoughts; firstly, that nothing felt as good as Milene's form wrapped around his. More than the physical though, was his hope that in time, the squalls that had raged in his mind since she'd left would subdue under her orderly countenance. Thomas knew that he functioned best under her instruction. The second was a nagging feeling that they were being watched.

Resisting the temptation to extend their reunion into the early hours, Milene insisted that, for this one night at least, they return to the rooms that Mira had prepared for them. Thomas agreed. Anything they had to share with Mira could wait until the morning.

Chapter 23 - Oprah Winfrey

The hall was narrow and dark. Its walls were bare and the only light he could see came from the open door at the end of the passage.

A familiar voice called to him.

Thomas continued down the hall and into the room.

Kaitlin?

Under the bed.

"Kaitlin?" asked Mira, sitting on the corner of Thomas' bed.

"Nightmare," he replied, instinctively.

"Don't get up."

Thomas reached for his phone but Mira beat him to the punch.

"It's gone nine," she said, snapping closed her notebook. "You must have needed that."

He had. "Is Milene…"

"She's gone already. A full day of meetings with prospective employers. You know what she's like. Once she makes up her mind about something…"

"How are *you* feeling today?"

"I'm fine," she replied, after a pause. Through sleepy eyes, he could see that she was already dressed for business.

"You want me to come into the office with you today? Help out around the place…"

"I'll be needing your input soon enough but in the meantime, take a few days. Relax."

"Thanks. Was thinking about going back to Kirkmalcolm. You did say that the old man wanted the MacMillan situation tidied up as soon as…"

Mira shook her head. She walked over to the shutters and unlatched them. For the first time in weeks, the sky was more grey than blue. "We spoke of many things on Sunday."

Thomas reached over awkwardly and picked up his t-shirt.

"If you'd like to share, Mira…"

"Oh, I'm sorry. I didn't realise I'd offered Oprah fucking Winfrey a bed for the night."

Instantly regretting his last sentence, Thomas bit his lip. As he did, Mira dialled down the caustic and began to open up. "Look, it's no secret that the old man and I had disagreements about the direction in which to take the firm. The property aspect was his idea but it did work. I'd been badgering him about downscaling the legal side of things but you know what he's like."

Mira caught herself.

"What he was like. I mean, is there any point in another costly refurb of a building that's seen better days when we can streamline the business and shift operations into any number of vacant, serviced blocks within a stones throw of where we are now?"

"And he disagreed?"

"Of course he did. The optics, Thomas. All about perception. The day to day running of the business he didn't give two fucks about, but someone had to."

Mira picked up Thomas' trousers from the floor and folded them over the chair in the corner. "Do you know when I finally realised that he'd already checked out?"

Thomas shook his head.

"During that last conversation."

"Come again?"

"After all we'd been through, the last thing Rothwell Glen asked of me was to find him someone to ghostwrite his fucking memoirs."

"He was writing a book?"

"Him and every other middle aged retiree in Kelvindale. Because all of his pals had started writing books, he thought the world needed to read three hundred pages of second hand golfing anecdotes, gripes about temples and the rising cost of fucking avocados. Needless to say, I talked him down off that ledge pretty quickly. After all we'd been through, too. You think you know someone."

"A wee ego buff. What harm could it have done?" asked Thomas.

Mira shook her head. "What harm could it have done? This was one big dog who'd clearly forgotten all the bones he'd buried in the garden. No, it was never going to happen. And that's how we left it. Within twelve hours, he was flat out on the floor of a jet that he didn't own, surrounded by people he didn't know, working to save a heart that was still set on sharing with the world his musings on cars, taxation and vegetables."

"Jesus."

"Let that be a lesson to us all, Thomas. A song is just a song. Jesus doesn't love all the little fucking children. So, as your employer, I'm directing you to take a few days and go into town. See a movie, play some golf or something. If you need a set of clubs, speak to Collins. The old man has a few sets over at Hurtwood that he's clearly not going to need anymore. Enjoy the here and now, Thomas. I want your mind clear for the journey ahead. I have big plans for the future and you're part of it. So, forget about Kirkmalcolm and forget about MacMillan. We're finished, and if Campbell Ames is to be believed, so is he."

Thomas didn't respond but he understood the implication perfectly. Angus John MacMillan had become an unnecessary inconvenience.

He watched from the balcony as Piotr held the door open for Mira. After a short and uncharacteristic moment of reflection, Thomas could feel Kunis Clement's cold brutal wheels starting to move again. He picked up his phone and searched his recent contacts. I can't believe I'm doing this, he thought.

"Listen, shut up. Do you have a car?"

Chapter 24 - Edelweiss Terrace

Suspecting that his movements were being monitored, Thomas cut through the back of Kelvin Drive and into the Botanics on foot. If anyone was watching, this would be considered a perfectly normal route to the heart of the West End. Derek was advised to wait in the car park above the supermarket. In his excitement, he'd left his flat immediately and was only seven minutes from overstaying his allotted time when Thomas arrived.

"Where to?" asked Derek, clearing his navigation screen.

"We won't need that. I'll show you where to go."

For almost the entirety of the journey, Derek Stobbie didn't stop talking. Ordinarily, this would have irritated Thomas no end but as his driver wittered on, he came to the realisation that it had been more than twenty four hours since he'd last taken any medication, prescribed or otherwise. The twinges and calf cramps he had initially put down to an uncommon day of physicality with Milene but his body was telling him to let go. A different kind of temptation was the smell of the latest batch of Mrs Derek's freshly baked produce. Thomas devoured the entire pack, as well as most of Derek's flask of coffee by the time they reached the gates of Kirkmalcolm.

"Mr Leven," said the sentry guards at the gatepost. "What can we do for you?"

"I just need a few minutes with my client."

Normally personable, the sentry guard didn't respond. He closed the window and turned to pick up the phone. Thomas watched him. A series of grunts before he put the phone down. "I'm afraid I can't grant you access today, Mr Leven."

"Why is that?"

"In light of recent events, Mr Armour and his staff, in conjunction with the Scottish Office and the Police, are undertaking a full review of prisoner access this week. All visitations, scheduled or not, have been suspended."

"Suspended? For how long?"

"Indefinitely."

"So when can I see him?"

"You can't."

"Can I at least talk to him? On a phone or something?"

"That would be out of the question."

"As legal counsel, it is my right to be able to freely correspond with my client, is that not correct?"

"You're the lawyer, Mr Leven."

"Exactly." Thomas turned to Derek and asked for a pen. Derek looked blank.

"You want to be a writer and you don't have a fucking pen? Christ almighty." Thomas looked back at the sentry with a sheepish grin.

Reluctantly, the guard handed over a biro.

Thomas wrote a single line…

> With a'thing that he doth see, hind the thicket or the
> juba stone…

"I insist that this is delivered to the prisoner at once. We'll pull over and await his response."

Derek slowly spun his car and parked on the verge. He took his phone and opened up the voice recorder.

"Date, Tuesday 1st of May. Time, 11.16am. Outlook, fair to cloudy. I'm here at the state's secure facility at Kirkmalcolm with Thomas Leven, the lawyer representing the convicted serial killer, Angus John MacMillan. Thomas, can you bring us up to speed with events?"

Unimpressed, Thomas shook his head and stepped out of the car. He checked his phone. Nothing.

Damn.

In the distance, the peak of Ben Alder was hidden by a veil of grey. Overhead, the solitary cloud which had been hanging over the prison since they arrived found that it had company.

"Thomas," called Derek. "Look."

The guard had returned.

"Well?"

"I did as you requested and passed the message on to the prisoner."

"And?"

"And what?"

"Did he respond?"

"I'm afraid not, Mr Leven. Will there be anything else?"

Thomas returned to the car.

"Where to now, boss?" asked Derek.

"Drop me in town," he replied. "I've got an appointment to keep."

****

"You're lucky to catch me," said Innes Guthrie, ushering Thomas in. "Between the garage and Crowley getting his jags, I've not even had the chance to put the kettle on once today. You're more than welcome to stay for some lunch."

"That would be perfect, thank you."

"Gives us another chance to delve deep into the murky waters of Westerwick. I have to say that I was quite thrilled by the interest you showed in my interpretations at the weekend. I know at the moment that MacMillan is big news again but most observers' interest tends to veer more towards the sensational than the scholarly though it's an approach that's served me well to now. Would you like tea with your lunch or something stronger?" asked Guthrie with a wicked grin.

"I'll stick with the tea for the time being, thanks."

"Probably best," replied Guthrie, slightly disappointed "Crowley isn't keen on day time drinking, if I'm being honest."

"Sounds like your husband is a wise fellow."

"Husband?" Guthrie laughed. "Whatever gave you that idea? Dear boy, Crowley is my cat."

Before Thomas had a chance to react, the professor placed a large cardboard box on the table.

"Right, to business," he said, removing the lid. "Notes, files and research relating to the island of Westerwick. Naturally, there are a few items pertaining to MacMillan, his alleged crimes and his trial. How would you like to proceed?"

Though amazed at the scope of Guthrie's archive, Thomas returned to the professor's words, "You said alleged?"

"It may not be an opinion that would meet with widespread approval, nor is it one upon which I'd stake my life, but I have always had a few questions as to the veracity of the official verdict."

"Can you elaborate?"

Professor Guthrie stretched back.

"How long have you got?"

As long as you need, thought Thomas.

****

"What do you mean when you say, 'sub-Hermetic'?"

"I'm sorry," said the professor, pouring milk into Thomas' tea. "Getting a bit ahead of myself again. Hermetic as pertaining to the thought that the world is governed by a primaeval, divine wisdom."

Thomas sipped his tea, none the wiser.

Guthrie continued. "Certain movements which sprung up in the mid to late 20th century bastardised these views, leaning heavily on the ideology of men such as Julius Evola, an Italian philosopher with a penchant for misogyny and fascism. Within these units, you'll generally find a figurehead at the centre of the movement. Someone who fed into the belief that we are living in what is considered Kali Yuga."

"And that is?"

"A dark age of unchecked materialistic appetites. As a self-styled l'uomo differenziato - a man who has become different - the coven's leader would seek to exert control over the devotees of the sect by anointing another as someone special. Now, this person may, as in MacMillan's case, be a true born of the ground they consider sacrosanct. Using substances like curare or old fashioned tannin root, this particular devotee will slowly begin to accept their exalted status within the group. The problem for the one who has been deemed most high is that once they have reached a plateau, for the good of the sect, they must be sacrificed."

"Literally or metaphorically?"

"Again, in MacMillan's case, both." Professor Guthrie reached into the box of files. "Look, here. You've studied the case. Where's the proof of MacMillan's guilt?"

The professor's large, cluttered kitchen was made more homely by an old but functioning hearth, by which he and Thomas discussed their respective findings. As the professor spread his workings over the dining room table, Thomas opened up a digital file which contained the pictures he'd taken of the man found hanging opposite the Kunis Clement building.

"The poor fellow from last week?"

Thomas zoomed in on the man's chest.

"Do those symbols mean anything to you?"

"The overlapping V's. Of course," replied Guthrie.

314

"Indulgentia, invocatio, vindicta. A not too subtle play on the University motto, but a clear indication you're on the right track."

"And its significance?"

Pursing his lips, Guthrie raised a finger and left for his study. Awaiting the professor's return, Thomas snapped a biscuit in half and put it in his mouth. Painfully sweet, Thomas felt the sugar kick in his head as if he'd swallowed a desiccated, honeyed mule. As welcome as the rush was, he had to admit that he preferred Mrs Derek's baking.

"Here we are," cried the professor, slamming down a thin volume on the table. "I should be more careful with this one. It predates me by a good forty years and is one of the few copies in existence."

"Burgon's Concise History of Executions," read Thomas aloud.

As Innes Guthrie leafed through the decaying pages, Thomas felt both confused yet captivated by the book's graphic illustrations.

"There," said the professor, stopping on page fifty seven. He placed a piece of paper over the two pages and traced around the image. "If we go with accounts less contemporary than what we're used to, this is how the crucifixion of Jesus Christ may have appeared."

Innes Guthrie took Thomas' hands and held them over his sketch.

"The stauros in Greek, or in Latin, the crux simplex was a more common method of execution than the one more familiar to modern Christians, the crux immissa. According to Burgon, the repentant thief, Dismas and the impenitent Gestas would each have been impaled on a crux simplex - a single stake - whereas Jesus Christ himself would've been tied between two stakes and tortured before being raised then executed. Still with me?"

As he nodded, the professor pushed Thomas' fingers together to make the symbol he recognised from the wounds of the impaled man.

"If Burgon is to be believed, *that* is The True Cross."

As Guthrie's premise sank in, Thomas exhaled. "Professor, in the car you mentioned that the pastor kept three people captive."

"That is correct, though according to McCandlish, the female slave was pregnant."

"I take it that none of them survived?"

"Miraculously, the child did. No name, no gender. Nothing is known of the child except that it was birthed and taken by Colville's men to England. The remains of its poor parents were buried in unconsecrated fields beyond the grounds of the parish. The cabin boy survived, albeit briefly. He was buried alongside the other white crew members that subsequently washed up on the shores."

"You said that I might be able to see those journals," said Thomas.

"I said no such thing," replied Guthrie with a chuckle.

Realising that any breach of the professor's resolve may require a lighter touch, Thomas knew he had to keep the conversation light while he plotted his next move. "Maybe I should concentrate more on Glasgow? I'm sure Westerwick hasn't got a monopoly on deviant weirdos."

Guthrie sniggered, almost choking on his biscuit. Unfolding the marker on the page of an old broadsheet, Thomas scanned the highlighted article.

"It says here that Cicely Telfer was arrested and actually charged. It clearly didn't stick. Why do you think that was?"

"Two dead husbands and an uncommon interest in the supernatural meant that when MacMillan went to ground, his landlady was their first port of call. Naturally, when the Police searched Mrs Telfer's flat they found, according to the original charge sheet, 'ritualistic paraphernalia' which turned out to be a ouija board and some old tarot cards. However, during a second, more thorough search beneath the floorboards, in between the joists, they found body parts belonging to a number of missing people, including a bag containing the skull and organs of what turned out to be Archie Broome. Understandably, Cicely Telfer was devastated. Though the evidence against her appeared to be overwhelming, she continued to swear her innocence. Then came the fire."

"Was MacMillan responsible for that?"

"Well, that remains unclear. What we do know is that some time in the early hours of the following morning, a fire broke out. Whether in Cicely Telfer's flat or in the unoccupied flat directly beneath, its origin remains a mystery and despite the attention of the eight fire trucks, two entire tenement blocks on Caird Drive were burnt to a shell. By lunchtime, MacMillan had handed himself in. His testimony and that of her nephew, Andrew, then on military training in Yorkshire, shifted the focus away from Mrs Telfer. Those statements probably saved her from indefinite incarceration."

"There appear to be a number of parallels between events onWesterwick and what occurred here in Glasgow," said Thomas. "Were you aware that Eilidh Broome was pregnant when she fell to her death?"

Innes Guthrie's reaction was not one of surprise. He shook his head and said, "Given that the details of her autopsy are inaccessible, it would suggest that there may be some truth in that."

"Even now, there are files we're not allowed to read."

"Ask yourself this. Why can't you access almost dead files? Who benefits from this, exactly?"

"The same people who aren't revealing much about that young doctor," said Thomas. "Do you think that there's a possibility that MacMillan may have been set up?"

"That is a question, Thomas. You know, my opinion of Angus John MacMillan is one that has been formed from a number of pieces but always, from a distance. My honest feeling is that he was involved, though to what extent I couldn't say. Given how intimate you've been with him, I'd say that your instincts on the matter would surely trump mine."

The professor picked up the pot from the hearth and topped up Thomas' cup.

Stirring the milk in, Thomas said, "MacMillan spoke in detail about the leader of the coven. A fellow named Sand. He said that…"

"I'm sorry. Who?" the professor interrupted.

"Sand," replied Thomas. "Are you familiar with him?"

"Follow me."

Not one wall in the large and dusty study was bare. Facing

the windows, from floor to ceiling were bookcases, with shelves heaving with the sheer weight of words. Upon the threadbare rugs were islands, formations of journals and clusters of magazines. The only clear space in the entire chamber was on Innes Guthrie's desk.

Standing beside Thomas, the professor shot him a look. "Don't tell a soul," he whispered. From a shoulder height shelf, Guthrie lifted five books and passed them to Thomas. Despite looking like any random selection, the books were not only bound together but hollow.

"I thought this only happened in the movies," said Thomas.

Guthrie didn't respond. He removed a small key from the pocket of his waistcoat and opened the box hidden in the wall. "Shall we discuss Mr McCandlish over something stronger?"

Back at the kitchen table, the professor began his ritual. Some clear, light plastic coated the surface. "If you wouldn't mind," he said, passing a pair of white, cotton gloves to Thomas. "The dirt."

As Thomas pulled the gloves tight around his fingers, Guthrie carefully placed McCandlish's journals on the plastic and said, "The authors' cursive takes a little getting used to but read from here…"

The professor was correct, thought Thomas, slowly following McCandlish's lines.

'We took the wide road then turned into Struan's Field and approached the residence of Pastor Sand with caution.'

"Holy shit."

"Indeed," replied the professor. "Continue…"

'Leitch sniffed the air and laughed. Sulphur, he shouted. Auld Joe was definitely around. I didn't believe him. I didn't want to believe him.'

"Auld Joe's the pastor, right?"

"No," said Guthrie. "While Pastor James Sand was the conductor, it was Auld Joe who called the tune. Colloquially, he is known by many names; Ifrit, Ilbis, Angra Manyu, The Goat of Mendes. The bringer of light or the father of lies personified. The choice is yours."

Thomas now understood.

"Many believe that he was an archetype, a paradigm of rebellion against injustice. The great visionary, William Blake also held views that were not too dissimilar to that assertion."

"And you?" asked Thomas. "Is that what you believe?"

"It matters not what I believe, Thomas. I'm just a curious traveller. Now tell me more about *your* Sand."

Though Guthrie was comfortable sharing some of McCandlish's secrets, Thomas felt his own curiosities would be safer hidden behind the cloak of MacMillan's inclinations.

"Obsession," said Innes Guthrie, firmly. "Some form of vulnerability will be at play but the obsession and desire will always cloud objectivity. And that is how they work themselves into a position where the …let's call it, the mark, where the mark is pliant and ready to carry out the task the group wishes."

"And MacMillan's desire for Eilidh Broome was strong enough to turn him from a reserved philosophy student into someone capable of murder?"

"Given the right circumstances," replied the professor, "anyone is capable."

Guthrie delved back into the box and spread a number of photographs on the table. "Eilidh Broome may not have been my cup of tea but one can see exactly why MacMillan fell for her."

From the moment Thomas saw the photograph until he dropped it on the table with the others, not a single breath left his body. He swallowed hard then looked again. In the files and paperwork handed to him by Kunis Clement, Thomas realised that there was little in the way of information about her, let alone a single image. He had seen photographs of Eilidh Broome before but in truth, not since he was a student.

"See what I mean? That's the kind of effect she had on MacMillan."

"This," said Thomas pointing at the picture, "isn't Eilidh Broome."

He handed it to Guthrie. The professor pushed his glasses further back onto the bridge of his nose and looked closely.

"No, that is definitely her."

"And this?" asked Thomas, picking up another photograph.

The professor's eyes narrowed, "I don't understand what you're getting at."

Looking back at Thomas from the picture was not the face of Eilidh Broome.

It was Kaitlin Ramsay.

Thomas felt a tightening around the collar.

"If you need to take a moment..." Professor Guthrie pointed Thomas in the direction of his bathroom. "Shall I pour you a cold drink?"

The long thin room with its brightly coloured tiles was reassuringly cool. Thomas turned on the tap and splashed some water on his face, instantly turning down the temperature on the blood vessels erupting through the epidermis. Eilidh Broome had been dead for three decades but Kaitlin Ramsay was real, in the here and now. Thomas could still taste her lips, feel the curve of her waist and see those birds on her back. Perplexed, he took out his phone and called Kaitlin's number.

The number you have called is not in service. Please try again later.

He checked her status on the app. As it had been since Sunday morning, it was offline. Maybe she's taking some time out to think. A lot has happened and boundaries have been crossed. Thomas scrolled down and tapped on another number.

As ever, Jacqueline answered.

In no mood for incidentals, Thomas got straight to the point.

"I need you to put me through to Kaitlin."

"Kaitlin?"

"Yes, Kaitlin."

"Are you ok, Thomas?" asked the receptionist, softly.

"Perfectly fine, Jacqueline. Will you put me through to Kaitlin, please?"

"I'm sorry but I don't..."

"Jesus," growled Thomas. "Kaitlin Ramsay, my paralegal. Used to be a mousey wee thing."

"I can transfer you to Sam Cleary, if you'd like? He's been supervising the paralegals but…" Jacqueline paused, "as far as I can recall, we've never had a Kaitlin Ramsay."

For the first time in days, Thomas felt the need for medication. Waiting for him by the kitchen door was Innes Guthrie.

"Are you okay, Thomas? You looked awfully flushed there. I know it can get a little warm in here at times but when you get to my age…"

Without a word, Thomas picked up the photograph of Eilidh Broome and left the professor's flat.

By the time he reached Gibson Street, the first drops of rain in a fortnight started falling from the skies. Just as its citizens had begun to acclimatise to the temperate, the city found a way, as it always does, of pulling the stool from under them. The almost forgotten sound of dried wiper blades scraping over the windshields moved everyone's eyes from the slate coloured sky to the slow moving traffic on the road, the diners at the restaurant on the corner, reluctant to succumb to an elemental defeat, urging the staff to prolong their stay by extending the awnings.

The rain felt sharp and it cut into his tender skin like liquified razorblades. Thomas removed his jacket and welcomed the pain.

His phone rang and he answered it without looking.

"Kaitlin?"

"Who's Kaitlin?" asked Milene.

"A paralegal … never mind. What's up?"

"Why didn't you collect him?"

"I don't know what you mean."

"You were supposed to pick him up from Carlos and take him to his tutor. We talked about this last night."

We did? Thomas asked himself.

"Thomas, if this is going to be like before, then maybe we…"

"No," he interrupted. "It's not. Just with all the shit that's going down with Kirkmalcolm and the old man, I just forgot. I'm sorry."

Thomas could hear Milene sigh.

"For this to work, I need to be able to trust you."

"It will. And you can."

"OK, pick him up from the tutor on Banavie Road at five? You got that?"

"Tutor, Banavie Road, five. Got it."

"And you can tell me all about this Kaitlin girl later," she added.

****

Under a coating of rain, the dusty red sandstone blocks around the bowling club looked darker than usual. On the scaffold, a muscular middle aged man unclipped the last of the poles around the windows of Thomas' flat. With the accuracy of a cocktail bartender, the scaffolder casually tossed a three metre length of aluminium to the strong, dextrous younger employee standing on the pavement below, who in turn caught the pole with the ease of a cheerleader catching a twirling baton. Given the length of time they'd spent working on the blond sandstone of his corner block, Thomas could see no significant improvement.

Sheltered under an oversize brolly bearing the name of the journal he compiled lists for, stood Derek. With his back to the bowling club railing and his phone by his mouth, Thomas' neighbour appeared to be recording and, unofficially at least, supervising the scaffolder's movements. If Thomas had to compile a list of the people he least wanted to see at this precise moment, Derek's place on the podium would be safe.

"How was your appointment?"

It took Thomas a second to recall his previous excuse to get away from Derek. "Yeah, good," he muttered.

"I'm on a group with a few of the journalists at the paper. That fellow they found hanging? It was outside your Kunis Clement building, wasn't it?"

"What have you heard?"

"Young doctor. Father of two."

"Shame."

"Word is, at the time of his death, he was being investigated for improper practices. I was thinking that we need to pool our resources and come up with a schedule that…"

Thomas stopped Derek. "Maybe later. I need to go check on the work being done."

"Good call," said Derek, "and you might want to remind them that internal building work after eight in the evening is strictly prohibited. That was some racket they made last night, I can tell you."

From his hall, Thomas could see the living room, curtains tied back with off white dust sheets over the table by the window and his recliner. He turned left into the bedroom and from the drawer of the bedside table, took out a small box and shook it. The sound suggested that its contents were meagre. Still, he thought, this is it. He checked his phone and seeing that he had two hours before he had to pick up the boy, he set the alarm and swallowed the capsule. Before he lay down on the bed, he reached into his jacket and on a stud, freshly exposed by the surveyor, he hung the picture he'd taken from Professor Guthrie on a snaggle nail.

Thomas closed his eyes and almost immediately, his drug starved body began to draw out the effects of the capsule he'd just swallowed. Sinking into the silence, his thoughts returned to Kaitlin.

Silent for weeks, the wind made up for lost time, picking up and swirling around the bricked up chimney breast at the south end of the room. From it, came movement; a tapping of sorts. Light at first but then more determined. Thomas closed his eyes again and wished it away. A bird trapped in the chimney. The same thing had happened not long after he moved in but Thomas, still heavily medicated, dozed through a few days of its feverish but ultimately futile attempts to extricate itself from peril. Once the flapping had become more subdued, the exhausted bird inevitably dropped to its death, broken.

While this bird remained at the frantic stage of its fight, Thomas gave some semi lucid thought to pulling back the sheets of plasterboard and tearing out the strips of insulation to give the creature a chance denied to his predecessor. Mira would understand. She can recoup the cost of the damage from the money she'd yet to pay him for his work on MacMillan. You're welcome. Just about to slip away…the flapping returned, and louder as if the bird knew what Thomas was thinking. If I could just keep him awake long enough. With its heart racing and wings scraping against the inner brick, the bird tapped out a message with its sharp, black beak. Save me Thomas. If you save me, you can save yourself. To Thomas, this made sense. No selfless act of kindness, however small, goes unnoticed in Heaven. His mother said that to him. Her voice, almost gone as a memory, had returned. Just enough for her to repeat her plea. Don't leave me, Thomas. It's dark and I don't want to die here, alone. I'm scared, son. Help me. Try as he wanted, he couldn't ignore the tapping, growing louder, moving closer until he could feel the brush of something against his cheek. That.

Thomas' body shook with fear.

There. Again.

The tapping stopped.

Thomas opened his eyes. On his chest, sat a blackbird. It had his mothers face. Their eyes linked. The bird shuffled closer to his face then turned its head.

"Don't leave me like you left that girl, Thomas. Thomas. Thomas. I will die here."

The bird cawed as it stabbed its beak into his eye.

Thomas sat bolt upright, the sweat dripping from his forehead. Wearied from another visitation, he covered his eyes with his fingertips. The alarm on his phone was becoming too loud and irritating to ignore any longer. Half an hour to get the boy.

He washed his face and after carrying out another check of his still intact ocular regions, he changed into clothing more suited to the less clement conditions. As he walked down the close and out onto the street, the viscera of the building was completely clear for the first time since he'd taken up residence there. A few feet above the functional black plated street name was a dark polished stone insert with elegant gold coloured lettering. Hidden behind tons of metal and wood for months, Thomas hadn't even noticed it was there. As he narrowed his eyes to read what it said, the nurse from the ground floor flat said…

"Edelweiss Terrace. Lovely, isn't it?"

Edelweiss Terrace? Cicely Telfer. Angus John MacMillan. Eilidh Broome.

"But this is Partickhill Road. It can't be Edelweiss Terrace."

"I think it comes from before the first world war," she said. "All the blocks on the street had their own designation. Derek could tell you all about it, he's the local expert…"

Edelweiss Terrace. Where Eilidh Broome lived. A flat which backed on to…

Without saying another word, Thomas darted to the corner of Partickhill Road. He looked down Gardner Street. A hundred metres to the left, was a turning. Ignoring the pain, he raced down the hill, the one he'd been driven down on so many occasions, and turned onto the street which ran parallel with his. Opposite the rebuilt tenement, the name on the lamppost said Caird Drive.

Thomas stopped an elderly man walking a dog. "Excuse me but do you live around here?"

"I do," he said guardedly.

"Can I ask how long you've been here?"

"A long time."

"Ten, twenty years?"

"Longer. Since I was about your age, I guess."

"This building. Was it always here?"

"No, they rebuilt it after the big fire, so probably thirty years ago. The old block was where that murderer lived."

Thomas cursed himself. As someone who prided himself on his attention to detail, to have missed this one key element was unforgivable. He started piecing and positing. Flat. Owned by the old man. Mask. The Red Room. Kaitlin and Eilidh. Hidden in plain sight. Of course. He cursed himself again. So much time wasted. Concentrate. Though still sluggish from the earlier capsule, Thomas' mind pushed through, connecting the pieces like a numbered jigsaw. IVI is W.

W is Westerwick.

I need to speak to Guthrie again.

He checked his phone. Less than ten minutes to collect the boy from his tutor. Quickest way was down the steep wynd just beyond the bowling club. The rain brings out a different type of person, thought Thomas, his mind racing faster than his feet. Happy, determined, serious people. Seems the topless drunks and the pavement dancing maniacs have been driven off the streets. For now.

Five minutes.

Past the serious joggers, bare legged and puddle splashed, almost vertical on the uphill climb. A red faced girl with a green woollen cap, balanced by two full bags of groceries, stopping for breath against the twisty rail. At the bottom, a toddler in a warm looking jacket ran towards the lane before his father tugged gently on his hood, diverting him towards a less exhausting route.

Two minutes.

Thomas opened the gate, climbed the stairs to the front door and pushed the bell. He recalled the tutor's husband. A bookish man who dealt with the parents and the issues pertaining to the financial recompense. Milene liked them both though Thomas couldn't shake the feeling that he was being judged for passing on the boy's extra curricular education to a stranger.

"He's been collected. You've only just missed him."

"What do you mean I've just missed him? *I'm* meant to collect him."

"No, it was an older gentleman. I've seen him here before."

Dread enveloped Thomas. His phone rang. He looked at the screen. Derek. Decline.

"Which way did they go?"

"I couldn't say but the boy was asking if he could go to the park."

As Thomas ran towards the play area, his phone rang again. This time it was Mira.

"Where are you?"

"I've gone to pick the boy up but…"

"Thomas, I don't want you to be alarmed," she said, "but MacMillan is gone."

Thomas stopped running. "As in dead?"

"No, gone. Campbell Ames has just informed me that he disappeared this afternoon."

"For a second time, a convicted murderer has just walked out of the country's most secure unit and on the same afternoon, someone has taken the boy from his tutor. And you're telling me not to be alarmed? Jesus fucking Christ..."

Silence on the line.

"Where is the boy?"

"That indeed is the fucking question, Mira. Actually, no. Who has him is probably more relevant. Did you send anyone to pick him up?"

"Let me speak to Milene."

As Thomas scoured the park, looking for a sign of Milene's child, his phone rang again. It was Milene.

"Where is he?"

"I was there, right on time to collect him, I swear to God, but the idiot who runs the place told me that someone else had beaten me to it."

"What the fuck is going on?" screamed Milene, hysterically.

"Stay calm. I will find him."

Given the change in weather conditions, Hayburn Park was much less busy than it had been on Saturday when Thomas last raced around the lane. "What was he wearing when you dropped him off?"

"His lemon jacket and jeans, I think. I don't know..."

About fifty yards down the crescent, Thomas could see a small figure wearing yellow holding the hand of a larger, hooded person.

"I think I see him," he said. "I'll call you right back."

"Hey!" Thomas shouted.

That's him.

For the first time in years, Thomas broke into a sprint. Despite running against light traffic, he struggled to make up enough ground before the pair turned left onto the steep, narrow climb of Partickhill Lane.

Keep going.

Push.

Knowing that this was one trial he could ill afford to lose, Thomas dug into his reserves and reached the top of the wynd. For a moment, he draped his arms over the railing and breathed through his teeth, filling his burning lungs with air. Though it felt as if the lactic acid was tearing holes through his calves and through his thighs, Thomas went again.

Towards the flat. The fucking flat. How could I have been so blind? No time now. Got to find the boy.

Ahead, seventy yards or so, on the pavement beside the entrance to the bowling club sat a familiar car. By its open boot stood Collins. Thomas froze. The driver looked at him before slamming it shut. Opening the driver's side door, Collins spoke with the passenger seated behind. Thomas could not see who the driver was talking to but with his mind on full alert, the scenario he feared most was one he considered the most likely. Thomas picked up the pace just as the limousine turned right down the hill.

Thomas looked at his phone. Given its age and condition, it was no surprise to him that its battery was almost out of charge. About to open the door to his close, he heard a car screech to a halt.

"Did you hear the news?" said Derek, leaning from the driver's window.

Thomas nodded.

"He could be anywhere," he added, excitedly. "Wait a minute. That note you passed him. Do you think that had…"

Thomas shook his head.

"So where would he go? You know him better than anyone, I suppose. But not like that. That's not what I meant. It's just, I mean if we…or another concerned citizen was to find him, before the police do, just think of the coverage it would get?"

As Derek's mind sped off in the direction of the Pulitzer, a realisation dawned on Thomas.

"I think I know where he'll go."

"What are we waiting for?"

Thomas got into the car.

"Hang on," he said. "You should probably tell your wife that you won't be home for a while."

"Of course," replied Derek, dialling her number.

Thomas put his hand across the phone.

"Probably best to tell her in person. We're going to be a while."

"Righto," said Derek. "How long, you reckon?"

"Not sure but get some of her bread and biscuits for the trip."

"Got you," said Derek.

"But leave the keys, I'll turn the car around."

"Why?"

"We need to go in that direction."

Derek's questions may have been reasonable but each one only served to irritate Thomas more. "Jesus man, do you want the story or don't you?"

Derek looked ahead and pondered. A series of slow but determined nods suggested that he did.

"Right, chop chop."

Thomas unlocked his door and walked around to the driver's side.

"Let me borrow your phone for a second. Mine has died."

Derek whispered, "The PIN's 1977"

Good man.

Thomas watched as Derek ran into the close. He made it to a mental count of ten before he released the handbrake and sped off.

Chapter 25 - Whippoorwill

The roads out of Glasgow that afternoon were much quieter than Thomas expected. Blocking the number of Derek's wife before he reached the blossom lined boulevard of the Great Western Road meant that the journey west would be considerably more peaceful than if he hadn't. Thomas considered how irked Derek's wife would be when she realised that not only had he surrendered their car but that he'd been keeping their joint debit card inside his phone's clear plastic case. The news bulletin on the hour laid the blame for MacMillan's disappearance firmly at the feet of the First Minister, something else, Thomas thought, his neighbour would just have to live with. The cheery sounding Englishman reading out the subsequent weather report mentioned that the north and west coasts of the country were at risk of localised overnight storms and heavy showers. None of this mattered to Thomas, free of the city's grip. He had to find MacMillan and return the boy to his mother.

As rebellious beams of sunlight poked through the low black clouds that hung over the loch's tree-line hamlets,

Thomas briefly allowed himself the luxury of a distraction. On a clear, straight section of the road, he slowed and scrolled through the music Derek had stored on his phone. On second thoughts...

By the time he'd taken the tight, puddle coated road through the village of Tarbet, it was already a quarter to eight. With the kirk's spire reaching skyward like a thick, craggy digit, warning the clouds to calm it, the rain gods ignored the appeal and sent it down harder. From the Arrochar turn, the radio signal was relinquished but given the forced bonhomie of the post drive time presenter and the formulaic playlist he offered up, Thomas wasn't too disappointed. To his ears, the sounds of mid-signal static was an improvement on both that and Derek's favoured lo-fi miserablism.

Last Ferry to Westerwick ... departs at eight.

Beyond the dozen or so cars and tourers queued at the departure jetty, sat a police van and a squad car. As the lights of the latter illuminated the harbour, Thomas checked Derek's phone. Still no signal.

Ahead, a pretty but forlorn looking teen was selling tickets. Smothered by an oversized orange jacket bearing the peeling decal of the company about to transport him across the water, Thomas's eyes were drawn to the worker's narrow shoulders and the motto spread between his blades; 'It's Closer Than You Think'.

As the teen reached Thomas, the driver of the motor home directly in front stepped from his cabin.

"Calm down," he shouted back into the vehicle. "I'm going to ask him now, alright? Here, pal. Is there wifi on the ferry?"

"There is," replied the teen. He turned to Thomas who

336

asked what was happening ahead.

"Police doing routine checks."

Thomas patted himself down. "I think I might have left my licence at home."

"That won't be a problem, Sir," he said. "They're just taking a quick look inside your car and your boot."

"Do they always do this?"

"Now and again. They've been doing it all afternoon."

"No worries."

"Just yourself?"

"On the way out. But I'll be bringing someone back."

****

Thomas left Derek's car and followed his nose, and the motorhome family, upstairs to the Captain's Cabin. As he'd not eaten since sharing some baked sugar with Innes Guthrie, the aroma of the freshly cooked fare made Thomas' mouth water.

After the motorhome family cleared out the last of the dry-ended macaroni, Thomas settled for a pie that contained more kidney than steak. Given that he didn't know what awaited him - and when he might have the chance to eat again - Thomas took up the cashier's offer of all the trimmings. Added to the tray, a couple of bags of gourmet potato crisps, for the final leg of the journey. Tapping the card against the reader, Thomas was sure Derek would eventually understand. Consider the spontaneous display of largesse a legitimate business expense. While the tourists seated at the observation tables strained through the elements for a view of the island, a group of travelling police officers were huddled under the larger of the two screens watching a rolling news bulletin.

Authorities have named the deceased as Richard Raymond, a thirty three year old guard at the Kirkmalcolm facility. Police Scotland have described this latest incident as 'unexplained'.

Thomas thought it wiser to pay his respects from the shadows.

One by one the vehicles left the ferry and drove the wide harbour boulevard of Port Fintan. As the wind swirled across the bay, blowing sheets of rain sidewards, the only light visible beyond the harbour was that from the Westerwick Hotel, set back from the port and located behind the obelisk, a memorial to those from the island who'd perished in long forgotten days.

Thomas' thoughts returned to Milene and her life before. Of how happy she'd been with him. Sexually and socially compatible. Satisfied here, by another and in a way he couldn't better. As Thomas continued to fixate on the manner of the boy's conception, he gripped the wheel tightly and squeezed his foot on the pedal, the increasing revolutions matching a rage which he could no longer mask.

The parallel roads that took him west in the darkness were less narrow and in far better condition than he'd anticipated. No superfast broadband out here, he thought. As the battery on Derek's phone had been drained of most of its charge, Thomas used the car's navigation system to locate Struan's Field and from that, the site of the MacMillan croft. Though not hungry, he had an inexplicable pang for a slice of thick white toast coated with marmalade. What was it called? Without the rind, though. Smooth. Just like his mother made. Mother's Pride. That's it. She would be proud of him. I'll make her proud of me.

Approaching the turning point between the Fintan and the Low Road, Thomas found that the less developed route was blocked by two red police signs. He got out of the car and, protecting himself against the elements, surveyed the area. Though there appeared not to be another living soul around, over the brow of the rise he could see only darkness, cleft by an intermittent light. In the near distance, the whirr of propeller blades broke the rural silence. Thomas returned to the car and zoomed in on the navigation screen which confirmed his location as being on the periphery of Struan's Field.

Maybe he's here and they've trapped him already, thought Thomas. Like Pastor Sand. Save the child first then drag the prisoner along the pebbles and over the cliff.

Over the cliff.

Thomas pressed the navigation screen again. Quickly, he scrolled until he found what he was looking for:

Point of Interest.

Until he spotted McLennan's lighthouse, only darkness and silence had kept Thomas company on the three mile drive to Scharr Point. He pulled into the narrow, low-walled car park where the road had faded to an end. Thomas opened the boot of the car and rummaged around for something sharp or something heavy. Using the torch on Derek's phone, he continued slowly over the uneven rocky moss, towards the cliff's edge.

Trading the faltering light for one less artificial, Thomas looked down to the shoreline and returned to an invocation from his youth.

> The moon like a flower
> In heaven's high bower
> With silent delight.
> Sits and smiles at the night.

As Thomas ended his descent, what filled his senses was markedly different from the mildly bubbling banks of the Kelvin or the cold sea salt flats of Skelmorlie. Unlike Blake's moon, here was no delight. No songs of innocence. Only the sea's wild choler and the faint scent of sulphur.

"Where's the boy?"

At the mouth of the inlet, sheltering beneath a canopy of deep lying knotted roots was a familiar presence. Seated low on a boulder and stoking a fire that had been burning a while, Angus John MacMillan didn't look at Thomas as he repeated his question.

"I knew you'd come."

"Final warning," growled Thomas cracking a sheared length of scaffolding pole against the rocks.

"How does this work?" MacMillan asked. "I say nothing, you brain me with that cudgel and you're still none the wiser as to the boy's whereabouts?"

As Thomas moved in on MacMillan, the escaped prisoner

raised his makeshift poker from the flame.

"That's close enough."

"Where is he?"

"I'd imagine he's tucked up in bed by now. Most nine year olds don't stay up this late."

"You don't have him?"

"What on earth would I want with a nine year old child? No, your driver picked him up and took him to the park. He was very insistent on that. I believe they shared an ice cream float before Collins drove him home. "

"Collins?" muttered Thomas. "How…"

"Those ties that bound us under Cicely Telfer's roof will never be broken. He says you're quite a talented artist. Birds and the like. Tell me, have you ever sketched a Whippoorwill?"

Confused, Thomas struggled to process the glut of information. MacMillan continued. "But that's North American, isn't it? They say that the Whippoorwill can sense the essence departing a body. And that its mournful cry is actually that of a soul, captured. I've never heard its cry, have you? "

"Is that what you've done to Collins? Captured his soul?"

"No, the essence of Hector Andrew Collins is quite secure. Yours however, remains in the balance."

Thomas considered MacMillan's words carefully. "Why did you return?"

"Because Sand broke our agreement."

"What agreement?"

"That one's will belongs only to the soul and that judgement be left to the almighty."

"Did you kill the doctor or was that Sand?"

"We all played our part."

"What about Rothwell Glen? "

"No, his demise, while necessary, was purely fortuitous."

"And poor Raymond? He meant no harm."

"Raymond will see eternity by our side."

"Who are you?" cried Thomas, tired and exasperated.

MacMillan returned to stoking the fire.

"I take it you're not my father?"

He shook his head. "In order to save you, I first had to convince you. No Thomas, I'm afraid that like me, you're all alone."

"We're nothing alike," Thomas spat, his grip tightening around his makeshift weapon.

"Our blood surges through this rock, Thomas. Like you, I am a child of duality, a cambion born of both the devils and the angels. A servant of the succubus."

"What does that even mean?"

"You were never in the least bit curious about where you're from?"

In the Leven household, the details of Thomas' adoption had never been openly discussed.

"Your birth mother left the island with you in her womb."

"Another lie," shouted Thomas as the waves crashed ever closer to the cove.

"Because I was of the island, I was chosen and primed.

Just as you were. The only difference is that I embraced the desires. In fact, I'd given in to them by the time I first reached the mainland with a teenager's yellow jumper on my back. But think about it, Thomas. The Leven's may have provided for the poor little damaged boy they inherited but since then, who has housed you and who has fed you? The question shouldn't be who helped you when you fell but who created the conditions for that fall? And who continues to benefit? Remember, Sand needed both Eilidh and I for that wicked circuit to be complete. But once she was gone…"

The cold sea water, no longer shallow, lapped against Thomas' feet. Though not yet strong enough to pull him in, he could feel the current growing. He took a step nearer to the fire. As he did, MacMillan reached into the flames and picked up a still blazing strand of the thickest jute.

"There's no trickery, no illusion. This is real."

"What do you want?" asked Thomas, through the tears.

"Same as you. To be happy. But you know that isn't possible. Fear is our companion. Sorrow is our lot."

MacMillan extended his hand towards Thomas and continued, "You've been guided as carefully as I was."

Thomas flinched from the touch of the glowing rope.

"But if they can't have me and they can't have you, who will Sand turn to next?"

As MacMillan tied the jute around their wrists, Thomas realised…

The boy.

"You see? I am the darkness but also the light. Your light, Thomas. That boy. By your actions only, you can save him and

343

break the chain. Without you, Sand can make no connection. The only being in your life that has ever loved you without condition is that boy. He does not reside in the fictions of your imagination, to be brought out as a crutch when needed. To him you will be no substitute but a hero, a real father, more than any sham of a man who'd let you sink. You think he doesn't know that? You think that I don't?"

With the surf breaking faster and more violently with each coming wave, Angus John MacMillan wound another length of the dense, searing rope around Thomas' chest and pulled tight.

"The time has come for you to sacrifice, Thomas Leven, with your broken body and poisoned mind."

Thomas rested his head on MacMillan's shoulder and began to sob. Tenderly, MacMillan kissed his cheek. "Do not worry," he whispered, "I will be with you. We both know that you were always destined for greater things, so sigh from the depths and give yourself to me. Soon your glory will be eternal and your soul will be secure."

"And Sand?"

"I'll deal with her myself."

Chapter 26 - Patient

Wearing a pair of oversized headphones, the boy rocked back and forth in his chair, connected to his electronic nanny, oblivious not only to the steady stream of people who came in and out of the room but to his mother, gently caressing the fingers of the patient.

Mira looked through the rain-soaked window to the pond directly ahead. Three floors beneath, a man attached to a tall monitor stood alone and smoked, untroubled by the danger posed by the proximity to his canister of compressed oxygen and the gusts of wind which lifted and billowed his pale hospital gown as though he was a damp, emphysemic Marilyn Monroe.

As she contemplated joining the rule-bending patient below, the door to the hospital room opened.

Milene stood and she and the doctor embraced.

"Don't worry," he whispered, "he'll be fine."

He flipped back the pages on his clipboard and asked rhetorically how the patient was doing. "We've scheduled him for surgery later tonight," he continued. "Dr Mills, as you probably know, is the best neurosurgeon in the country so if anyone can get to the bottom of this, it'll be her. Bleeds like this are actually quite common."

"And the burns?" asked Mira.

"Mainly superficial but the one around his neck may require a graft. We'll see…"

Milene spoke. "The consultants earlier reckoned that the bleed may have predated his accident and that he might have been suffering with this for quite some time."

"It's not common but it has been known for an acute intracerebral hematoma to develop weeks if not months after the initial cause of the trauma. I'm just glad that they picked up his signal in time."

"Isn't technology wonderful?" said Mira as Milene fought her emotions.

The doctor continued, "Thomas might not be responsive at the moment but he is perfectly comfortable. So, in the meantime, try to get some rest. You'll be no use to him if we have to admit you too. If there's anything you need, Milene, please don't hesitate to ask. You don't need me to tell you exactly how highly all of the staff here regard you. And your family, of course."

Once the medics had dispersed, the room returned to a state of quiet. The boy, no longer rocking, was now curled up on the seat with his legs dangling over the arm. Twisting a strand of hair, his eyes remained glued to the screen.

Mira joined Milene at the foot of the bed.

"I've thanked the neighbour on your behalf," she said. "He

was very helpful. And Campbell assured me that there won't be any charges pressed."

Mira placed her hand over Milene's and whispered, "Do as the doctor said and get some rest." Milene nodded as if the thought had never crossed her mind.

Turning to get the boy's attention, Mira let out a low but sharp whistle.

"Come and say goodbye to Thomas."

The boy removed his headphones and did as he was instructed.

Milene stood and embraced her stepmother.

"I'll fill a bag for you, gullet mitt."

"Gentle," said Milene, as the boy cuddled into Thomas' chest. As he did, Thomas moaned.

The unexpected sound shook the boy.

"It's ok," said Mira, taking the now concerned child away from the bed.

"Thomas, you're fine," said Milene softly. "We're all here. Just rest."

Attempting to open his eyes, he moaned again.

"Hey," she said, brushing back hair from his forehead. "It's ok. You're safe here."

"We'll leave you to it," said Mira, putting the boy's belongings into his rucksack.

At the third attempt, Thomas' eyes flickered then opened. As Milene reached over and tenderly kissed his cheek, a thin smile appeared.

The boy, realising that he had nothing to fear, returned

WESTERWICK GEORGE PATERSON

to the bedside. Thomas' eyes closed again but his smile widened. Slowly, he reached out his hand to the boy. Thomas squeezed his fingers and as he reached up towards his face, his eyes opened fully.

No.

He moaned again, this time very different from before.

From deep inside, he repeated.

"No."

With his breathing becoming more rapid, Thomas tried to pull himself up.

"We should go," said Mira.

Milene leant over to press the emergency button. Thomas pulled the oxygen tube from his nostrils before ripping the cannula from his hand. As Milene tried to calm him, a spray of blood from Thomas' open vein hit her cheek.

The nurse who arrived shouted for immediate back up as she and Milene struggled to restrain the patient.

Silently, Mira and the boy left the room. With every available medic racing towards the source of a noise more disturbingly primitive than developed, Mira placed her grandson's headphones over his ears and led him towards the elevator. As she was about to press the down button, the boy pushed in front and beat her to it. He stifled a giggle, Mira shook her head with mock disdain.

In the lift, the boy's eyes widened at the numbers on display. The look from his grandmother suggested that he'd be unwise to push any further buttons.

"Nana, what was happening? In the room?"

"Thomas is very sick and sometimes when you're sick, you

act a little crazy."

"Is Tom crazy?"

Mira shrugged but declined to offer a definitive answer. She took out a cigarette.

The lift door opened.

"Exit?" she asked.

"This way," he replied. "Can I have some ice cream, Nana?"

"No. It's too late for ice cream. Maybe at the weekend."

"Will Tom be ok?"

Mira took a long draw from her cigarette and nodded to her driver.

****

The rain had ceased by the time Piotr pulled into Mira's driveway on Kelvin Drive. There was no sign of the press encamped outside the house, but with a convicted murderer at large, Mira thought it prudent to keep her driver in the guest house for the night.

"Let's see who can get ready for bed the quickest," she said. The boy, as competitive as his mother, raced into his room and changed into his pyjamas. As he flushed and washed, Mira poured herself a large glass of wine. She had no intention of slipping into nightwear just yet.

"Let me check those teeth," she asked. "How long did you brush for?"

"Ten minutes," he replied, confidently. Mira arched an eyebrow and the boy instantly folded.

"Ok, five minutes."

Mira showed her teeth and the boy mirrored her. She took his brush and slowly worked on the areas he'd missed.

"Nana?"

"Wait … done."

The boy spat into the sink then said solemnly, "I'm worried about Tom. Is he going to be ok?"

"I've no idea," she replied. "I'm a chemist, not a doctor."

The boy's brow furrowed.

"Yes, he's going to be fine," she replied. "Right, time for bed."

"What are we doing tomorrow?"

"You're going to school…"

The boy groaned.

"Then afterwards, I'm going to make your favourite."

"Slices?"

"Don't tell your mother," Mira smiled.

The boy clenched his fists and said, "Yes!"

"Shall we?" she asked.

"We shall!" he replied.

Mira took the boy into his bedroom.

"Can I have a story? Please."

"Sure but first, say your prayers."

The boy knelt beside his bed and closed his eyes.

"God is dead and magic is afoot.

God is dead and magic is afoot.

God is dead and magic is afoot."

Mira kissed his head.

"Good boy."

George Paterson is a writer, broadcaster and musician whose work has been featured in film as well as on the London stage. His first novel, 'The Girl, The Crow, The Writer and The Fighter', published by Into Books, was shortlisted as Bloody Scotland's Best Debut in 2022.

He is based in Glasgow, Scotland.